P9-CMA-873

"Do you love him?"

Josie swallowed. "Yes, Gramps, I do. I love Mack."
In her answer was the certainty that had eluded her
for so long. "I only wish I knew what to do about it."

Gramps eased back in his chair, a beatific smile
lighting his face. "If you love him enough, something
will occur to you. Yep, you'll discover what to do."

"But I've made so many mistakes with him. I'm still
not sure how we can resolve our differences.
And," she said on a sudden note of panic, "what if
he thinks of me only as a friend?"

Gramps chuckled softly and from the table beside
his chair picked up a small framed photo of her
grandmother as a young woman. "Friend? I hope so.
The very best kind of love grows between friends."
A long comfortable moment of shared silence was
broken only by the crackling of the fire.

"Sometimes friendships go on forever, don't they,
Gramps?"

"Sometimes they go on for a lifetime." He looked
up, and his eyes found hers. "Trust him, Josie. And
trust yourself."

ABOUT THE AUTHOR

Laura Abbot says that "as a girl growing up in Kansas City during the 1940s, I was blessed by the presence in our home of my maternal grandmother. A storyteller and lover of language, she filled my ears with the sounds of poetry and my imagination with wonders." Laura's love of family, of home and of storytelling is reflected in *Mating for Life*, her first Superromance novel.

Laura taught English to junior and senior high school students in Kansas and Oklahoma for almost twenty-five years. She says that she "vowed to retire early from teaching (which I dearly loved) to devote myself to the full-time pursuit of a writing career." Which she's done, and very successfully, too.

Laura and her husband, Larry, live in Arkansas, where they built a home overlooking a beautiful clear-water lake—"about as close to heaven as anyone could be."

Laura Abbot

Mating for Life

Harlequin Books

TORONTO • NEW YORK • LONDON
AMSTERDAM • PARIS • SYDNEY • HAMBURG
STOCKHOLM • ATHENS • TOKYO • MILAN
MADRID • WARSAW • BUDAPEST • AUCKLAND

If you purchased this book without a cover you should be aware
that this book is stolen property. It was reported as "unsold and
destroyed" to the publisher, and neither the author nor the
publisher has received any payment for this "stripped book."

ISBN 0-373-70639-1

MATING FOR LIFE

Copyright © 1995 by Laura A. Shoffner.

All rights reserved. Except for use in any review, the reproduction or
utilization of this work in whole or in part in any form by any electronic,
mechanical or other means, now known or hereafter invented, including
xerography, photocopying and recording, or in any information storage
or retrieval system, is forbidden without the written permission of the
publisher, Harlequin Enterprises Limited, 225 Duncan Mill Road,
Don Mills, Ontario, Canada M3B 3K9.

All characters in this book have no existence outside the imagination of
the author and have no relation whatsoever to anyone bearing the same
name or names. They are not even distantly inspired by any individual
known or unknown to the author, and all incidents are pure invention.

This edition published by arrangement with Harlequin Enterprises B.V.

® and TM are trademarks of the publisher. Trademarks indicated with
® are registered in the United States Patent and Trademark Office, the
Canadian Trade Marks Office and in other countries.

Printed in U.S.A.

To Larry, my mate for life,
in heartfelt appreciation for the
constancy of his love and faith in me,
and in loving memory of
Grandmother B

CHAPTER ONE

THE LATE-AUGUST SUN beat down on the ribbon of concrete, creating shimmering mirages. Josie Calhoun gripped the steering wheel, fighting both the glare off the car in front of her and the fatigue of the six-hundred-mile trip. Shifting position, she stretched her long legs and squinted at the approaching road sign: Maizeville, 8 Miles. Elation and sadness warred within her.

Maizeville, Kansas. Josie gulped as memories of her grandparents, MJ and Gramps, washed over her. Digging in the moist black earth of MJ's vegetable garden, riding on the John Deere tractor with Gramps, helping turn the crank of the ice-cream freezer on a sweltering July day. The farm, nestled among the low-rising hills, had always been her sanctuary, her grandmother and grandfather always her anchors.

Tears smarted as Josie recalled her last visit—the bleak cold day last February when they'd buried MJ. The Kansas wind had ripped through the denuded branches and torn at the shroud. Josie, too, had felt ripped and torn. The barren landscape had offered no solace, and she, like the pitiless winter sky, bore the loss stoically, her frozen exterior masking her anguish.

And there it was, the massive ancient oak tree under whose leafy boughs pioneers had found shade and shelter on their long westward trek. Josie could hear MJ saying, "You always know you're home when the oak whispers to you."

Home, oh, yes, home. But a home without oatmeal raisin cookies, air-freshened sheets. A home without MJ.

A suppressed tide of grief rose through her, and the highway, lost in a sudden mist of tears, seemed to waver. With a great wrenching sob, she swerved to the shoulder of the road, braked sharply and, putting her head in her arms, gave in to the storm of emotion.

MACKENZIE SCOTT yawned and looked at his watch. It was nearing the end of his shift. Better check in with headquarters. After a long uneventful day patrolling the eastern sector of the county, he was ready for an invigorating shower and a hot meal. Routine stops—a traveler with a flat and two speeding offenders—had made for a boring shift, but boring sure beat some kinds of excitement.

As he started his radio transmission, he noticed a gray Honda weave across the center line and then, just before the Pioneer Oak, bounce to the shoulder.

The Pioneer Oak! *Dear God, no! Not again!* Mack stomped on the gas, his frenzied mind racing. *Sarah, no! Stop, Sarah!* He could still see the crumpled metal, the left rear tire spinning and spinning, could still be deafened by the horrible silence, unrelieved except for the hissing of the mangled radiator. He choked on the remembered stench of burning oil. Not his small dear Sarah. Not the oak!

"Mack, are you all right?" The radio crackled and the dispatcher's voice interrupted his nightmare.

"Yeah, sorry. I've got a stop. Check you later." Mack wiped his brow on his sleeve, turned on his patrol light and pulled in behind the parked Honda, noting the redheaded female driver slumped over the wheel.

JOSIE HICCUPED, drew a tentative breath and turned to fumble in her purse. She sniffed and wiped her eyes. Just as she located the empty tissue container, a sudden movement in the rearview mirror caught her eye. The flashing red light of the sheriff's slowing patrol car seemed the final straw.

"Damn! This is all I need," Josie muttered as she wiped her face with her fists and tried to regain control.

In the mirror she could see the deputy striding toward her, his tall muscular body suggesting order and authority. He rapped on the window. "Ma'am?"

Josie rolled down the window and felt a blast of Kansas heat.

"Yes, officer?"

"Are you all right?" Taking off his sunglasses, he stooped to peer at her. "I noticed you were having difficulty controlling your vehicle and wondered if you need help."

Josie looked into the deputy's clear brown eyes, set deep in his tanned face. His straightforward gaze was tinged with concern. Did she need help? Oh, yes, but not the kind he could give her. "I'm sorry. I just saw the Pioneer Oak and all these thoughts went through my mind and..." She felt the burning in her throat again; her hands were shaking. "Oh, dear, I'm afraid I'm not making sense. It's just..." The stifled sobs erupted.

He observed the dampened coppery curls sticking to her temples and the faint but generous sprinkling of freckles on her tearstained face. "Is there anything I can do to help?"

She attempted to pull herself together. "I...I'm so sorry to bother you. It's just that this is my first trip back since my grandmother died, and when I saw the oak, all of a sudden I missed her so much and...I just lost it." Josie wiped her face again and tried to sniff away the tears. "If you have a tissue...I seem to be out."

"I can do better than that." With a warm lopsided grin, he reached into his pocket, pulled out a clean linen handkerchief and offered it to her.

"Grief has no season," he said softly as he looked up at the offending oak. He turned and searched her glistening emerald eyes. "You just need some time to sit. I know how you feel."

She stared at him and saw that his eyes were swimming with compassion. "I'll just go wait in my vehicle," he said, "and keep an eye on you. You never know who might come along the highway. You take all the time you need, ma'am." And then he was gone.

MACK OPENED his car door, took off his hat and rubbed his broad hand through his wavy brown hair. A mighty attractive young woman, despite the tears. "First trip back," she'd said. He couldn't recall ever seeing her before. If he had, she'd be hard to forget.

He adjusted the seat so that he could lean back a little as he sat and waited. He squinted against the sun's glare to read the small print of a sticker attached to the left rear bumper of the Honda: "A bird in the bush is worth two in the hand." What was that supposed to mean? Oh, great! One of those antihunting, save-the-wildlife fanatics. He looked up. She was still hunched over the wheel. He rested his arm on the back of the passenger seat and, discreetly looking beyond the distraught redhead, he found himself staring at the oak tree.

For him it was no longer a landmark promising cool shade to the sun-weary traveler, but a symbol of that awful night eighteen months ago. It had been so dark and cold, the remnants of a March blizzard dotting the dormant fields. Mack felt his stomach tighten and his head begin to throb as he remembered.

Why, oh why, hadn't he insisted on driving Sarah home? She'd unexpectedly had to work the late shift at the hospital in Topeka, so rather than miss their date altogether, he'd driven to meet her for a midnight breakfast at an all-night truck stop. Tired though she was, she'd insisted on driving her car back to Maizeville so he wouldn't have to take her to work the next day. They exchanged a long lingering kiss to warm them for the lonely trip home. "Be careful on the bridges," he told her as he blew her one last kiss.

He followed her on the deserted highway, daydreaming about the happiness he'd found with her. Sarah. So tiny, so loving, so perfect. He was a lucky man indeed to be engaged to her.

His cozy reverie had jolted into nightmare. He'd watched helplessly as her little Chevy hit a patch of ice and slid sickeningly sideways. Then, out of control, it turned end over end and thudded into the unyielding trunk of the two-hundred-year-old oak....

My God, how he still missed her! Why couldn't he have saved her? Would the searing pain never stop? Could he ever again put himself in the position of being vulnerable to such unrelenting grief?

Joining the Sheriff's Department had been an instinctive and immediate reaction to the accident. He'd had to do something! If he couldn't change the past, maybe he could work to prevent someone else's loss. But every stretch of highway, and especially this one with the Pio-

neer Oak, was a grim reminder of his guilt and aching
loneliness.

The revving of an engine and a short honk returned
him to the August reality. As the Honda pulled back onto
the highway, he was cheered to see the young woman
waving a grateful salute. Pain knew no boundaries, he
supposed. Poor kid. Such beautiful red hair and vulnerable, big green eyes. She'd break someone's heart one
day. Yep, pain was no respecter of persons.

He sighed as he put his car in gear and picked up the
mike. "Headquarters? Mack here. I'm heading for the
barn. Ten-four."

JOSIE TURNED OFF the highway onto the county road,
warmed by the kindness she'd seen in the deputy sheriff's deep brown eyes. Tenderness from such an unexpected source! She felt strangely calm, as if the
maelstrom of tears and the handsome young man's gesture had primed her to savor the late-afternoon glory of
the fertile countryside. Acres of fields being prepared for
winter wheat stretched in rich brown symmetry. Graceful cottonwoods shaded the gravel road, and old stone
fences paid silent tribute to the backbreaking labor of
clearing the land. As she crossed the rickety wooden
bridge spanning Persimmon Creek, she began searching
the horizon for her first glimpse of Frank Calhoun's
white two-story farmhouse.

Although she hadn't seen Gramps since the funeral, his
frequent letters assured her that, although he was devastated by MJ's death, he still lived his oft-repeated ax-
iom: What really matters is what happens *in* us, not *to* us.
As he'd said in his last letter, "Dear girl, of course I'm
lonely. It's hard after forty-five years with your grandmother to wake up each morning without her. But she

wouldn't want any moping. She'd say, 'Frank, you just get on with life. Life is for the living.' So that's what I'm trying to do. It isn't always easy, but your visit will be just the tonic this old man needs.''

There it was! Off to the left she spied the silo, the stone chimney, and then the pitched roof. Finally her beloved farmhouse, square and reassuring, framed by two tall elms, came into view. As she turned into the lilac-bordered lane past the weather-beaten mailbox, a flood of memories threatened her control—MJ standing in the yard greeting her arrival with a flapping of her flowered apron, MJ running to swoop the lonely little girl up into her arms, MJ holding out her hand to guide Josie up the porch steps with a "Well, now, young lady, I want to hear all about your school year while we eat some chocolate cake."

Gulping, Josie maneuvered the Honda alongside the rear picket fence. The back door slammed, and Gramps hurried along the walk toward her. His craggy face seemed more furrowed, but his steel blue eyes were shining with anticipation. As she stepped out of the car, he held out his arms, and next thing she knew, she was smothered in a bear hug. Enveloped by the clean, laundry-soap smell of his chambray shirt, she said tearfully into his shoulder, "Oh, Gramps, it's so good to be home!"

BEFORE JOSIE LOADED the last supper plate into the dishwasher, she looked at the familiar Blue Willow pattern and thought of all the hopes and secrets that had been shared in this kitchen. When she was seven, she learned she'd been named after her grandmother, whose initials stood for Mary Josephine. From that day on, Josie had quit wishing she'd been named something more exotic, such as Lori or Sabrina, because to have MJ's name might mean she could be like her. No dumb kid would ever again get away with teasing her about being named after a horse. Hers was a special name indeed!

After starting the dishwasher, Josie got two glasses out of the cabinet and filled them with iced tea. She carried them out to the front porch where Gramps sat quietly rocking in the dusk. "I thought some tea might help cool us off," Josie said as she handed him his.

"Thanks, honey. It's kind of nice to be waited on. I know you had a long drive today. You must be bushed. Sit down and share my favorite time of the day with me."

Josie stretched out her lanky body on the ancient porch swing, leaving one leg on the floor to push herself gently to and fro. James Cagney, the fat old orange cat, jumped into her lap, curled into a ball and purred a welcome. The companionable silence was broken only by the creak of the swing, the clink of the ice cubes and a chorus of cicadas tuning up for their nightly concert. A gentle southerly breeze brought relief from the day's heat. In the western sky, the evening star signaled the approach of night.

She glanced at her grandfather. "Gramps, why is this your favorite time of day?"

"Well, for one thing, it's a chance for me to look back over the day's accomplishments while I rest my weary bones. For another, it was always the time your grandmother and I sat and visited. Talking things over, dreaming a little…sharing the beauty of this place. Look over there." He pointed to the western horizon, where streaks of violet, peach and orange rioted above the rolling hills.

Living in Chicago had made it easy for Josie to forget the vastness of the plains and the immediacy of sunrises and sunsets. She shivered with pleasure. "It's truly wonderful, Gramps. I'd almost forgotten."

"I remember how you and your grandmother used to wish on the evening star. How'd it go? Star light, star bright..."

Josie joined him. "...I wish I may, I wish I might, have the wish I wish tonight."

He leaned toward her. "What's your wish tonight, Josie?"

Among the rush of responses crowding Josie's brain appeared the face of an earnest brown-eyed deputy sheriff. Josie mentally erased the surprising image and contemplated the question. What would she wish? To have MJ back of course, or to finish her thesis and earn her master's degree, or to find the perfect job after completing her education, or...

"Gramps, I think above all I wish to find a love like yours and MJ's, a love strong enough to withstand pain and loss, a love that serves as an example to others." She paused. "A man to sit with quietly, as we're doing now. A man who appreciates this—" she gestured expansively "—gift of creation."

"I wish that for you, too, honey." Gramps studied her. "Know someone who might fill the bill?"

Josie blushed. Tom's bookish face came immediately to mind, his graying hair, his neatly trimmed mustache, the intelligent gray eyes behind the steel-rimmed glasses. Yet, could the energetic, city-bred Tom slow down long enough just to sit rocking and listening to the night sounds of the prairie?

"Well, maybe. Tom, Dr. Tom Hatcher, is one of the professors on my thesis committee. Right now, we have mainly a teacher-student relationship, although we've been out to dinner a few times and he's been very supportive and attentive. It could develop into something, I suppose.''

Josie had been attracted by Tom's wide-ranging knowledge of ornithology and his persistent work ethic. Complimentary of her papers and field research, he had encouraged her to pursue her thesis topic. His approval and interest meant a great deal to her; she felt safe under his direction.

"You'll know by the sparks, Josie. Always wait for the sparks. Sparks alone aren't enough, but without the sparks, life is very long." As if to emphasize his point, a mourning dove cooed in the distance.

Josie sat quietly, noting the sudden slump of Gramps's shoulders. "How are you, Gramps, really?" she asked. "I know you must be very lonely."

The old man sighed and turned back to face her, his eyes misty. "When your grandmother died, it was like the sun had set permanently. Suddenly there was no MJ. And since I'd just leased the fields to Marvin Haggerty and only kept a few head of cattle, there wasn't much work, either." He sat quietly, barely rocking. "Every reason I had to get up in the morning was gone. MJ. Work. Everything." His gnarled hands folded and refolded in his lap. "But I'm making it, honey. Slowly but surely."

They heard the plaintive call of a second dove, responding to its mate. Gramps rose and stretched. "Early to bed and early to rise. That dove just said it's my bedtime." He leaned over the swing and patted Josie's shoulder with his callused palm. "It's mighty good having you here, honey. Sweet dreams."

BUT DREAMS WOULDN'T come. Sometimes you're just too tired to sleep, Josie rationalized. Besides, a flood of sensations kept her mind racing. The wind soughing through the elms, the faraway hoot of an owl, the glow of the yard light making shadows on the far wall. Josie turned on the bedside lamp, slipped out of bed and opened her suitcase. Earlier, when exhaustion had overcome her, she'd decided she was too tired to finish unpacking. Now she was restless. She'd read somewhere that a sure cure for insomnia was to get up and do something productive. Getting settled—that was productive.

She opened the deep bottom drawer of the bureau, and as she put away her sweatshirts and sweaters, her hand came into contact with a hard rectangular object. She set the clothes on the floor, and reaching into the back of the drawer, pulled out a framed photograph.

Holding it up to the light, her breath caught in her throat as the familiar face gazed out at her, familiar from the many times she'd studied it on MJ's dresser. The face, ever the same—strong-jawed, the expression serious but with just a hint of mischief in the blue eyes, the high forehead crowned by the flight cap set at a jaunty angle. Kevin Patrick Calhoun, her father. The father she'd hardly known.

Josie stood up, clutching the photograph. She traced the inscription with her index finger: "To Mom and Dad with love as big as the Kansas sky, Kev."

Still clutching the photo, she settled into the wooden rocker by the south window. The breeze ruffled her long curly hair as she bent over the frame to search those eyes. How different would her life have been if he'd lived?

She'd been barely three when the doorbell had rung and two tall strangers dressed in blue had made her mother cry. "Killed in action." The words echoed in her ears even now. The moment was one of her few vivid early-childhood memories. "Killed in action over North Vietnam." Afterward she'd suffered nightmares of a sil-

ver plane, spinning endlessly in the sky, trailing smoke.
The dense green of the tropical jungle would loom closer
and closer, but the plane would just keep spinning until
she'd finally jolt awake, sobbing, "Daddy, Daddy!"

This photograph, showing him eternally young, eternally twenty-four, was all she had of him. Twenty-four.
Even younger than I am now, she mused. How she'd
longed for him as a child, longed for him still.

Perhaps if he *had* lived, Cheryl—her mother had never
wanted Josie to call her Mother—wouldn't have started
staying out late, wouldn't have married infantry captain
Gus Kovak, wouldn't have dragged Josie halfway around
the world from one army base to the next. Cheryl—always looking for the fountain of youth, the next adventure, the exciting new place—hated to be reminded that
she was old enough to be someone's mother. Besides,
who wanted a kid with her at the officers' club pool?
Who wanted to hunt for a sitter in the evenings? Cheryl
was always more than happy to dump Josie on MJ and
Gramps, and Josie spent almost every summer and
school vacation with them.

Thank God for her grandparents. The pain of being
the new kid at school, of feeling embarrassed to ask
playmates over, of constantly hearing, "Hey, Red, how's
the weather up there?" was somehow tolerable because
of the certainty that June would deliver her to the safety
of the farm.

Oh, Lord, it was good to be here and staying for a
while. The best years of her girlhood had been the two
when her mother and Gus had been stationed at nearby
Fort Riley and she'd been permitted to live with MJ and
Gramps. To go to the same school with the same friends
for two whole years was a piece of heaven. And now, here

for four whole months, a semester off to complete her thesis.

The breeze coming through the open window was turning cooler. Josie shivered, rose and stood the photo on the top of the bureau. Her fingers brushed across a bit of crumpled white fabric lying on the embroidered runner. Picking it up, she realized that she had driven off with the deputy's handkerchief. Carrying it to the light, she noticed the monogrammed *S* in the corner. She laid it on the bedside table and crawled under the sheet.

She'd have to return the handkerchief. What a fool she'd made of herself! Blubbering and hiccuping, she must have seemed like a big baby. And, Lord, how she must've looked! And yet, he'd been so kind and considerate. She kept seeing those warm brown eyes and his handsome face.

As she reached up to turn out the lamp, her fingers once again closed on the handkerchief, and she fell asleep with it balled in her fist, next to her cheek.

CHAPTER TWO

THE DRONING VOICE of the radio farm reporter awakened him, and Mack struggled to extricate himself from the sheet wadded around his legs. Sitting at the edge of the bed, he ran his fingers through his short hair, yawned, stretched, and then reached over to shut off the radio.

"C'mon, Stranger. Time for our morning run." The rangy black Lab was already standing by the bedroom door, wagging his tail in anticipation. Mack had had the dog only a few months. He'd found him, just a puppy, hanging around the rest area on Interstate 70. He'd loaded him into his patrol car and taken him into headquarters. When, after several days, no ads appeared and no one in the vicinity responded to inquiries, Mack concluded the dog had been abandoned by some traveler passing through. It was just as well no one stepped forth because Stranger, as Mack had dubbed him, decided that Mack was totally his master.

Mack pulled on a pair of gym shorts and his running shoes, went into the kitchen to start the coffee, and then whistled to Stranger to follow him through the back door and out onto the dirt road.

What a lucky break it had been for him to rent the old Britton place. Deputy Wells had told him that Frank Calhoun, after his wife's death last February, had been looking for someone to rent the house his hired hand used to live in, and Mack, cramped in the small, second-story apartment above the drugstore, had jumped at the chance.

Starting slowly and then settling into a comfortably challenging pace, Mack let his mind roam. He'd been tormented yet again last night by a dream that repeated incessantly just after the accident and that periodically hounded him still. Sarah reaching out to him from a distance, then a gradual zooming in to her face, the awful panic etched in her wide blue eyes, her voice crying, "Mack, Mack!"

He increased his pace, his feet pounding the dusty ground. When would it end, this suspension of time? Rationally he knew he should be getting on with his life. Yet he felt paralyzed, going through the motions and following a routine that kept him trapped by the past.

Just last week Sheriff Miller had talked with him about an opportunity to get some additional training from the Kansas Highway Patrol. While Mack always tried to be conscientious about his duties, he knew that, in the long run, he was not cut out for a career in law enforcement. At the time, the job had seemed a productive way to try to atone for Sarah's death and his own responsibility in it; lately, however, he'd felt an increasing need for something, anything, to knock his life onto a meaningful path. He had to start thinking about the future. The old wisdom of taking things one day at a time could get you through the worst times, but eventually you needed to get on with whatever you're meant to do. But he didn't feel ready yet.

Stranger darted up the road, then wheeled in his tracks to bark at Mack. "You silly fella. That's just a bunch of crows. Come." Stranger rejoined him as they turned at the fence corner onto the gravel road leading past the lane to Frank Calhoun's place.

Sweat gathering at Mack's neck beaded his broad heaving chest. He reached into the pocket of his shorts, withdrew a faded blue bandanna and wiped his brow. The early morning heat promised another scorcher.

"Okay, boy," he said to Stranger. "Let's go down to the bridge, rest a minute and head for home."

As Mack turned to retrace his steps, the racing of his blood and the pounding in his temples were invigorating. He'd always thrived on exercise. His work in the oil fields just after high school, as well as his construction jobs in college, had hardened his body and strengthened his muscles.

Back at the house, Mack stripped off his damp running gear and turned on the shower. The steamy water drilled his shoulders and slid over his body in soothing streams. As he reached for the towel before stepping out, the phone rang. "Damn," he muttered, knotting the towel around his waist.

"Hello? ... Oh, hi, Beth Ann.... Yeah, I just got out of the shower.... A week from Sunday? Let me look. No, I'm not on duty then.... A barbecue at your house? ... Sure, I'll be there around five. Thanks."

Count on Beth Ann. Always trying to look after him. Beth Ann Johnson, Sarah's older married sister, had latched onto him after Sarah's death, treated him like a member of the family. He appreciated it, he really did, except...sometimes it just seemed as if she was using him to help keep Sarah alive. As if, as long as she could see him and talk with him, Sarah might simply be waiting in the hallway ready to enter the room. And every now and then, when the light was just right and Beth Ann turned her back to him, he'd momentarily see Sarah, and the pain would sear him anew.

He went into the living room to shut the windows and draw the shades against the heat of the day. Reaching across his desk, he noted the dust on the vinyl cover of his computer. When was the last time he'd touched it? A few pages of his uncompleted manuscript were scattered randomly on the desk. He gathered them up and slipped them into the bulging folder marked The Changing Faces of the Flint Hills.

As he did so, several photographs fell out. He picked them up and idly studied them. One, taken at the highest elevation in the Flint Hills, was of the panicked cattle crowded in the loading chute on Interstate 35; another was of the Knute Rockne Memorial shown in stark relief against a gathering summer storm; and, oh, God, there was the one of the crumbling stone wall offset by the vivid crimsons and wines of the vibrant sumac. That day, when the light was just right and the crisp October air promised nothing but abundance and he'd been with Sarah.

He replaced the photos in the folder, crammed it into the desk drawer and turned his back on the room.

JOSIE STRUGGLED down the stairs with the bulging laundry basket, gratefully setting it on the kitchen table. Gramps looked up from his cereal. "Only home two days and you've dirtied all that?"

Josie poured a cup of steaming coffee. "You know me, Gramps. I'm no clotheshorse. This is all laundry I didn't have time to do before I left Chicago."

Dark circles underlined Josie's eyes. Her blazing mane was drawn into a loose ponytail, and her shapely figure, no longer that of a young girl, was concealed by her jersey nightshirt. "Sleep well?"

"Finally. I confess to having trouble drifting off."

"New place takes some getting used to. Do you have plans for the day?"

Popping a piece of bread into the toaster, Josie grinned and indicated the laundry basket. "First I've got a date with Maytag. Then I thought I'd finish unpacking my books and set up my computer."

"Could you use the old sewing room upstairs for a study? There's a table and a big old desk in there that might be just the ticket."

"That'd be great, Gramps. I'll need to spread out my field notes and books and stuff. Thanks."

"So how's that thesis coming along?"

Josie buttered the toast, shoved the laundry basket to one side and sat down across from her grandfather. "I've gathered all the data I need, but it's time to organize it. I've loved the research, but I'm not looking forward to the writing."

"You always did love birds. I remember when you were a little bit of a thing and tried to climb the mulberry tree to see the 'baby birdies.'" Gramps smiled fondly. "Now you're into bigger birds."

"When I was in Manitoba the summer of my first field excursion, I fell in love with the Canada geese. They were so incredibly graceful and seemed so human in their habits. Selecting a thesis topic was easy. Courtship rituals of the Canada geese. They mate for life, you know."

"Oh, yes, they do indeed. Just like some people." Gramps was quiet.

He was thinking of MJ, of course. To change the subject, Josie extracted a pencil and note pad from the table drawer. "What's on the grocery list? I thought I'd go to town this afternoon, stop by and see Amy, and pick up some groceries."

"You might buy some Milky Ways for my sweet tooth. Other than that, just suit yourself. Frankly, I'm looking forward to your good home cooking and maybe even a little entertaining. It's been a long time since I had folks in. Why don't you ask Amy and Les to supper Saturday evening? That'd be a start."

Later, as Josie loaded the washer, she recalled how good it had been to talk with Amy on the phone the night before and how much she was looking forward to seeing her this afternoon. Amy McDowell, now Peterson, had been her best friend in Maizeville ever since the day in seventh grade they'd both gotten the giggles at the way Miss Lovell, the English teacher, pronounced literature—"lit-er-ah-tooer." Josie couldn't imagine how Amy, who was so petite, would look seven months pregnant, but she'd soon find out.

Funneling the clothes into the roiling water, Josie noticed the wadded, monogrammed handkerchief slip into the suds. She decided she'd better drop it off at the Sheriff's Department that afternoon. The deputy's handsome face swam into her mind as she closed the lid of the washer. She'd probably feel a bit embarrassed if he saw her—her, the walking, talking waterfall. But, she thought, it would be nice to see him again. It'd been a long time since she'd experienced such old-fashioned Midwestern kindness. Yet...was it only his kindness that caused her shortness of breath?

CLUTCHING THE THICK envelope, Josie scampered up the steps of the courthouse. Her hair, swept up with a tortoiseshell clasp, glinted in the sun. After the morning's chores, she'd showered and changed into a pink sleeveless blouse and freshly ironed khaki shorts. The air conditioner hummed as she scanned the lobby directory. There it was—County Sheriff, Room 103.

The elderly woman behind the desk looked frazzled, one hand adjusting the desk radio, another reaching for the ringing telephone. With an arched eyebrow, she acknowledged Josie's presence. "Sheriff's Department . . . Yes, can you hold?" She cupped the phone on her shoulder and looked at Josie. "May I help you?"

Josie proffered the envelope. "Do you have a deputy with the last-name initial of *S?*"

"Oh, sure, you mean Ma—" Just then the sheriff strode briskly into the room.

"Alice, I need the Anderson file ASAP."

Alice gestured helplessly to the phone, then to Josie. "What do you need?"

"Please, if you'll just see that he gets this envelope, I'd appreciate it." Josie handed the envelope over the counter and left the office, feeling, she had to acknowledge, more than a little disappointed.

AMY'S HOUSE, a tan brick 1950s ranch-style, lay toward the edge of town. How far their lives had diverged since those days when their greatest thrill had been fawning over the lifeguard at the municipal pool, Josie reflected. She'd always wanted to go on to college, and Amy, true to Les since her sophomore year in high school, had wanted only to be Mrs. Lester Peterson. Now they both had their dreams. Josie just wished she had a better idea of what she was going to do with hers. She certainly couldn't afford to stay in graduate school forever.

A blue-and-white heart-shaped sign by the front door spelled out Welcome, Friends. A tinny Westminster chime reverberated as Josie pushed the doorbell.

"Josie, it's really you! I can't believe it!" Amy, her round pixie face wreathed in smiles, flung open the door and held out her arms to Josie.

"Hold on. Let me look at you." Josie surveyed her friend's rounded stomach. "No doubt about it. You are going to have a baby. Is there any room for a hug?" Giggling, they fell into each other's arms.

Amy led Josie into the pine-paneled family room and settled her in the recliner-rocker by the picture window overlooking the backyard. "Would you like some lemonade?"

"I'd love it. Did you make all those?" Josie pointed to the entry-hall wall covered with framed cross-stitched pictures of birds and flowers.

"Oh, sure. I enjoy handwork. Right now I'm making a quilt for the baby." Amy went into the kitchen and came back with two tall icy glasses of lemonade. She handed one to Josie. "Would you like to see the nursery?" After the nursery tour and a laugh-filled game of "remember when," the topic turned to Amy's pregnancy.

"Josie, I can't wait to hold this baby. It's what I've wanted my whole life. But...I'm kind of scared about the labor and what life will be like after it comes." Her dark eyes betrayed the depth of her anxiety.

"That's only natural, Amy. All mothers-to-be feel that way." Josie smiled. "Is Les excited, too?"

"Oh, I guess so. He keeps acting like some dumb cock rooster. As if he did this all by himself. I'd like to claim part of the credit. After all, I enjoy the process of making babies, too." Amy smiled wistfully. "But I wish Les would take more interest in how I'm feeling, what kind of car seat we'll need, things like that. He keeps saying I shouldn't have planned a baby to arrive during hunting season, and that if it's a girl, he'll drown it. I know he's just teasing, but..."

Josie winced under the glassy stare of the stuffed mallard mounted over the fireplace. "Les hasn't had a baby before, either. Maybe underneath he's scared, too, and all that talk is just bluster."

"I hope so." Amy sighed. "But to tell you the truth, sometimes I don't know if he even wants the baby. He's preoccupied right now with some big scheme he has to lease some farmland and start a sportsmen's club. He spends more time with his friend Mack riding around looking for just the right property than he does with me." Amy's lower lip quivered. She sighed again. "I'm sorry. Pay no attention to me. I've just got the baby blues. At least that's what my mother tells me."

Josie caught Amy's hand and squeezed it reassuringly. "Just wait until the baby comes. I'll bet Les'll change his tune. Right now the baby probably seems kind of unreal to him."

Amy settled heavily on the sofa. "I hope you're right. Let's change the subject now and talk about you. How's Chicago? Please tell me that Mr. Right has come along."

Josie laughed. "Chicago is just Chicago. Mostly I keep my nose in the books, so I rarely stray far from campus. Oh, a few Cubs games and a concert or two, but nothing very exotic. As for my all-too-dull love life, there hasn't been much excitement since Cal Kerwin back in seventh grade. Remember when we played post office?"

"Yuck! I'd forgotten. Cal was the only one without braces." Amy closed her eyes and mocked a moist first kiss.

"Right now I guess you could say I'm seeing a man. He's one of my professors, so his behavior toward me so far is circumspect but promising."

"Skip the circumspect part and cut right to the promising. I want to hear all the details." Amy adjusted her plaid maternity top over her ample stomach.

"Well, there's not much to tell. He's about forty, never married. He has lovely silvering black hair, nice gray eyes, a trim mustache. He's about five ten and incredibly intelligent."

"Ooh, a mustache. Sexy. How does it feel when he kisses you?"

Josie considered. How *did* it feel? "We've only been out on a few official dates and he's kissed me maybe two or three times. How does it feel? Prickly, I guess."

"Not the mustache, stupid. I mean when his lips touch yours, does electricity zoom through you? Do his experienced hands make you go limp in his arms? Do you think about, you know, doing it on the lab table?"

Josie laughed and threw a crocheted pillow at Amy. "You're too nosy. Anyway, nothing may come of it."

"Well, old friend, you better keep me posted. I love a good romance. Try to recall the graphic details. In my stage of pregnancy, vicarious thrills are about all I can get."

As the clock in the Methodist-church steeple chimed four, Josie stretched her legs and stood to embrace her friend. "Thanks for the chat, and if there're any late-breaking romantic developments, you'll be the first to know. Oops, I almost forgot. Gramps wondered if you and Les could join us for supper Saturday evening."

"I'd like that. Les always plays golf on Saturday afternoons, but if we could come around six-thirty, the answer is yes."

"ALICE, MY LOVE, 'and the hunter is home from the hill.'" Mack strode through the office, tossed his hat on his desk and unstrapped his holster. "Anything I need to know before I head home?"

"Pete Wells is checking on a cow that's been reported loose on Route 3, but that's about it," Alice replied. "Oh, before I forget, there's an envelope on your desk. Nice-looking young lady brought it in." Alice eyed him expectantly. "Mackenzie Scott, is there something you haven't told me?" Mack's genuine bewilderment wilted her hopes. "Nice attractive man like you ought to have more fun."

Mack picked up the envelope. "'Deputy Sheriff S'?" Why just the initial?

He slit the seal with his letter opener. A neatly folded ironed handkerchief fell onto the desk. A piece of note-paper remained in the envelope. Extracting it, Mack read, puzzled at first. Then he reread. "Usually it's the lady who drops her handkerchief. Thanks for dropping yours. With appreciation, Gray Honda."

Mack stuffed the handkerchief and note into his breast pocket and broke into a grin as he recalled the brimming green eyes of the attractive redhead. "Alice, there's nothing to tell." He turned the note over in his hand, disappointed to find no clue as to Gray Honda's identity.

JOSIE CLOSED the cattle gate behind her as she started up the pasture behind the house. The old wall at the far end was the highest point on Gramps's land and offered a panorama of the nearly lake-size farm pond, silvering in the setting sun, and of fields sprawling to Persimmon Creek where a windrow of dark green cedars bordered the horizon.

All through their supper of cold cuts, potato salad and watermelon, Josie had anticipated the moment she would sit once again by the wall, her special place. She wouldn't feel that she'd truly come home until then.

Carefully avoiding the cow patties, she crested the hill. A shiver of delight ran through her as, looking in all directions, she reacquainted herself with each remembered detail—the Haggertys' red barn, the north milo field, the huge mulberry tree down in the draw, the duck blind on the far shore of the pond. Of all the places on the farm, it was here that she most belonged, here that she felt she was indeed mistress of all that she surveyed, and here where those childhood seeds planted by MJ had most taken root.

She sighed with contentment as she sat down, leaning against the warm stones of the fence. Home at last. At least for a while. She recalled her last conversation with Tom in Chicago. He'd asked her about her plans after she finished her degree. And though she knew it made sense to try to find a teaching position at a college, she'd responded that what she really wanted was an outdoor job, particularly one in waterfowl management. Tom's answer had disturbed her.

"That's really hard work, and most of the jobs go to men, but if you think you'd like to apply at some colleges, I could help you. Besides, if you were off in the wilds of Canada, how could I see you? And I like seeing you."

She remembered the gray eyes, liquid with promise. Darn. Life had been safe and uncomplicated as long as she was going to classes and studying. Perhaps these months on the farm working on her thesis would help her find some answers.

A hawk whirred overhead and swooped toward its prey, hidden in the tall grass near the edge of the pond. Josie, admiring his grace and strength, watched the age-old ritual of predator-victim. Although an acknowledged, even necessary, part of nature, it nevertheless always caused her to shudder slightly.

Her gaze was drawn to the dam at the end of the pond. A man and a dog stood on top of it, the pair silhouetted against the setting sun. The man signaled the dog to sit and then he threw a stick into the water. He gave a hand sign and the dog, a black arc, leapt into the water and swam toward the object. She could hear the man clap and yell something. The dog turned and, with stick in tow, swam to shore.

While they continued repeating the maneuver, Josie pulled a foxtail, stretched out on her back to enjoy the changing colors of the sky and thought again about that last evening with Tom. He'd leaned across the dinner table, enclosing her hand in his dry cool grasp. "Josie, dear girl, how can I help you with the answers? I do want to, you know." She'd felt like such a fool. The wise older man and the dewy-eyed ingenue. "And I think I have at least one very good idea for your future." Josie had felt a frisson of panic and hadn't dared to ask the nature of his "very good idea."

She bit into the succulent stem of the foxtail, remembering the tide of conflicting emotions she'd felt—hopefulness, uncertainty, relief, fear. Why fear? And what had Amy said today? "Let me know all the graphic details." What were they? A feeling of security and safety when she was with Tom, as if she could once again be a little girl. His embraces comforted her, as did his kisses, formal and circumspect. There was that word again— "circumspect." It hardly caused one to—how had Amy put it?—go "limp in his arms." In all fairness, Josie thought as she chewed on the stem, she and Tom needed more time.

The sounds from the pond were coming closer. Laughter, splashing and barking. Josie sat up, slowly brushing the dried grass from her back. On the near bank she noticed a pile of clothes. In the water she could see two figures, a black dog swimming side by side with a man whose powerful strokes were keeping pace. Treading water, the man stopped and splashed the dog, who swam to him, licked his face and then turned to shore. The dog scrambled up the bank and stood shaking himself with pleasure. The man breaststroked toward the shore and when it was shallow enough, stopped swimming and stood.

Josie gasped. Wading toward her through waist-deep water was a well-built man, his broad shoulders and chest tanned a golden honey, a V of brown-gold hair drawing the eye toward his taut waist—and beyond. Josie was mesmerized. Her limited experience had not prepared her for this sudden rush of embarrassment and pleasure.

She sat still as a stone, aware of a powerful, even alarming, aliveness within her—almost primal in its urgency. As the initial shock and thrill subsided, Josie dared to look down again at the man. The short curly brown hair, the honest face, the deep-set eyes, all seemed very familiar. Josie's breath caught in her throat.

S. Dear Lord, it was the deputy! She hoped he wouldn't spot her. Sitting motionless as a statue, her pulse pounding, she prayed for premature darkness. A sudden breeze raised goose bumps on her skin and made her nipples tauten visibly against the fabric of her blouse.

"Come on, Stranger. That's enough for tonight." The man stepped into his shorts and pulled a T-shirt over his well-muscled shoulders. As the sun sank over the pond, man and dog walked across the dam and into the trees, disappearing from view.

Josie, disturbed by her involuntary arousal and fear of discovery, took her time crossing the pasture back to the house. She was aware something definitive had happened, though she couldn't for the life of her say what or why. She let herself quietly in through the back screen door.

"Josie, that you?" Gramps called from the living room.

Josie composed herself, wiping her damp hands on her shorts, and walked into the room. "I'm back from my walk."

Gramps turned the volume of the television down momentarily. "Say, before I forget, I was down to the mailbox today and saw the feller who rents the old Britton place. He's been kind of lonely, so I invited him to join us Saturday night for supper when Amy and Lester come. Hope that's okay."

MACK RUBBED a hand over his sandpapery jaw as he stood at the mirror. He plugged in the razor and pulling his skin taut, ran it over his cheek.

He was looking forward to dinner with Frank Calhoun, whose company he enjoyed. Since moving to the Britton place, he had spent several late-summer afternoons with Frank up at the pond fishing. Frank had stocked the pond with bass and catfish and allowed only a few select pals to fish there. Mack had felt privileged.

The loss of his wife had clearly been a blow to Frank, an emptiness Mack felt echoing in himself. Drawing the razor over his chin, he remembered Frank's advice when Mack had asked him how he got through each day.

"One foot in front of the other, son. I'll always miss her. She was the other half of me. MJ and I were sort of like the wild geese, together in all seasons." Frank had pointed to a hillock at the far north end of the pond. "See over yonder? That's where the geese nest in the spring. Same pair every year. Amazing. Geese mate for life. When one dies, the other one keeps calling and swimming in circles, searching for the mate."

He paused. "Some days that's what I think I'm doing, just swimming in circles." Mack knew that feeling all too well. "But men aren't geese. We can't keep swimming in circles, much as we wish the impossible would happen and the mate would return. There are no easy answers, son. But you're young and have so much ahead of you. Sarah's gone. She would want you to make room in your heart for another woman—a mate to share your journey."

Now from the image in the bathroom mirror, Mack's eyes reflected both the gratitude he felt for Frank's wisdom and the doubt that he could ever again love as he had loved Sarah.

After splashing on some after-shave, he scooped up his change and keys and dropped them into his pocket. All he needed now was his handkerchief. It was still in the envelope and sitting on top of the bureau. With the trace of a smile, he took out the handkerchief and stuck it in his hip pocket.

JOSIE PUT the last setting of silverware on the table and stood back to admire the arrangement—Blue Willow on white linen, stemmed cobalt goblets and a colorful centerpiece of zinnias and marigolds. Mentally reviewing the menu—chicken tetrazzini in the oven, green salad in the refrigerator ready to be tossed, rolls rising, peach pie cooling—Josie smiled in anticipation.

Whistling "Little Brown Jug," Gramps stuck his head through the doorway. "Looks nice, honey." Resuming his whistling, he wandered out to the front porch to wait for the company. Josie was touched by the twinkle in his eye and spring in his step. Much of the time he seemed at loose ends, bravely trying to conceal his pain. The dinner party had been a good idea.

Interrupted in checking the progress of the rolls by the shrill of the telephone, Josie picked up the receiver.

The caller was Amy. "Josie," she said. "I'm sorry to cancel out on you at the last minute, but Les isn't home from the golf course yet. I expected him around five, but...sometimes he hangs around the grill room and plays cards."

Josie chewed on her lip as she detected the disappointment and hurt in her friend's voice. "Listen, Amy, why don't you leave a note for Les and come on by yourself?"

Amy hesitated. "I don't think Les would like that. He gets upset when I go off and do something on my own. I'm really sorry, Josie."

"We'll try it another time, then. We'll miss you." Josie replaced the receiver, her jaw tightening as she thought of Les's total lack of consideration for his wife.

Peeking once again at the rising dough, Josie heard a car coming up the lane. Must be Gramps's guest, the fellow renting the Britton place. Gramps hadn't told her much about him, just that he seemed lonely and the two of them had done some fishing together. As she untied her apron and started toward the front porch, she heard Gramps saying, "Glad you could make it, Mack."

Josie laid the apron on a chair and strolled onto the porch. The men had their backs to her, Gramps pointing out the view to a tall well-built man dressed in sharply pressed denim pants and a short-sleeved plaid shirt. They turned to face her.

Josie stopped dead in her tracks, swaying slightly as she felt the blood first drain from her face and then return with a colorful rush.

"Mack, this is my granddaughter, Josie. Josie, may I present Mackenzie Scott, our neighbor." The buzzing in her head made Gramps's words sound as if they were muffled in flannel.

The young man extended his right hand, clasping hers in a warm firm grip, and then covered their entwined hands with his left. "Miss Gray Honda, I presume." The brown eyes hinted of laughter.

"How do you do, Mr. Mackenzie, er, Mr. Scott." With difficulty, and, she had to admit, reluctance, she removed her hand and lowered her head to hide the blush suffusing her face.

Gramps stared from one to the other. "Do you two know each other?"

"No!" Josie said.

"Yes," Mack said simultaneously.

Gramps chuckled. "Well, which is it?"

Mack searched Josie's face and seemed to read her concern. "Let's put it this way, Frank. We've seen each other on the road." Josie signaled a silent thanks with her eyes. "But please, do call me Mack," he said to her. "Everyone else does."

As soon as she could tactfully withdraw, Josie made an excuse about the food and fled into the kitchen. *S.* Scott. Mackenzie Scott. Oh, Lord! She put her hands on the counter and leaned over, willing her heart to stop pounding. Those eyes, that face and, great Jehoshaphat, that body!

Get hold of yourself, girl. He's just the nice deputy sheriff who helped you over a rough moment. But then the thought came again. *He's just the nice deputy sheriff*

*who helped you over a rough moment and who has the
most incredible naked body you've ever seen.*

It was only with difficulty that she managed a pass-
able attempt at conversation during dinner. Gramps and
Mack didn't seem to notice her problem. They talked
politics, farm prices, prospects for the hunting season. As
she cleared the main-course dishes, she could hear
snatches of their conversation. "Hunting lease . . . forty
or fifty members . . . extra income." Men! Hunting! But
the dinner party was going smoothly. Why ruin it by giving them a strong dose of her antihunting sentiments?
Another time maybe.

Cutting into the warm pie, Josie perked up as she heard
Gramps ask, "How long did you work in the oil fields?"

"When I graduated from high school, I didn't have a
clue what I wanted to do with my life. The boom was at
its peak and a kid could make great money working in the
oil fields. I spent three years, back in the early eighties,
thinking the money'd go on forever. Then came the
bust."

Josie had no difficulty imagining his young body, back
bared to the sun, assembling a rig. She saw his thick wavy
hair damp with perspiration as he removed his hard hat,
heard his deep laughter in response to a co-worker's jest,
smelled the man smell of—

"Isn't that right, Josie?" What had Gramps just been
talking about? "Looks like that girl's been woolgather-
ing." Gramps winked at Mack. "I was just telling Mack
you'll be starting on your thesis this week."

"The thesis? Oh, yes, I've got a big job in front of
me."

"Your grandfather tells me you're doing research on
the Canada geese."

"Yes, on the courtship rituals." Courtship rituals! Good heavens, she needed to get onto a safe subject, one that didn't cause her to turn as red as the Haggertys' barn. "What did you do, Mack, after the oil fields dried up?"

"After three years of hard labor, I thought I was entitled to a bit of fun, so I went out to Colorado and worked for a couple of years doing whatever I could— waiting tables, operating ski lifts, working construction—until I decided it was time to get on with my education. Then I came back to Kansas and eventually graduated from Kansas State."

Josie was about to ask him what sort of degree he had when Gramps interjected. "Mack's a deputy sheriff here. Doing a good job, too, according to his boss." Gramps smiled approvingly.

A deputy sheriff. As if she didn't know. Here was the most attractive man she'd seen in a good long while, and at their first meeting she'd been a pathetic sobbing wreck.

"Great pie, Josie." Mack's appreciative eyes fixed on her. "We single guys don't usually get good home-cooked meals."

Josie flushed with pleasure. "Why don't you two go on out to the porch? I'll join you when I get the dishes cleaned up."

"My mother always used to say, 'Don't leave the table empty-handed.' Let me clear the table and then I'll sit on the porch with Frank." Mack shoved back his chair, picked up their three pie plates in his capable hands and followed Josie into the kitchen.

As she rinsed the plates and silverware, the lingering presence of Mack's woodsy after-shave filled her with a peculiar uneasy longing. When he'd set the dishes on the

counter next to the sink, she'd had to resist the temptation to reach out and touch the hard solidity of his
shoulder. What in the world had come over her? She
dawdled over the dishes, delaying the inevitable moment
she would join the men on the porch.

When at last she did, she sat at the other end of the
porch swing from Mack and observed the two men.
Gramps, rocking slowly back and forth, was well into one
of his favorite hunting stories—the one about the time he
fell through the ice. Mack, gently pushing the swing with
one foot, listened attentively, chuckling at the appropriate points.

Josie studied his profile—well-defined eyebrows ac-
centuating his deep-set gentle eyes, a slightly crooked
nose, perhaps the result of some injury, full lips and a
resolute jaw. His fingers, laced together in his lap, looked
strong and capable. The veins on the back of his hand
stood in clear relief against his tanned skin.

Mack turned to look at her. "Do you miss Chicago,
Josie?"

"Not really. I guess I'm a country girl at heart." She
gestured with her arm at the expanse before them. "Look
at that. The rolling hills, the profusion of growing things,
and that immense sky. When I was a little girl, I thought
that everything I could see from this porch belonged just
to me."

"You know," he said. "I really liked Colorado. The
skiing and trout-fishing were great and the scenery was
spectacular—snow-covered peaks, rushing streams, fields
of columbine. I enjoyed living there. But always there
was something pulling me back to Kansas."

Gramps stopped his rocking and looked at Mack.
"Funny thing, some folks can't understand why we love

it here. They speed through the state in such a goldarned hurry that all they see is flatness and dust. They don't take the time to appreciate the special beauty."

"Kansas is a land of nuance and subtlety," Mack observed. "Just the play of light and shadow on a ripe wheat field is a picture in itself."

"I couldn't sell that in Chicago." Josie laughed. "Let's just keep Kansas a secret for the special few." She felt herself relaxing, enjoying the thread of harmony among them.

A scarf of blue-pink clouds partially shrouded the setting sun, and a mourning dove sounded its three-note call in the distance—hoo-hoo-hoooo, the last syllable hanging in the dusk.

Gramps resumed rocking. "This daylight savings time seems out of kilter with nature," he said. "Used to be a man would get up with the cock and go to bed with the sun. Nowadays, I have to think about what time it is."

"It's only a little past eight-thirty, Gramps."

"Eight-thirty?" The rocking ceased. "Well, I'll be. Almost my bedtime." He stood up.

Mack, too, rose to his feet. "I'd better be getting on home."

Before she could stop herself, Josie reached out and touched his tanned arm. "Please don't go yet." Good grief. Why had she blurted that out?

"Josie's right. Please don't go on my account. Stay and keep this granddaughter of mine company for a while." Gramps shook Mack's hand. "We enjoyed having you for supper, young man. Hope you'll come again soon." Josie detected a sparkle in Gramps's eye as he sauntered into the house.

Now that Mack and she were alone, she was desperate for conversation. Why had she asked him to stay? What could they talk about? "Would you like another piece of pie?"

"It was mighty good, thanks, but I'm full up to here." He leveled his hand in front of his Adam's apple.

He continued pushing the swing in a slow rhythmic motion. The cicadas' drone became almost deafening. Neither Josie nor Mack spoke, and Josie began to feel desperate.

"I wanted—" she began.

"Do you—" he began at the same time.

They both laughed. "You first," she said.

"No, ladies first." He gazed intently at her.

With a voice full of all the frogs in the pond, she croaked, "I wanted you to stay so...so I could thank you for the other day. And for realizing that I hadn't told Gramps about going to pieces when I saw the oak."

He smiled. "Helping damsels in distress is part of the job. I'm glad I was there."

Josie could feel the warmth emanating from those delicious brown eyes. He seemed to empathize with her need to cry that day. "Well, at any rate, I appreciated it."

"I didn't know then," he said, "that your grandmother was MJ Calhoun. Although I didn't know her very well, she was always kind to me, and I've heard many fine things about her." He paused. "Would it help to talk about her? You must have loved her very much."

Josie felt warmed by his sympathy, yet wondered about the hint of pain she saw in his eyes. "Yes, I did love her very much, and I'll never stop missing her. She and Gramps were about all the family I had. Cheryl, that's my mother—she hates me to call her anything but

Cheryl—loved me in her own way, I suppose. But after my father was killed, she just felt...overwhelmed, and couldn't cope with a daughter. My happiest times growing up were here on this farm." Why was she telling him all this? She was babbling.

"What do you remember especially about your grandmother?"

Josie considered the question. "Everywhere I look, she's here. In the flowers I cut for the centerpiece, in the recipes I pull from her old cookbooks, in the photo albums on the shelf in my bedroom. She made this place a home for me, not just with her great cooking or the things she made, but with her hugs, her scoldings, our late-night talks on this porch—everything." Josie shrugged. She could feel the sting of tears behind her lids. "You know what I mean?"

"Yes." Mack reached over and took her hands in his. "I don't know whether it's any comfort or not, but I know how it feels to miss someone who's gone."

She saw the grief in his eyes. Just as he said, "Say, this is getting a little heavy," Josie felt a telltale tear trickle down her cheek.

"Oh, no, here I go again, the Lady of the Lake." Josie struggled for composure and then grinned through her tears as Mack stood up, sketched a little bow and whipped an all-too-familiar handkerchief out of his hip pocket.

"May I possibly be of service?" he asked as he offered her the square of white linen. Gratefully she accepted it and then blew her nose in a loud most unladylike manner. "Now tell me all about being a deputy sheriff."

"Not until I get that piece of pie. I've gotten a second wind."

NEAR MIDNIGHT, with James Cagney curled at her feet, Josie lay in bed listening to the sound of the breeze in the elm tree and the occasional bug hitting the screen. She found herself resurrecting every detail of the evening. The casualness, the warmth, the comfort of Mack. Yet buried just below the surface of his vigorous masculinity was an undeniable sweetness and vulnerability.

After he'd finished the pie, they'd sat, swaying back and forth in the swing in companionable silence watching one brilliant star after another begin to flicker in the blue-black sky. Then quietly, as if to himself, he'd recited, " 'It is a beauteous evening, calm and free,/The holy time is quiet as a Nun/Breathless with adoration; the broad sun/Is sinking down in its tranquillity...' "

She'd raised her brows questioningly. "William Wordsworth." He'd smiled, and then looked contemplative.

Moved by the recollected words, Josie threw off the sheet and let the breeze caress her body. What a strange and wonderful night! A deputy sheriff, an oil-rig worker, a fisherman, a poet and...a model for Michelangelo. She felt the heat of desire rising within her as she turned over, determinedly socked the pillow and once again reached over to the nightstand to retrieve a white handkerchief.

CHAPTER THREE

THE FOLLOWING SATURDAY, just after dawn, Josie sat straight up in bed, startled awake by the sound of shots fired from the draw between the house and the county road.

James Cagney jumped to the floor and scooted down the hall as Josie flung on her robe and ran to the window. Through the branches of the elm, she spotted the camouflage hats and vests of three hunters standing near the south fence line, emptying the shells of their shotguns. A liver-and-white Brittany spaniel cleared the big cedar tree, a blue-gray dove dangling from its mouth. The dog circled its master and dropped the bird, lifeless, on the ground.

Josie ground her teeth in frustration. What a start to the Labor Day weekend! Men, puffed up with their own importance, proving themselves by killing defenseless birds. Each animal had a special purpose for which it was created. Who did these arrogant hunters think they were to interfere with that life cycle?

As the men shouldered their shotguns and started up the fencerow toward the pond, she turned abruptly from the window and pulled on jeans, sweatshirt and running shoes. Damn them! What presumption to hunt here! They could hunt if they must, but *not* on Calhoun land. The nerve!

Huffing and puffing, she set off through the pasture in hot pursuit, her heart pounding with exertion and indignation. She saw the three figures pause at the corner fence post to raise the barbed wire to let the dog through. She cupped her hands.

"Stop right there," she hollered. Their broad backs to her, they appeared to be ignoring her as she raced over the last intervening yards. "Get off this land! What are you doing here?" Breathless, she faced them, hands planted on her hips.

As they turned toward her, tilting the bills of their hunting caps back on their foreheads, Josie gasped in surprise. Mack, Les Peterson and a blond sullen-looking teenage boy stared at her with irritation.

"What's it look like? Mack, Clay and I are dove-hunting, that's what." Les curled his lip in annoyance. "That is, if you haven't scared off every dove in the county."

Josie, aware of Mack's silent contemplation, found herself wilting. But, damn it, they had no business being here! "Look, this is Calhoun land, and as long as I'm here, there'll be no hunting on it. Period." Josie felt her anger mounting.

"Well, little lady, you just may have to rethink that." Les turned to hold a strand of barbed wire for the boy to climb through the fence.

Mack stopped him with a hand on the shoulder. "Hold it, Les. There's obviously been a misunderstanding here." Les paused. The short wiry teenager leaned cockily against the fence post as Mack turned back to Josie. "Are you aware that your grandfather gave us permission to hunt here?"

Josie dug in like a rebellious eleven-year-old. "No, but that doesn't change the fact that I want you off this land." She looked into Mack's troubled eyes, noting the determined set of his jaw. "I will not tolerate the shooting of birds. It's sadistic and pointless."

"I'm sorry you feel that way, Josie. I'd have thought that a zoologist would have been taught about the importance of culling the flocks."

Josie grimaced as she recalled the words of her wildlife-ecology teacher: "Nature is cruel and the flocks will be culled, whether by predators, disease, starvation or hunters. Controlled and responsible hunting, though protested by some, is nevertheless perhaps less cruel than some of the other forms of flock reduction."

Intellectually she understood his statement; emotionally she couldn't accept it. Especially with the geese. Watching a gander search for a mate, court her, nest with her, guard her and their eggs during the brood, soar together on the cold autumnal winds, she'd developed a reverence for them, felt a unique bond with them. No way would she put up with these three oafs killing doves. And just let any hunter even try to blow her beloved geese out of the sky!

"Look. You've had your fun. Why don't you just leave?" Josie refused to back down.

Les rolled his eyes. "Give it a rest, Josie. Who's in charge here? You or Frank?"

Mack took off his cap, wiping his wrist over his damp hair. "As a matter of fact, Josie, we're through hunting for the day. We have our limit. Right now we're just walking over to the pond to take a look. No shooting, I promise. May we have permission to cross your land?" His tone, she sensed, was faintly mocking.

Josie felt his scrutiny. Was he disappointed in her? Had she overreacted? She stifled the thought that she'd made a fool of herself. She was right, she knew she was. But... if Gramps had given permission?

"Okay. Sounds fair enough. I apologize for my behavior. I had no right to be such a shrew. But you need to understand I have very strong convictions about the cruelty of hunting. I'll talk with my grandfather, but until then, I'd appreciate it if you'd find another killing field."

She heard the teenager mutter, "Jeez, get a life, lady."

Mack draped an arm around the boy's shoulder. "Easy, Clay. Let's do like the lady says." They moved to where Les was again holding the fence for them.

With as much dignity as she could muster, Josie turned and strode toward the house. *Men!*

As the kitchen screen door slammed shut behind her, James Cagney padded in from the hallway, eyed Josie and set up an insistent meowing. She looked down at his bulging sides. "Think it's time to eat, do you? Okay, fatso, let's get some breakfast."

As she opened the refrigerator, Josie grimaced as a cluster of shots from the direction of the Haggerty farm broke the tranquillity of the morning. More damn hunters.

ROLLING THE OLD swivel chair away from the desk, Josie stretched her arms over her head and hunched one shoulder, then the other, to ease the cramp at the base of her neck. Looking at the computer screen, she felt a sense of triumph. There before her was the first statistical graph for her thesis, in correct form at last. After pushing Save, she left the document and went to a blank screen. "Dear Tom..." she began.

What could she say? "I'm finally settled here to the point that I have spent the last couple of weeks dutifully working on my thesis." How sophomoric! Of *course* she was working on her thesis. He was the teacher and that was what he expected her to be doing.

She pressed Delete and started again. "I'm finally settled here and relishing the peace and quiet after the busy summer-school session." That sounded neutral. "My grandfather seems to enjoy having the company after those months alone following my grandmother's death...."

She completed that paragraph with a quick summary of recent events. Lifting her fingers to massage the back of her neck, she considered telling him about her dove-hunting outburst. Would he sympathize or merely grin wryly at her emotionalism? In truth, even Gramps had remonstrated with her gently when she'd confronted him about the three hunters.

"Honey," he'd said, "fellers in these parts have been hunting ever since they were little tykes. The good times they have talking and tramping through the fields together are worth more than the few birds they kill."

Despite Gramps's endorsement, Josie still couldn't see how thinking people, especially people she cared about, could sanction slaughter.

Hunching her shoulders, she placed her fingers on the keyboard and stared at the computer screen. Probably she should ask Tom about himself. "You must be getting ready for the start of the fall term, aren't you? I'll be interested in hearing about your classes and how you feel about your chances to be named head of the department."

Dear Lord, the whole thing sounded so blah. It was hard to find just the right balance between formality and familiarity.

How to end the letter? The one she'd received from him, vivid and whimsical in its description of his vacation trip to the Maine coast, had been signed, "Love, Tom." Now what did that mean? Lots of people signed letters "Love." But if she did it, wasn't that a bit presumptuous of her as his student and premature of her as his...his...whatever she was?

Finally she settled for "Affectionately," activated the printer and watched her lame words clatter into permanence.

MACK LEANED ACROSS the steering wheel to adjust the volume of the old Dan Fogelberg song "The Leader of the Band."

The day had been cooler, hinting of autumn. When Beth Ann had called to remind him about the barbecue this evening, he'd welcomed the prospect, wedged as it was between two demanding patrol shifts over the busy Labor Day weekend. Yesterday had not been so bad, but tomorrow would be intense.

Easing his Ford Bronco to a stop at the intersection of the highway, Mack looked in both directions before pulling out. From the corner of his eye as he glanced left, he caught sight of the broad leafy branches of the Pioneer Oak, burnished golden green in the rays of the setting sun. It had been just about this time of day when he'd first seen Josie Calhoun, her emerald eyes awash with tears.

She was an interesting mixture: sad little girl, missing her beloved grandmother; ambitious capable young woman, bent on proving herself as an ornithologist; and obstinate temperamental firecracker single-handedly taking on causes. He winced as he recalled their confrontation over the hunting yesterday morning. Life would never be dull with her around; Frank's open delight with her and his new lease on life made that apparent.

Mack smiled as he remembered her confusion when she'd recognized him that night on the porch a week ago. The blush had spread becomingly upward from her generous mouth to her straight slightly flared nose, past those wide green eyes to the roots of her naturally curly red hair. Her momentary disorientation had given him pause to take in the tall loose-limbed young woman before him, dressed in a simple full-flowing denim skirt topped by a scoop-neck peasant blouse, which revealed full breasts tapering to a slim waist.

He'd enjoyed the hearty home-cooking and the easy natural conversation with Frank and Josie. The perfection of the quiet summer evening wrapping about the three of them had brought him a sense of peace. It was good to be with people who valued simple things.

As he turned onto Chestnut Street now, the Johnsons' large Dutch Colonial house loomed before him, dominating the block. The deep front yard, almost totally shaded by three ancient oaks, looked refreshingly cool. Mack pulled to a stop at the curb, noting the royal blue Dodge Ram pickup carelessly parked facing him on the wrong side of the street. As he turned off the ignition, he was struck suddenly by a disconcerting thought. Tonight was the first time he'd seen the Pioneer Oak without automatically thinking of Sarah and feeling overcome by a sense of loss and guilt.

"Mack! It's so good to see you." Beth Ann swung open the front door. The top of her immaculately coiffed blond head reached only to his shoulder. Standing on tiptoe, she gave him a sisterly hug and a kiss on the cheek, then tucked her arm in his and led him through the entry hall into the kitchen-family room.

"Now sit right down there," she said, indicating a bar stool drawn up to the counter, "and tell me all about what you've been doing while I finish tossing this salad." Moving lightly like a dancer across the room, Beth Ann smoothed the skirt of her flowered polished-cotton sundress, which fit her small-boned figure like a doll's costume. "What would you like? Lemonade or beer?"

Before Mack could answer, Beth Ann's husband, Ralph, balancing a roasting pan, hot pads and tongs, slid open the patio door and barely made it to the counter without spilling the heap of barbecued ribs.

"Close call." He grinned, wiping his hands on a kitchen towel before shaking hands with Mack. "Long time, no see. We're glad you could make it." Ralph's high forehead and thinning hair made him look older than his forty years, but his engaging grin and gentle eyes suggested a warmth of character. "Give this man a beer, woman."

"Did I hear somebody say 'beer'?" Clay Johnson bounded into the room, relieved his mother of the open bottle in her hand, took a healthy swig and then grinned puckishly as he handed it back to her. "Hey, Mack. Great to see you, man." The two exchanged high fives.

"Fifteen-year-olds have no business drinking beer," Ralph said firmly.

Clay faced his father. "Hey, Dad, it was only a sip. Chill out. It's no big deal."

"For starters, son, it's against the law."

Beth Ann slid over and put her arms around Ralph's waist. "It *was* only a sip, sweetheart. I'd rather he try it at home than somewhere else."

Uncomfortable with the potential for disharmony, Beth Ann redirected the conversation. "Mack, did you see Clay's new truck?"

"You mean the one that's illegally parked out front?" Mack couldn't suppress his grin.

"Jeez, Mack. Give me a break. I'm leaving again in a minute." Seeing the dubious upthrust of Mack's eyebrows, he added. "I know, I know. I have to have a licensed driver with me." He rolled his eyes. "Sometimes, buddy, it's a big pain your being a deputy sheriff. Jeff Bramledge—age *seventeen*—is going with me."

Deliver me from ever again having to be a fifteen-year-old, Mack thought as he trailed the youngster to the front door. Fifteen was a tough age. He'd always liked Clay. He was basically a good kid, but he had his mother buffaloed. "Take it easy out there, fella." Mack waved Clay on his way.

Later, sitting at the dining-room table, Mack could see past the archway into the family room. There, on the grand piano, were three framed pictures. From one of them, Sarah's lovely timeless gaze pierced his heart.

Beth Ann leaned over to him, placing a delicate manicured hand on his forearm. "She was beautiful, wasn't she? I know you miss her as much as I do."

Mack mumbled the expected response. This was a ritual he and Beth Ann followed at each encounter, Beth Ann finding a way to begin a discussion of Sarah, fixing her eyes on Mack so as to prolong and nurture her own pain by feeding on his.

"Her birthday is coming up soon. She would have been twenty-eight. I still can't believe she's gone. Just think, Mack, you two would probably have been married by now." Beth Ann's lashes, fringed with mascara, closed over her blue eyes.

Mack shifted in his chair, picked up his fork and, head down, attacked the remains of the scalloped potatoes.

"For God's sake, Beth Ann, let the man eat his meal. This kind of talk won't bring Sarah back. It's been a year and a half and, sure we miss her, but we all need to get on with our lives."

Beth Ann's body stiffened and became strangely still. She slowly turned to pin Ralph with a cold stare. "Don't you ever minimize my love for my sister." Still glaring at her husband, she moved her right hand to Mack's left and absently patted it, as if including him in her ultimatum.

After dessert, she pulled her organizer notebook out of a kitchen drawer and opened it to a November calendar page. Pointing an index finger triumphantly to a date, she announced in no uncertain terms, "Mack, on this Saturday, you are going to do me a tremendous favor."

"I am?"

"You are. It's already settled. I've told the Harvest Festival Committee, so you can't back out on me now." She smiled smugly.

"Hold on a minute, Beth Ann. What are you talking about?" Mack felt stirrings of discomfort.

"You, brother dear..."

Did she have to call him that? He knew why she did, but it still made him cringe.

"...are going to exhibit your photography at the arts-and-crafts show at the Harvest Festival." She glowed in triumph.

"What the hell? You've got to be nuts!"

"Never more sane, brother dear. You've been hiding your light under a bushel for far too long. Sarah showed me some of the pictures you took of her and of the Kansas landscape. They'll be just the thing for the festival."

"Beth Ann, I haven't touched my camera in months. And even if I had, I don't think what I've got is exhibit caliber."

"Nonsense. It's about time you shared your talent instead of just riding all over the county with a gun on your hip."

"No. It's out of the question."

She moved to perch beside him on the sofa, one arm draped across his shoulders, effectively pinning him to the seat. "Please don't disappoint me, Mack. Sarah would've wanted you to do this. She wanted the world to see your talent. If you won't do it for me, do it for her."

At the end of the evening, as Ralph followed him out to the curb, Mack asked, "Where did Clay's truck come from? He's not even sixteen."

Ralph shook his head. "I know. Beth Ann dipped into her trust fund. She can't seem to deny him anything. 'An early sixteenth birthday present,' she said. When I take a different position from hers, like I did with this truck, it always sends her into a tailspin that ends up in a discussion about how I don't understand her feelings about Sarah's death."

"That's tough, Ralph," Mack said sympathetically.

"I noticed tonight, Mack, that you got some of the brunt of Beth Ann's preoccupation with her grief. I'm sorry. I don't know what gets into her. Some days everything seems to go along all right, but then she dredges it all up again. She just can't seem to leave it." Ralph sighed and stared for a long moment into space. "I see she's trying to hold you captive to her grief, but, man, you're young. You can't live forever with only a memory." Ralph patted Mack's shoulder forlornly before saying good-night and walking pensively up the sidewalk.

Driving home through the inky moonless night, Mack tried to put his finger on what made him so uncomfortable about Beth Ann. At first, resurrecting their mutual memories of Sarah had served as a kind of catharsis. Beth Ann had hung so attentively on his every word about Sarah, forcing from him words pulled from the depths of his grief. And the pictures she'd painted in his mind with her stories about Sarah had, for a while, kept Sarah alive. With time, however, the stories became set pieces, and the images turned from flesh to cardboard. Rather than bringing Sarah closer to him, Beth Ann's insistence on shared sorrow pushed the real Sarah farther and farther away.

As the headlights focused on the Persimmon Creek bridge, Mack wondered why, in heaven's name, he'd agreed to Beth Ann's preposterous request about the festival. He cursed himself. No one but Sarah and one or two others had seen his photography since college. Now he'd agreed to have it on display for the whole county. Damn!

THE NORTHWEST WIND whipped the Stars and Stripes around the flagpole and swirled the dust underfoot as Frank and Josie threaded their way through the cars parked in the pasture adjacent to the football field. The lights illuminating the field were beacons, drawing the crowd of jostling students and townsfolk to the time-worn bleachers for the first home football game. In the west end zone, Josie could see the band members poised to march onto the field.

"Hi, Smitty. Just watch these Tigers!" Gramps waved at his buddy from the feed store. Scanning the crowd, Josie noted grade-school kids running back and forth under and behind the bleachers, bundled grannies

planted beside their husbands, proud fathers of the
players huddled on the sidelines discussing game strategy, and rosy-cheeked giddy Pep Club girls anticipating
the arrival on the field of their heroes—the Maizeville
Tigers.

Sitting in the the student section were several high
school boys, including the slightly built blond youngster
who'd been hunting with Mack and Les that day, sporting wrestling letter jackets and teasing the girls in front
of them.

Josie followed Gramps to seats high on the back row.
As she settled in, she smiled contentedly to herself—the
Friday-night football game. Some things never change.

The drum majorette blew her whistle and hoisted her
baton, as the fifty-member band, in wavering lines,
marched onto the field playing the school fight song with
gusto. At the final crescendo, the black-and-gold-clad
Maizeville Tigers appeared from the east end zone. The
bleachers rocked with stomping and cheering.

Josie noticed, during the excitement, that Mack Scott
had joined her grandfather. He leaned around Gramps,
stuck out his hand and said, "Good to see you, Josie.
Great night for a game, isn't it?"

Was it the contagious excitement of the crowd or the
touch of Mack's hand that made her heart pound?

She could hear Mack and Gramps discussing the mer-
its of the new quarterback and the awesome defensive
record of the opponents, the Park City Pirates. She
leaned forward and glanced surreptitiously at Mack. Below the black Tigers ball cap, his face glowed with boy-
ish anticipation.

After the kickoff, she became absorbed in the game,
cheering wildly with the rest when Maizeville scored a
touchdown. Yet, even as she followed each team up and

down the field, a part of her was aware, keenly aware, of Mack's warm presence just on the other side of Gramps. Observing his body language, she noted the intensity with which he watched, planting his feet, hunching over his knees and tensing his muscles at the snap of the ball, never taking his eyes off the field until the play was over.

During a time-out, she grinned across Gramps at him. "Okay. Confess. You must have played football yourself. Right?"

"Is it that obvious? Yeah, I was a tackle four years out at Great Bend. Whenever I come to a game, the old adrenaline just takes over."

It was easy to imagine those strong legs and taut hips encased in football pants, easy to picture the already broad shoulders enlarged even further by pads. How she'd have loved watching him take his helmet in those strong hands, strap it on over that wavy brown hair and run determinedly onto the field!

A roar from the crowd shattered her reverie and then caused her to flush slightly as she realized the direction her thoughts had taken.

At halftime, Mack left to get them coffee from the concession stand. Josie, idly looking about, noticed Les, wearing his state-championship letter jacket, swaggering through the crowd, hailing first one friend and then punching another on the shoulder. Trailing behind and occasionally forced to jump up and down to keep sight of Les was Amy. Finally she caught up to him, taking hold of his sleeve. After a whispered conversation, they both scanned the crowd. When Amy spied Josie, high in the bleachers, she waved and mouthed, "See me after the game!" Josie nodded and returned the wave.

When Mack arrived with the steaming coffees, he sat down next to Josie and handed her and Gramps their cups. "What a crowd! I think I spilled more than I kept!"

She could feel the rough wool of his plaid shirt through her thin cardigan as the crowd settled again into the bleachers. The solidity of his body next to hers was both comforting and disturbing. As he leaned across her to comment to Frank, she could see the tanned skin drawn over his cheekbone and the generous curve of his mouth. She longed to touch the soft skin of his earlobe.

As he sat back, a scent of wood smoke lingered in the air. Only by an act of will did Josie keep herself from snuggling against him. She would have liked that strong arm around her, protecting her from the chill in the air. As he tensed for a play on the field, she watched his thigh muscles bunch and harden, desperate to reach out and lay her palm there. *Admit it, Josie, you're attracted to him. You're as giddy as the girls in the Pep Club.*

A thrilling goal-line stand at the end of the fourth quarter prevented the Pirates from scoring, and the game ended in a 7-0 victory for the home team. As Gramps, Mack and Josie reached the sidelines, Les and Amy sought them out.

Les, eyes glittering, put his hand on Frank's shoulder. "Listen, Amy and I are having a little victory party at the house. Few folks are coming over, kind of spur of the moment, you know."

Amy looked up at Les and then added, "You're all invited. Please do come."

"Well, now, that's mighty nice of you." Frank reached into his pocket for his watch. "Josie'll tell you that I'm up way past my bedtime. I'll have to say no." He turned to Mack. "No point one old man spoiling your fun, though. Would you mind bringing Josie home, Mack?"

"That's okay, Gramps," Josie said quickly. "I'll just go on home with you."

"Josie, please come." Amy looked at her with such pleading that Josie was slightly alarmed. "We really do want you there, don't we, Les?"

Les staggered slightly. "Sure do. See you at the house, Mack." He turned toward the parking lot and Amy hurried after him.

Mack took Josie's elbow. "It's really no problem. I'll be happy to drop you off afterward."

"Sure you don't want me to go with you, Gramps?" What was she looking for? An out?

"Don't be silly," Gramps said. "I'm fine on my own. Take care of her, young feller." And with that Gramps waved and walked away.

Amy grabbed Josie the minute she came into the house, crowded with noisy laughing adults exulting over the Tigers' win. Cigarette smoke hung heavy in the family room, and several of the men were standing on the patio, beers in their hands, rehashing the game.

Pulling her into the kitchen, Amy hissed, "I'm so glad you're here. Can you help me get the chips and dip out? Les just started inviting people at the game. I wasn't prepared for this. In fact, I don't even know how many are coming." Josie looked at Amy with concern. There were big blue circles under her eyes, and she moved slowly, unconsciously reaching to cradle her abdomen every few seconds.

"Are you all right?"

"I'm just tired, that's all."

"Then why are you having this party?"

"Oh, Josie, this happens all the time. Les has a few drinks, starts feeling his oats and then has to play the big-time host. I'll rest tomorrow."

Josie opened the dip and spooned it into the dish with a vengeance. That insensitive clod!

Sidling through the crowd, Josie held the chip and dip bowls high to avoid having them knocked to the floor. Safely arriving at the dining-room table, she saw two women casting baleful glances in Amy's direction. She overheard one say, "Poor thing, she just lets him walk all over her. Talk about a chauvinist."

"He wouldn't last long at my house," the other agreed. "Do you suppose she knows what all he's doing 'at the golf course'?"

Raucous laughter from the men in the kitchen drowned out the rest of the conversation. Josie's stomach churned.

She felt a hand on her shoulder. Turning, she found herself staring into Mack's amused brown eyes. "You didn't know you were coming to a party to work, did you?"

Relaxing under his touch, she smiled. "It's okay. Amy's exhausted."

"Well, Mack, who's your date?" A petite woman, dressed in an elegant black pantsuit accessorized with a wide gold belt and black-and-gold silk scarf, stood before them, her lips forming a smile, but her eyes devoid of warmth.

"Josie, I'd like you to meet Beth Ann Johnson."

Josie mumbled a greeting, feeling like a great awkward giraffe next to this bandbox figurine.

"Josie is Frank Calhoun's granddaughter," Mack offered by way of explanation.

"How nice to meet you. Aren't you the one who has something to do with birds? I'd love to hear all about it sometime." Beth Ann threw Josie another frozen smile and put her arm possessively through Mack's.

"What's Clay up to tonight?" Mack inquired.

"Oh, he told me there was a party somewhere. I'm not sure just where." She laughed indulgently. "Boys will be boys, you know."

"Yes, I know all too well," Mack responded dryly. "You might want to check on his whereabouts."

"Don't be such an old worrywart, Mack. It's a small town. There's not much mischief the boys could get into here." She disengaged her arm, pecked him on the cheek and sashayed toward the bar.

Mack shook his head and rolled his eyes at Josie. "I'm afraid that's one mother ostrich with her head pretty deep in the sand."

Just then Les, his face flushed, ambled toward them, thrust a beer into Josie's hand, clamped an arm around Mack's shoulder and dragged him off. "You gotta come hear some of the great ideas Bud Smaltz has for the sportsmen's-club lease."

Josie sought refuge in the kitchen, helping Amy slice carrots and celery to add to the hors d'oeuvres tray. In the family room, they could see some of the guests rifling through the CDs and finally pulling out the sound track of *The Big Chill*. Soon, several couples were dancing enthusiastically, including Beth Ann Johnson and a man Josie presumed was her husband.

Amy nodded in the gyrating little blonde's direction. "Did you meet Beth Ann?"

"Yes. I can't exactly say her greeting was cordial."

Amy frowned. "It figures. We all try to excuse her behavior, but it's not easy."

"What are you talking about?"

"Oh, I guess you don't know. Beth Ann's sister, Sarah, was killed in a freak auto accident about a year and a half ago. Beth Ann just can't seem to put it behind her."

"I'm sorry."

"Tonight she probably was ticked off when she saw you come in with Mack."

"Whatever for?"

"Because, my dear friend, Beth Ann doesn't think Mack should have anything to do with another woman. You see, Sarah and Mack were engaged."

Josie felt as if someone had just knocked the wind out of her. Engaged! To lose someone so tragically... No wonder he'd understood her grief. Embarrassment flooded her as she remembered her girlish speculations at the ball game. She'd mistaken compassion for interest, kindness for possibility.

MACK HANDED Josie into the Bronco, then walked around to the driver's side, drawing welcome breaths of the cool night air, and hopped in beside her.

In the glow from the street lamp, her hair was almost golden, curling loosely on her shoulders. He fought a sudden impulse to wrap one of those soft flaming tendrils around his finger. Turning on the ignition, he glanced at her again, noting her downcast eyes and the stillness of her body.

"Were you as ready to leave that party as I was?" he asked as he drew away from the curb.

She sat quietly, staring into her lap.

"Did I say the wrong thing?"

She turned and looked at him, her beautiful eyes troubled. "No, of course not. I...I'm just concerned for Amy. She looked so fragile and tired."

"Les is not numbered among the world's most considerate men, that's for sure."

"Mack, I really wish there was something I could do for her, but..."

"You can. Just be her friend, Josie. She needs one."
Then, in an afterthought, he added, "We all do."

They drove in silence for a few minutes. Then Mack
said, "Your grandfather has been a good friend to me.
Although I don't see him often, when I do, his common
sense and wisdom help me a lot."

Josie nodded, then touched his shoulder tentatively.
"I'd like to be your friend, too. Mack... Amy told me
about Sarah. I'm so sorry."

Mack slowed the Bronco and pulled over to the side of
the road, scraping the passenger-side fenders along a row
of sunflowers. He shut off the engine and turned to look
at her. "Josie, I appreciate that offer. It means a lot
coming from you, because I know you've suffered a loss,
too." He took her hands in his. The longing and vulnerability in her eyes made him ache. "I can always use another friend. Maybe so can you."

Her eyes filled. "Then friends we are." She made a
slight movement to withdraw her hands from his, but
paused as he gently squeezed her fingers before reluctantly releasing his grasp.

Her funny sweet freckled face was dominated by the
deep pools of her eyes, alive with compassion. The
promise in them seemed to seal their friendship, and
Mack found it difficult to look away. But finally he
turned to roll down his window, letting the cool night air
wash over them. The breeze rustled the dried sunflower
stalks, and the lowing of distant cattle provided a counterpoint.

"That day you stopped on the highway," he said hes-
itantly, "reminded me of... of Sarah's accident."

Josie's eyes betrayed bafflement.

"This is difficult for me to talk about." He sat quietly
for a moment, struggling with his emotions. "She... Her

car slid on the highway and crashed into the Pioneer Oak.''

A pained gasp of realization escaped Josie. ''So when I...''

''Yes, when I saw you there, for a moment, I relived the terrible night of the accident.''

''Oh, Mack. How awful. Of all the places I could have picked.''

''You know, in a way, maybe it helped. Your grief was very real that day. It made me think about the fact that I'm not the only one who's ever suffered. Perhaps that's an important step in healing.'' He looked thoughtful. ''That day, you said something about the oak, how it reminded you of...?''

''Oh, yes. Of MJ. Of the many times she told me stories about the oak and the people on the wagon trains stopping there before they set off for Indian territory. For me, the oak was always a symbol of shelter, security and, most important, of home. Every year just before I'd come from wherever my mother and stepfather were stationed, MJ would write and say, 'You'll know you're home when the oak whispers to you.' ''

Mack smiled. ''It's good for me to think about that. Maybe those words will help me view the oak as something other than an agent of destruction.'' He restarted the engine and pulled away from the shoulder. ''Thanks for listening.'' Intent upon the road, he didn't see her glowing eyes and wistful smile.

At the house, when Mack helped Josie out of the Bronco, he took her hand. It was warm and fit palm to palm, finger to finger, into his. As they strolled up the walk, he continued to hold her hand, noticing only as they got to the back door that he'd done so naturally, without thinking. It felt good.

Standing on the first step, Josie turned to him. "Thank you for bringing me home. I really appreciate it."

He grasped her by the shoulders and gazed into her eyes, feeling a thaw beginning somewhere deep within him. He lifted one hand to her cheek. "Josie, I..." His voice thickened. "I needed a friend tonight."

He continued to look at her, feeling a sort of surprise. He started to draw her nearer, but she pulled away. "Wait right here a minute," she said. "I have something for you." And she was gone, swallowed up by the dark farmhouse.

Mack took a deep breath, trying to control the long-buried feelings rising within him—a tremulous lightness in his chest, an ache deep in his groin, a shaky sense of life stirring within him. Josie's openness, her vulnerability, even her feistiness had all affected him in ways no one had since...for a long, long time. Did he dare to risk closeness again? But if he didn't risk, would he always be a hollow man, just going through the motions?

The back door opened, and Josie stood framed in the kitchen light, her glorious red hair spreading like an aureole about her smiling face. She held something behind her back. Walking toward him, she said, "I have something for you." She held out her palm on which lay a crisply ironed white handkerchief. Her eyes sparkled. "I don't think I'll be needing this anymore."

He took the handkerchief, aware of powerful emotions sweeping over him as he stared at the beautiful woman standing before him. Before he could check himself, he pulled her into his arms and bent his head to whisper in her ear, "And I have something for you."

He probed her eyes with his for a moment, then gently placed his lips on hers. The kiss, light and tentative at first, soon grew more insistent. He felt her arms creep up over his shoulders, until at last they locked around him.

Josie was the first to pull away, her eyes like those of a puzzled child. "Mack, I—"

Mack cupped her face in his hands. "Every friendship should be sealed with a kiss." He kissed her again, lightly and fleetingly. "Good night, Josie." And he turned and strode back down the walk.

As MACK OPENED the back door to his house, he let Stranger out for a run and walked into the living room. He moved into the bedroom, emptying his pockets on the dresser and laying the white handkerchief to one side.

"I don't think I'll be needing this anymore," she'd said. No more tears. And for the first time, Mack admitted to himself that maybe his own grief was slowly dissipating.

He went back into the living room, restlessly pacing between the bookcase and the desk, too wide awake to sleep, too energized to settle on reading or television. Her lovely face, soulful eyes offering so much; the feel of her long clean body molded to his; her soft breasts finding a home against his chest ... Oh God, for the first time in a long while he wanted a woman. No! Not just any woman. *This* woman.

Hearing Stranger scratch at the back door, Mack stepped into the kitchen and let the dog in. Stranger jumped up on Mack, wagging his tale in a frenzy of delight. "Down, boy. Are you glad to see me?" Mack knelt, wrapping his arms around Stranger's neck and burying his face in the dense black coat. "I'm glad to see you, too, fella."

Dog and master walked back into the living room where Mack paused at the computer. Slowly he removed the vinyl cover, flicked the On switch and eased into the desk chair. Words, which had abandoned him for months, crowded to the surface of his consciousness.

He sat back, gathering his thoughts; and when the blank screen appeared, he started typing, tentatively at first, and then with an outpouring of words.

In the winter, the Flint Hills are gray desolate monoliths, stretching barrenly to the borders of the known earth. Lifeless, unyielding and formidable, the January hills echo that in man which is anguished, lonely and desperate. But with the gradual warming of the southern winds, with the arrival of the first songbirds, with the first tentative buds on the sparse wind-battered bushes, hope stirs the aching heart and spring becomes a promise....

It was nearly three in the morning before Mack, spent at last, turned off the computer and went to bed, falling into a deep dreamless sleep.

CHAPTER FOUR

TUGGING THE KNEE-HIGH rubber boots on over her running shoes wasn't easy. Josie wrestled the left boot, thrusting her foot deeper toward the toe. Finally! She stood up, pulled her cream fisherman's sweater over her faded jeans and smashed Gramps's old leather cowboy hat over her unruly hair. As an afterthought, she plucked the stiff jean jacket off the peg, then grabbed the keys and walked toward the barn. Gramps had asked her this morning to feed the cattle in the east pasture if he didn't get back from the doctor by five o'clock.

The pickup was already loaded with the hay bales. All she had to do was deliver them. She carefully backed the truck out of the barn and rattled across the rutted yard to the first cattle gate. What a nuisance it was getting in and out to open and shut the gates! But as a child, she'd learned the importance. Only once had she left a gate open. The long night Gramps, MJ and she had spent corralling the missing cattle had convinced her she would never again be so careless.

She liked these September days, with their exhilarating fresh mornings tempered by the sun's warming rays at midday and ending, as now, with a northwest breeze, which brought color to her cheeks and made her thankful for her sweater.

Reaching the pasture, she giggled as she watched the cattle, strung out one by one, hurrying toward the truck.

They lumbered along like tour-group travelers at a noon buffet. The exertion of unstrapping the bales and pitching them into the trough reminded her of the necessity of getting more exercise. She was spending too many hours hunched over the computer and not enough outdoors walking and running.

As she climbed back into the cab, leaving the cattle contentedly munching, she saw in the distance a black Ford Bronco turning onto the gravel road to the south. Mack! She watched as the familiar vehicle passed the Calhoun lane and turned up the narrow dirt road to the Britton place.

She sat for a moment, the engine idling. Not for the first time these past few days, she conjured up that wonderful confusing evening. Hugging herself against a sudden chill, she reached over, picked up the jacket and wrapped it around her shoulders.

What had that kiss meant? She remembered every detail, the warmth of his hands on her shoulders, the fathomless depth of his eyes, the spontaneity of his embrace and, best of all, the sweetness and promise of his eager lips.

But what was it he'd said? Something about sealing their friendship. *Friendship.* She supposed that was what this was all about. He'd told her about Sarah. Maybe all he'd intended was a thank-you for listening. Certainly there'd been nothing romantic about their conversation that night. Just two friends talking.

She knew, however, what the kiss meant to her. Gramps had said, "Wait for the sparks." When Mack had kissed her, she'd felt an explosion of sparks piercing her from the inside out. Sparks, yes, she knew sparks.

With the flat of her hand, she hit the steering wheel in frustration before easing off the emergency brake and starting across the bumpy pasture. What a ninny she was being! Of course he only meant friendship. That was probably all he was ready for. She mustn't get her hopes up.

But as she drove the pickup into the barn, she felt again that aching longing....

IN THE DARKNESS of the early morning a couple of days later, Mack pulled up quietly to Frank Calhoun's back walk. Only the kitchen light was on. The big orange tiger cat was perched on the windowsill watching him. He eased open the car door, strode up the walk and tapped gently on the screen.

Frank opened the door and wordlessly beckoned him in. Frank handed Mack a hot thermos of coffee, stuffed some shells into the pocket of his camouflage jacket and picked up his shotgun. Turning off the kitchen light, he pulled the door shut noiselessly and followed Mack out to the Bronco, where Stranger sat expectantly in the back, sensing the upcoming adventure.

Only after they'd started down the lane did either of them speak. "Opening day of teal season is always a thrill for me." Frank sighed with satisfaction. "No matter how old I get, I feel just like I did when I was nine years old and my father took me duck hunting for the first time. My hands shook with excitement then just like they are now."

Mack grinned at him. "We could be in for a good day. Stranger and I were up at the pond late yesterday, and there were fifteen or twenty blue-wings going out to feed."

"Let's start there, then. After that, we could hit Haggertys' pond, maybe go into town for a big chicken-fried steak, before heading over to the Randolphs' place. Then if we haven't gotten our limit, we could end up back at our pond."

"Sounds good to me." Mack swung the Bronco onto the side of the road and stopped for Frank to get out and unlock the pasture gate. As Frank hauled himself back into his seat, Mack paused before accelerating. "Maybe over lunch we can talk some more about Les's idea of a sportsmen's club on your land."

JOSIE CROSSED the cold floor to her bed just as the first hint of orange teased the eastern horizon. Gramps had tried to be so careful not to wake her, but she'd awakened before him, on pins and needles until she heard the Bronco pull into the lane.

She'd left the warmth of her covers to tiptoe quietly to the hall window, which overlooked the back of the house. Crouched beside it, she'd watched Mack eagerly approach the house, hunting boots echoing on the walk. She'd strained to hear what the two men were saying, but failed. Then, too soon, they were leaving, Mack easing the Bronco down the lane.

Even after she could no longer hear the engine, she'd stood at the window, heart pounding. Their camaraderie, their heightened expectation, had been communicated to her. On the one hand she could smile indulgently and dismiss them as overgrown boys; on the other, as they set out for the hunt, she envied their distinctive male bond.

But appealing as all that was, she was profoundly disturbed by what they were deliberately setting out to do—kill birds! At dinner last night, Gramps had offered a justification. "You're not going to change tradition. Men hunt, period. Always have, always will. Maybe it's something women just can't understand." Josie had stifled the liberated-woman's response that rose instinctively to her lips. The last thing she needed was to hurt Gramps. And it was too late to change tradition for him. But, damn!

Back under the comforter now with James Cagney purring against her, she vacillated between envying the male bonding and protesting the wanton destruction of even one brilliantly feathered teal.

Just as the rim of the sun reddened the morning sky, she dozed off, oblivious to the far-off report of a gun.

AFTER INDULGING HERSELF by sleeping late, and with the house all to herself, Josie vowed not to let the idea of the hunt ruin her mood.

She spent a full day on her thesis, putting the finishing touches on the third chapter and outlining the fourth. Humming with satisfaction, she turned off the computer and went into the kitchen to treat herself to a Coke before putting the chicken in the oven for supper.

The late-afternoon breeze stirred the organdy curtains at the kitchen window, and she thought absently that soon she'd need to close some of the windows before the cool of the evening. She mixed the bread crumbs with the onions and celery she'd sautéed in butter, added a sprinkle of sage and spooned the stuffing into the breast cavity.

Leaning over the stove to put dinner in the oven, she noted the time. Five o'clock. Where were those men? Probably waiting for one last chance as the birds went out at dusk to feed. Gramps would be tired when he came home. His enthusiasm for the hunt had been that of a ten-year-old, but his seventy-four-year-old body would be aching with fatigue. Maybe she'd go ahead and feed the cattle and save him the effort.

Standing in the barn alongside the pickup, Josie eyed the bales stacked up to the roof. She hadn't counted on the challenge of loading them onto the truck. As she climbed onto the first layer of the pyramid, she determined that the easiest way might be to climb to the top and then roll each bale down.

Several hens protested, squawking and flapping their wings, as she disturbed their roosts on the hay. Steadying one foot on the lower bale, she grabbed for the wire of a higher bale and hoisted herself onto the second layer. One more to go. A barn cat shrieked and jumped over her arm to safety as she reached for a handhold on the highest bale. Just a little farther...

"Hi, Red, how's the weather up there?" Like a high-voltage current, anger surged through her, remembered humiliation choked her, and her hand, clawing for a purchase in the prickly unyielding straw, grasped air. One foot slipped on the slick packed surface of the lower bale, and she felt herself falling backward.

"Damn you!" she wailed as the childhood feelings of inferiority aroused by the familiar taunt swept over her.

She landed against something solid, which then cratered to the ground, carrying her with it. The air momentarily knocked out of her, she opened her eyes to find herself lying on top of Mack.

"What are you...?"

Lifting his head a couple of inches off the ground, he grinned dizzily. "I had no idea you'd fallen for me so hard."

As she reared off his chest to protest, she felt his strong arms wrap around her. He reached one hand up to cradle her head gently into the curve of his neck. She could smell the sharp scent of metal, mixed with the freshness of clean autumn air. His other hand caressed the small of her back as he pulled her even closer into the bedrock of him.

"Shh, shh," he murmured. "Just lie here and get your breath for a minute. You're okay."

Lie there and get her breath! *I may never breathe again,* she thought, *but it won't be because of the fall.* She wanted to inch her way along his body, feeling every nerve and muscle, from their entwined legs to their joined hips, up to where she could feel her nipples chafed by the buttons of his hunting jacket, to the secret softness of the skin lying beneath the stubble under his chin.

His right hand strayed to her buttocks as he pulled her still closer. "Josie, I..."

She lifted her head and read the apology and desire in his eyes. He sat up enough to twist to one side, rolling her gently onto her back as his right hand explored her ribs. She was heedless of the dirt floor, the bits of straw and chicken feathers clinging to her hair, the dust motes swirling in the light coming through the open barn door.

She was consumed by the intensity of his gaze, by the warmth of his fingers tenderly tracing the curve of her waist. She didn't move. She floated in some glorious suspension of time, only the tingling of her body reminding her that this was not a dream.

"Mack, ready to clean those birds?" Gramps's silhouette filled the barn door. Surveying the situation, he stopped abruptly. "Everything, er, okay here?"

Mack cradled Josie's shoulders and helped her to a sitting position. "Josie took a header off the hay bales. I think she's all right."

Momentarily Gramps's figure swayed in Josie's vision, then cleared. "Wow," she said. "I think I'll live. It's a good thing Mack was here to catch me."

Mack stood up and pulled her to her feet, leading her to a seat on the lowest hay bale. "I don't know how grateful you should be. Could be I startled you and made you lose your balance."

Josie smiled weakly. "It wasn't your fault. How could you know that the kids in grade school used to tease me unmercifully about being tallest in the class? And red-headed and freckled to boot. I thought I'd outgrown those feelings, but I guess not." She looked Mack up and down. "How about you? Are you all right?"

"No complaints. After all, it isn't every day a beautiful girl throws herself at me."

Gramps chuckled and shifted to the other foot. "She never did take too kindly to teasing. Guess all that moving around with her mother and stepfather was hard. It's tough being the new kid. Always a target."

Mack grabbed her hand, pulled her up, circling her waist with his other arm and walked her behind Gramps toward the house. "Well, for what it's worth, I've never seen a more attractive dirt-covered farmhand in my life. By way of apology and because I intended to anyway, may I invite you to be my guest next weekend for a trip to Kansas City? It's the least I can do to demonstrate that tall redheads with tempers have an appeal all their own. Anyway, you might enjoy the retriever field trial we'll be attending."

While the men sat on the back steps cleaning the teal, Josie luxuriated in a hot steamy tub. Her back was sore, and she knew she'd have an ugly bruise on her knee, but the lilac-scented bubbles cascading over her skin were gentle reminders of Mack's hands smoothing over the curves of her body. Had Gramps not come into the barn when he did, who knew what she might have done?

She bent her knees and slid her back down the tub till only her face remained above the water. Poor Mack! Her anger had surprised him; certainly he hadn't intended to get her goat with his "Hi, Red. How's the weather up there?"

Why was she still so sensitive? She'd always felt like a plain Jane, a grackle amid the peacocks. She made a mental inventory. Unruly red hair. Freckles from head to toe. Okay eyelashes, but skin that turned salmon pink in the sun. No beach goddess here! Wide mouth, big teeth. Long legs, knobby knees. Adequate boobs and a slim waist. But the hands. "Capable hands" was what her mother had called them as she'd sighed and suggested, not too tactfully, that spending money on a manicurist would be a waste. All in all, yes, a plain Jane.

Josie told herself to stop it. She was her own worst enemy. And Mack did seem to like her. She had to face it— when he touched her, she forgot all about what she looked like.

"Mmm…" she murmured. He did make her feel good. She dribbled tantalizing droplets from the washcloth over her firm abdomen, which quickened instinctively as she recalled the feel of his long hard body beneath hers.

A loud knock brought Josie quickly to a sitting position. "Who is it?" she called.

"It's Gramps, honey. Do we have enough chicken for Mack to join us for supper?"

Josie felt a rush of pleasure. "Sure, please ask him to stay. It's the least I can do for bowling him over." She stood up and caught her grinning reflection in the mirror. She stepped carefully out of the tub onto the deep plush of the mat and reached for a towel.

A retriever field trial? Not your garden-variety kind of date, but in her current mood, she'd go to a hog calling

if he invited her. She rubbed her legs with the thick towel.
Would they be going to Kansas City just for the day? No.
He'd said the weekend. She stopped in midmotion. What
if...? Surely they wouldn't be... She found herself
blushing at the fantasies flooding her thoughts.

CHAPTER FIVE

ROLLING HILLS, gilded by the early-morning sun, rose on either side of the river valley. Oaks, maples and elms, hinting of the brilliant foliage yet to come, bordered the harvested fields and sheltered the well-kept farmhouses along the route. Cresting a long hill just east of Bonner Springs, Josie and Mack saw silhouetted on the horizon the hazy Kansas City skyline, veiled in the morning mists rising from the confluence of the Missouri and the Kaw rivers.

"Pretty," said Mack. "At this time of day and from a distance, cities always look tranquil. But the rest of it—the noise, the dirt, the crowds—you can have. How do you stand living in Chicago?"

"It's not so bad. I'm so involved with my work that where I am doesn't seem important. But I confess that when I do get out in the country or when I'm at the farm I wonder myself how I stand it."

Mack twisted in his seat, reaching into his hip pocket for his billfold. As he braked for the tollgate, Josie noted, not for the first time, his strong square hands on the wheel. He did everything so competently, so gracefully.

"Nice day," Mack observed to the tollgate attendant, pocketing his change. Accelerating, he tossed the Missouri map into Josie's lap. "Okay, you're the navigator. Get us to the James A. Reed Wildlife Area. It's somewhere near Lee's Summit."

As Josie struggled to unfold the map, she asked, "How did you get interested in field trials, anyway?"

"Blame it on Stranger. After I brought him home, I started reading about Labs. They're amazing animals, instinctive retrievers. Then one day at the vet's office, I met a lady who raises and trains Labs for field trials. She got me interested and suggested I might enjoy seeing one. And the rest, as they say, is history, and here we are. Or will be if you ever get the dang map deciphered."

"I beg your pardon, Mr. Scott. If I can follow the journeys of migrating waterfowl, I can surely get one human being to his destination. As a matter of fact, sir, if you'll follow the signs now for I-435, you'll save us an unnecessary trip to Des Moines."

He reached over with his right hand to give her a mock slap on the knee, but instead, let his hand settle on her thigh. Giving her leg a squeeze, he said, "Great date, huh? I'll bet you never guessed you'd be going to the dogs."

She groaned. "Some sense of humor you've got there. Puns seem to be a habit of yours. To what do we attribute such sadistic behavior?"

"Dear lady, to the fact that I love words. I was an English major."

"What?" She never had gotten around to asking him what he'd studied at university. Now she could hardly control the shriek in her voice. "An English major? You're kidding." It didn't compute with her image of him.

"I kid you not. Cross my heart."

"But...but," she stammered, "how does an English major get from college to the sheriff's office?"

"By car. Ford Broncos are good." He chuckled at his own cleverness.

"No, seriously."

"Seriously, you could call it a detour from my intended path. My parents were voracious readers. My mother was the town librarian. I grew up with books and always liked writing. In fact, my goal is to be a writer. Majored in English, minored in journalism. Actually that's why I landed in Maizeville. Cheap rent, close to Kansas State U. I was planning to take a year, live on the money I'd squirreled away and give free-lance writing a try."

"But?"

"But...when Sarah was killed, the words just dried up. Nothing came. I needed action. One of my part-time jobs at Kansas State was working for the campus police, so it wasn't too much of a reach to sign on with the sheriff. It was at least a way to try to make some sense out of the accident."

In the silence that followed, Josie found herself covering his hand with hers. After a moment or two, he turned his hand palm up and laced her fingers with his, squeezing her hand gently in silent gratitude.

He changed the subject. "Have you been to Kansas City often?"

"I flew in and out of the airport whenever Cheryl and my stepfather unloaded me on Gramps and MJ. And several times MJ and Gramps brought me to Kansas City for special events like a baseball game or a shopping trip. My favorite memory is the time MJ drove me in to see the Christmas lights on the Plaza. For a little girl, it was spectacular to crest the hill on Wornall Road and see that fairyland of lights laid out before me. It was snowing big round flakes, the kind that stick to your tongue. 'Silent Night' was playing on the car radio and MJ was humming along. It was one of those magic moments that's frozen in detail in my memory. Christmases weren't always good times for me, but the ones on the farm with MJ and Gramps were special."

Mack disengaged his hand, reached up and traced his index finger across her cheek. "Such a sad little girl." He paused. "And such a lovely grown one."

She laid aside the reminiscence to bask in his approval. He saw into her in a way few had bothered to do. No matter how hard she tried to rationalize the neglect and pain of her childhood, it had a way of resurfacing and rendering her vulnerable. No wonder as a child and adolescent she'd been accused of being aloof. But Mack—Mack seemed to see something else in her.

"If you don't mind my asking, how do you feel about your mother now?" He looked over his shoulder, then changed lanes to merge with the exiting traffic.

She gave his question serious consideration. "Most of the time I think I'm very adult about the whole thing. I excuse her because I know my father's death was a devastating blow. She was young, saddled with a three-year-old and didn't know what she wanted. MJ told me that she and my father had a whirlwind courtship. Cheryl had always wanted to get married, the Vietnam conflict was weighing on everyone's mind, and it just seemed the thing to do. I guess when her dreams were shattered, she kind of went to pieces. From that time on, it just seemed that all she wanted was to stay young. To stay desirable. I always felt like an embarrassment to her or living proof that she was growing older. She tried, I guess. In her own way, I think she loves me."

"But it wasn't enough."

"No, it wasn't. Part of me is still very angry with her."

"Do you see much of her?"

"We talk long-distance on holidays and birthdays. When Gus, my stepfather, retired from the army, they bought a house in Portugal. I've only visited them once, just after college. I may be her daughter biologically, but now we're just two women whose paths have crossed."

He reached down to squeeze her hand, noting the wistful expression on her face. "No wonder it's the oak that whispers 'home' to you."

WELCOME TO THE KANSAS City Retriever Club Licensed Trial, the sign at the entrance to the wildlife refuge read. It did not prepare Mack for the number of pickups, motor homes, dog trailers and cars parked in uneven lines at the edge of the park, nor for the license tags indicating competitors from as far away as California and Georgia. "Wow, this is a bigger deal than I thought."

"Look, Mack." Josie pointed to several handlers working their dogs in an open area behind the parked vehicles. She clapped her hands together excitedly. "Black Labs, yellow Labs, even that golden over there. I've never seen so many handsome dogs in one place in my life."

Mack draped his arm around her shoulder. "They're great, aren't they?" He backed the Bronco between a station wagon from Louisiana and a pickup from Texas.

The sun had burned off the morning mists and the midfifties temperature promised a comfortable day. The wheat-colored sedge lining the banks of the glittering ponds and the trees turning crimson, gold and orange were overarched by a brilliant blue autumnal sky. As Mack steered Josie through the parking area, he couldn't help noting that she matched the late September day—khaki jeans molding her firm legs and buttocks, gold turtleneck and paprika-colored sweater fitting loosely over her generous breasts, and the whole concoction topped with those burnished red-orange curls. He was finding it hard to concentrate on the dogs.

After getting coffee at the concession stand, they stood trying to get their bearings among the hubbub of the crowd. "I've never seen so many different kinds of people," Josie remarked. A bearded young man in dirty jeans, scuffed cowboy boots and a faded red shirt stood talking to a statuesque blonde, clad in jodhpurs, polished riding boots, safari jacket and jauntily cocked digger's hat. Two teenage boys dressed in camouflage hunting gear stood at the back of a pickup getting an excited golden retriever out of his wire kennel. A wizened dwarf of an old man in baggy tweeds, complete with a jacket patched with leather at the elbows, sidled up to them, his face crinkling into a warm smile.

"This your first field trial?"

"Does it show?" Mack extended his hand. "I'm Mack Scott. This is Josie Calhoun."

"Glad to meet you. I'm Harry Orwig. My dogs aren't competing at the moment. Let me show you around, introduce you to some folks and help you get oriented." He steered them toward a crowd of people grouped near the edge of one of the small ponds. "This is a derby stake for dogs under two years old. You'll notice the puppy enthusiasm makes up for some of the mistakes they make." Harry handed Mack a program listing the different stakes and the names of the competing dogs, owners and trainers.

Just then the crowd stilled as a man in a white jacket leading a black bitch stepped into the cleared space and gestured for the dog to sit and stay. A shot rang out in the distance, and an object tumbled to the far bank of the pond. The dog sat, quivering with eagerness.

"Back!" The man made a forceful gesture with his arm toward the fallen object. The dog took off on a dead run, plunging without so much as a break in stride into the water, and churned her way straight across the pond. She picked up the object, then, as her owner gave several sharp blasts on his whistle, swam back, climbed onto the shore, circled her master and sat, delivering the object to her master's hand. Only then did she stand to shake off the water clinging to her coat. The crowd applauded politely.

Josie tugged Mack's sleeve. "Mack, it's a duck." She gestured to the object, which had appeared to be just a shackled bunch of feathers.

Harry leaned over to her. "Retrievers have an instinct for retrieving game, especially waterfowl. Birds are used in training only as necessary, but in the field and for a trial like this, smell has a great deal to do with the dog's performance. The best dogs are not only strong and well-trained, but have a keen nose."

Josie shuddered. "I appreciate what you're saying about the dogs, but as a bird lover, I'm having difficulty with all this."

Harry chuckled. "If you love birds, you also love seeing animals doing well what they were born to do. Watch the dogs, and by the end of the day, see if you don't think they should be given a chance to show off."

Mack put his arm around Josie, drawing her against his body. He'd looked forward to the trial and was enjoying it, but it paled in comparison to the exuberance he felt being with Josie. The mix of little girl and defiant woman, of vulnerability and independence, of freckles and radiant smile, made him weak in the knees.

He watched her chatting with Harry, catching only shreds of the conversation—"blind retrieves," "amateur stakes," "line breeding"—as he marveled at the sun weaving golden threads through the wisps of her hair lifted by the breeze and felt the softness of one rounded breast pressing against his rib cage.

"One of my pups will be on the line soon," Harry said. "Nice talking to you folks." He gave a jaunty salute and disappeared into the spectators.

By early afternoon, Mack and Josie had seen dogs cross long distances through a variety of terrains to retrieve fallen birds, some older dogs retrieving as many as three different birds in one test and picking up planted birds, which they hadn't seen fall. Mack had found the owners and trainers friendly and forthcoming with information and advice.

Around two o'clock, Mack asked, "Hungry?"

"I've been so intrigued I haven't thought about it. But now that you mention it, I'm starving!"

Later, munching on hot dogs stuffed in buns spilling over with sauerkraut and mustard, they perched on a rock wall. Josie looked at Mack inquiringly. "Could Stranger be trained as a field-trial dog?"

Mack wiped his mouth on a paper napkin. "He could be trained, but he couldn't compete. Field-trial dogs have to be purebred stock, registered with the American Kennel Club. I'm pretty sure he *is* a purebred, but without papers, he's no good for this. But I plan to train him as a hunting dog, and maybe someday I'll have a registered Lab."

Josie carefully swallowed the last pungent bit of her hot dog. "Mack, why do you hunt?" She stared intently at him. "Please don't think I'm being judgmental, but in this day and age we certainly don't need to hunt in order to survive. I understand the point about culling birds, but hunters do it for the sport. How can it be 'sport' to kill beautiful living things, or for that matter to use them in competition like they're doing here?''

Mack frowned at the edge in her voice. "I might ask a question, too. Why are you so opposed to hunting? After all, your grandfather hunts."

"Okay, I guess that's fair." She took a swig from her soft drink as she considered his question. "There's more to it than being a bleeding heart, save-the-whales sort of person, although I am passionately committed to preservation. If I'm honest, though, part of it has to do with my stepfather."

"Tell me."

"When I was about seven or eight, Gus took me hunting with a friend of his and the friend's little girl. At first I was happy to be going on such a big adventure. It was teal season, but after a while, the blind got hot. I remember the weeds kept scratching my face. The mosquitoes were thick. Finally several birds flew in and landed about thirty feet away. I thought they were beautiful with their graceful bodies and chalky blue wing feathers. Then Gus aimed his shotgun. He was going to kill them! I remember shouting, 'Don't shoot, Gus. Don't shoot!' But he got angry and brushed me aside. I'll never forget that blast reverberating in my ear. He shot the bird on the water. Its head flopped down, and the other birds sprang off the pond in a frantic escape."

Mack noted the faraway pained look on Josie's face. He waited for her to continue.

"Then he waded out and brought the bird back, throwing it at my feet. 'Don't be such a sissy, Josie,' he said. 'It's just a dead bird.' He was practically snarling. I remember choking on tears as I smoothed the sleek wet feathers with my finger and watched its blood pool on the dry grass. All the way home in the car I kept asking over and over in my head, Why did you have to kill it? Why did you have to kill it?"

Josie ran her finger around the rim of the plastic cup in her hand. Finally she looked up, sadness etched in her face. "It seems senseless and cruel to destroy such lovely creatures all in the name of sport."

She eased herself off the wall. "I'm sorry I brought up the topic. I was having a good time. Let's not ruin our day with controversy."

He stood beside her, gazing at the cloud bank in the north. "Even if I don't agree with you, I understand why you feel the way you do. I owe you an answer to your question because I do know why I hunt. Rather than talk about it, though, try this on for size. When we get back to Maizeville, I'd like to *show* you my answer, if you're willing."

She looked up, the frown melting into a small grin. "Okay. You've got a deal. Truce?"

"Truce. Come on, Red, we have just enough time to watch the open stakes before checking in at our motel."

Funny, she didn't seem to mind his calling her Red. Maybe she could hear the warmth and genuine affection he intended. She smiled as he took the napkins and hot-dog wrappers and threw them into a trash container, then grabbed her hand and took off toward the far pond.

THAT EVENING, riding back to the motel following a bountiful lobster dinner at the Savoy Grill, a venerable Kansas City landmark, Josie felt relaxed and contented.

The accommodations had turned out to be a two-bedroom suite, a fact that both calmed her apprehension about the sleeping arrangements and, if she was truthful, resulted in a hint of disappointment. She thought of the intensity of his interest in the field trial, his eyes dancing in delight as he watched the uncanny performance of the champion retrievers, and his pine-scented closely shaved skin raking her cheek as he had nestled her closer to whisper in her ear. She'd had to fight to keep from pulling him to her and melting into his soft sweater or from letting her hands drift down to the tantalizing firm curve of his behind.

Mack reached over to change the radio station, filling the interior with mellow light rock. She glanced over at him, savoring his profile. She'd been bowled over in the motel when he appeared in a camel sports jacket, brown flannel trousers, cream-colored dress shirt and hunter green-and-crimson paisley tie. She'd always pictured him in his uniform or casual clothes; now she had a new image for her mental file. Shivering with pleasure, she remembered the goose bumps erupting on her skin when he'd taken her by both hands, twirled her around and with smiling eyes approved her long-sleeved, V-necked kelly green wool sheath. "Miss Josie, you *do* clean up well!"

Lost in her reverie, she was taken by surprise as the Bronco slowed and stopped. "Are we here already?" she asked, her heart leaping into her throat as she projected the delicious possibilities of the next few moments.

Mack turned in his seat, cupped her face in his warm hands and leaned to kiss her tenderly and lingeringly. "Time flies when you're having fun, Red." With a light brush of his thumb across her lower lip, he released her, climbed out of the Bronco and came around the car to escort her inside.

Wrapping her to him with his left arm, he pulled her along to their door, fumbling with his right hand to insert the key. "Let me try that again." He paused and gave her another light kiss. "Yep, just as I suspected. The ever so delicate taste of lobster and lemon butter."

She elbowed him in the ribs, pulling away to face him, laughter bubbling just below the surface of her voice. "Gee, Prince Charming, you sure know how to make a girl feel good."

He shoved open the door, propelling her ahead of him, then kicked the door shut behind him. He folded her in a hug, nuzzling her neck with his mouth. "That's just what I aim to do. Make this girl feel good."

His lips caught hers in a deep hungry kiss. Her body arched into his, reveling in the contact at knee, groin and breast. Her hands traced up the soft sleeves of his camel jacket sensing the muscles coiling beneath, circled his broad shoulders and clasped behind his neck in a movement that pulled him closer. When at last he withdrew his lips, she shuddered breathlessly, stepped back and looked into his face, illuminated by the outdoor light shining through the window.

"I think you succeeded," she breathed.

He released her, turned on the table lamp and helped her out of her coat. "If you don't mind, I'll get rid of my jacket and tie. You sit right down here on the sofa. I've got a surprise." He crossed the sitting room to the tiny kitchenette. Opening the under-the-counter refrigerator, he extracted a bottle. "I hope you like champagne."

"Rarely do I get any on a graduate student's income. But, yes, I do like it."

He poured two flutes and handed her one. Sitting in the corner of the sofa, one leg drawn up so he could face her, he said, "I propose a toast." She looked up expectantly. "To my friend Josie and to more happy times."

He clinked his glass to hers, locking her eyes with his as he drank.

Josie was the first to look away, aware of both euphoria and self-consciousness. What could this big dear wonderful man see in her? It was too good to be true, too good to last. Her toes knuckled under in her pumps, tension starting to rise from her feet, up through her midsection, paralyzing her breathing.

"Mack, I..." She gulped. "I hope I'm your friend. I want to be." She took another sip of the champagne, feeling it bubble in her throat. Was that still all it was? Friendship? She didn't feel like just his friend. She felt like a quivering mass of desire. If they were just friends, what must he think of the intensity of her response to his kisses? God help her. What if she was making a fool of herself?

"I'm not sure friendship is all I'm feeling," he whispered as if reading her mind. He set his glass down, gently removed hers from her icy fingertips and, straightening his legs and propping his feet on the coffee table, pulled her over beside him, snuggling her against his shoulder. As he idly stroked her hair, he began in low measured words, "Josie, I want to be fair to you. For a long time my feelings have been confused. I can't rush things. Hell, I'm not even sure how you feel about me. I do know that when Sarah died..."

Sarah! Was she going to hear more? Maybe she was only a pale substitute for his lost love. Didn't he know how much she wanted him?

"...I thought I'd never feel anything again. I couldn't even think about other women, about dating. It all seemed impossible. I'd dream about Sarah, about the wreck. Even in my sleep, I couldn't give her up." He stopped talking, his hand resting on her head.

Josie held her breath, afraid to move, afraid to speak. Slowly his fingers started working through her hair again, repeatedly stroking, entwining, disengaging. Every pore in her being was directed to those meandering fingers.

"And then you came along. You're one of a kind, you know that?" He turned and put his other hand on her cheek. "A rare bird, indeed." He pulled her to him. "Oh, Josie, help me to go slow. Not to hurt you." His mouth sought hers in a frenzied search for reassurance, his tongue exploring the inside of her mouth, plunging, retreating, plunging again.

She felt explosions within as his hand fell from her cheek to caress the soft skin of her neck, languorously explored the length of her arm and came to rest on her thigh. As his other arm drew her closer, he swung his legs off the coffee table, stretched his body under hers, eased against the pillow, running his hand over her thigh as he repositioned the two of them.

She was dimly aware of her skirt hoisting higher on her leg as she broke away long enough to nestle into him, entangling her fingers in his thick hair. Her breasts seemed to fight against the constraint of her bra as she leaned over him, her mouth hungrily seeking his.

"Oh, Josie," he moaned as he ran his hands up and down her back, palming her buttocks to pull her into him. Her breath came in ragged gasps as she felt his iron hardness. He shifted her onto her side, her back against the sofa, and drew away to look at her, his caramel brown eyes sweet with desire. His right hand, the palm searing her, traveled from her hip to her waist, exploring.

As he leaned closer to nip at her exposed ear, then planted tiny hot kisses on her neck, she felt electrifying pinpricks of longing. As the kisses moved lower, she could feel her arteries throbbing under the assault of his

mouth. Moving across her chest then gently beneath the
cloth of her dress, his fingers cupped one lush breast, ripe
beneath the lacy cover, and found the engorged nipple.
Josie was drowning in a sea of sensation.

He moved back against the arm of the sofa, pulling her
on top of him. His hands fumbled with the zipper at the
back of her dress. He slowly pulled it down as he cradled
her head with the other hand, drawing her mouth to his,
drinking her in. She felt the hooks of her bra give way to
his nimble fingers.

He moved her to one side, sitting up and raising her
with him. He searched her face, as if for permission, then
reached up to her shoulders and slid the dress down over
her arms. For a fleeting moment she felt embarrassed and
exposed as he removed her bra and laid it aside, but the
adoring look on his face silenced her doubts.

With each hand he lifted a breast, allowing his thumbs
to rub gently over the taut pink nipples. His eyes swam
as he released her, then savagely pulled her to him,
crushing her breasts against the wall of his chest. "Josie, my God, you're beautiful."

She stopped, feeling herself go rigid against him. "Wh-
what did you say?" she stammered.

He pulled back, holding her at arm's length. "You're
beautiful," he repeated.

She felt the tears course down her cheeks before she
was even aware that she was crying. Great sobs of air
were stuck in her throat.

Concern flooded his features. "Josie, what the hell?
Are you all right? Did I do something?"

Her shoulders shook. "It's just . . . no one's ever said
that to me." She pulled the dress up over her bare shoulders. "You don't have to say it, you know." A sob es-

caped. "I know I'm not beautiful." Humiliated, she swiped ineffectually at the tears.

"Come with me." He stood up, pausing long enough to reach in his pocket to hand her his white handkerchief. He guided her to her feet, reaching behind her to zip up her dress. As he lifted the mane of coppery curls outside the fabric at the nape of her neck, his eyes sought hers. "So. You don't think you're beautiful?"

She lowered her gaze, shrugged, and then shook her head.

With one hand on the small of her back, he guided her to the mirror above the credenza. With his hands firmly planted on her shoulders, he stood behind her. With one hand he tilted her chin, forcing her to look at her image. "Tell me what you see."

She faltered. "I see a mess. A pale tearstained blotch." She tried to turn away.

"Not so fast." He made her face the mirror again, then lowered his arms to encircle her from behind, cradling her body against his, his arms crossed beneath her breasts. "Slowly. In detail. Tell me what you see."

Aware he meant business, Josie scrutinized herself in the mirror. "I see a tall gangly carrot," she began slowly. "I see white skin marred with funny red-brown splotches. Pale eyebrows and lashes. A long pointy nose. Big mouth. For some reason this handsome man is holding me, making me take this awful inventory." Her chin came up in defiance. "I see a plain Jane, an ugly duckling."

She twisted in his grasp. "Please, do we have to do this?"

Once more he turned her to face herself. "Yes, we have to do this. Now. I want to tell you what *I* see." He nuzzled her temple with his chin. "I see a swan." Josie

squirmed, fighting his grasp. "Yes, a beautiful swan. I
see a woman who has no idea how lovely she is. Tawny
carefree hair. Glowing skin that's been kissed by the sun.
A mouth rich with laughter. And eyes. Ah, the
eyes."

He turned her to face him. "The poet says eyes are the
window of the soul. I believe it. In your eyes I see loneliness, yes. But I also see honesty and compassion. Josie, I see beauty."

He embraced her gently, reaching down to take her
hand. "I never again want to hear you call yourself ugly.
When you look in a mirror, always see yourself as I see
you." He lifted her fingers to his mouth, kissed them
gently and deliberately, and removed the handkerchief
from her clutched fingers. "Last time you told me you
wouldn't be needing this again. No more tears, remember?" He winked at her as he planted a light kiss on her
cheek. "Good night, beautiful swan." He walked into his
bedroom, shutting the door softly behind him.

JOSIE HAD TOSSED and turned all night, the memory of
Mack's sweetness and powerful masculinity mingling
with the aching traces of her arousal. She relived the
warmth and passion in a clenching deep in her inner-
most being. To sleep would be to diminish the wonder of
it all, the wonder of feeling . . . Did she dare say it? The
wonder of feeling cherished.

Even now, as they approached Maizeville, she wanted
him to keep driving, to prolong the euphoria that had
enveloped her these past few hours.

As if on cue, Mack slowed the Bronco as he reached
the last mileage sign before Maizeville and said, "Just for
the record, Josie, I want you to know that I was planning on asking you to join me this weekend even before

you knocked me over that day in the barn." He turned to grin at her. "I was breathless then, and after yesterday and last night, I'm still breathless."

She flushed with pleasure and tried to think of a light comeback. But somehow her lungs weren't working very well, either. "Mack, I had a wonderful time. You made me feel very special."

"We aim to please, ma'am."

"I want you to know, though, that you don't need to spend that kind of money on me. It must have been an expensive weekend."

He put his arm around her shoulder. "You let me worry about that. When a guy hasn't had more than two or three dates in eighteen months, he can justify a big night or two. Besides, it's tough to compete with Chicago when the most exciting local event is the Elks' Club bingo night."

She giggled. "Even I can beat that. Why don't you come over a week from tomorrow night for homemade vegetable soup and a fast game of gin rummy?" Her heart was thudding in her chest. Could she wait until then to see him again?

He turned onto the road leading to the farm. "I'll have to take a rain check."

Her heart plummeted. Had she been too forward? Was she rushing him? "Well, maybe another time."

"Count on it, Red. That Monday night is a meeting of all the hunters interested in the sportsmen's-club project. And the next ten days or more are going to be really busy at work. I'm on duty extra hours to help cover for Pete Wells while he takes some highway-patrol training in Salina." He ruffled her hair. "But as soon as I have some free time, you'll be the first to know."

She felt a smile warming her from the inside out, but how could she endure so many days without seeing him? Without kissing him? Without feeling his arms around her?

He drove up the long lane to the Calhoun farm. "Say, how's this for an idea? Why don't you come to the meeting that night? Whether or not I agree with it, you have a viewpoint about hunting that deserves to be heard. I'll set it up." As he slowed to a stop by the back walk, he removed his hand from her hair and switched off the ignition. Then he faced her expectantly. "How about it?"

She turned the idea over in her mind. Why should she put herself in the position of letting a group of hunters use her for target practice? Yet she knew of no other way to get their attention. It might be tilting at windmills, but damn it, she should at least try.

"I'm not sure it'll do any good, Mack, but it's very fair of you to offer me the opportunity. I'll give it my best shot." She paused and then realized what she'd said. She laughed. "See what you've done? Now I'm punning."

Grinning delightedly, he picked up her left hand and held it in both of his. "Josie, you're something else, you know that? You've made me feel alive again. Be patient with me." He caressed the back of her hand and tenderly massaged each fingertip, filling her with pleasure.

She looked into his strong gentle face. "Thank you, Mack, for a very special time."

"I want to give you something to remember me by."

Before she could ask what he meant, she noted the merriment rising in his eyes.

"As a token of my affection, Red, please do me the honor of keeping my handkerchief." Chuckling, he pulled out the handkerchief and wrapped her palm around it. Then he leaned over, kissed her on the cheek and hopped out of the Bronco.

He escorted her to the kitchen door, set her bag down and held her at arm's length, drinking her in. "No question about it. You *are* beautiful." He started back down the walk. "See you soon, lovely swan."

She watched his retreat, happiness and disappointment warring within her. Reluctantly she turned her back, picked up the bag and went into the house, the screen door banging behind her.

"That you, honey?" The eagerness in Gramps's voice was unmistakable.

"I'm home." Josie left the small suitcase at the foot of the stairs and went into the living room to drop a kiss on Gramps's balding head. She collapsed onto the sofa.

"Did you have a good time?"

"A wonderful time."

"Care to elaborate?" A hopeful smile played over his features.

"Not really." She noted the disappointment that doomed his smile. "But, Gramps, I know about sparks."

The sun rose again in his eyes. "Ah. You'll tell me what I need to know in your own time. Fair enough."

Josie tucked one foot under her. "Are you going to that meeting of the sportsmen's group next week?"

Gramps laid aside the newspaper he'd been reading. "Thought I would. Why?"

"Mack's invited me to speak to them."

"Oh?" Gramps's tone was guarded.

"You know how strongly opposed I am to hunting. Mack suggested it was a perspective that needed to be aired. Not that I think it'll do any good or change anybody's opinion."

Gramps sighed and locked his hands behind his head. "No, it probably won't and you're not apt to make yourself very popular. In fact, it'll be like volunteering for the lion's den."

"So?"

"So...even your old grandfather doesn't agree with you about the evils of hunting, but I'm proud as hell that you've got the guts to stand up for your beliefs."

"Can we go together?" Josie asked uncertainly.

Gramps winked. "Wouldn't have it any other way."

She rose to her feet. "Now, I'm going to go unpack and try to plant my feet on solid ground so I can make some progress on my thesis."

"Josie? You have some mail. I picked it up yesterday and put it on your dresser."

In her bedroom, she hoisted the suitcase onto the bed, hung up her jacket and reached for the letters. The first was from Maizeville. Slitting the envelope, she withdrew a colorful stork-shaped invitation. A baby shower for Amy. How nice! She opened the card and felt her excitement ebb. She read the last line again. "Hostesses: Marcia Schwartz and Beth Ann Johnson."

Picking up the second, a legal-sized envelope, she identified Tom's familiar handwriting, cramped and precise. Tom. She hadn't given him a thought this whole weekend. As she tried to picture him, his slight body, silvering hair and gray eyes faded into the image of an athlete with brown naturally wavy hair and deep brandy eyes filled with desire.

CHAPTER SIX

CLUTCHING TOM'S LETTER, Josie sank into the rocker by the window. Why did she have this twisted feeling in her stomach? The voice of reality shattering the illusion of romance?

She chastised herself. Tom was a caring decent human being. Only a few weeks ago she and Amy had speculated about his importance in her future. Now all she wanted was to luxuriate in the reflected glow of Mack's approving eyes. To feel again his finger tracing the planes of her face, to curl snugly into the warmth of him, to burn under his hands tenderly sculpting the curve of her breast. With a reluctant sigh, Josie lifted the flap of the envelope and extracted the two-page typed letter.

Skimming the first page, Josie was relieved to see carefully documented suggestions for editing the preliminary chapters of her thesis. It was like Tom to be so thorough. The scientist in him. His painstaking approach to his research and his insistence on precision made him a topnotch ornithologist and an excellent teacher.

The second page moved to more personal information—his chances for being named head of the department, his frustration with one of his graduate assistants, an invitation to address an audience of Audubon Society members. Just as her heart was beginning to lift, she saw the ominous words—"Dearest Josie." Oh, no.

Dearest Josie, as I worked on this letter, I realized I was trying to picture you in your setting. Are you standing by a mailbox, or sitting at a kitchen table, curled up with a good book? Reading the rough drafts of thesis chapters is a poor substitute for a newsy letter or, better yet, having you here in Chicago. I must confess I miss our visits in the faculty lounge, our collaboration on research and our quiet dinners at Luigi's. I hope you will find time to give me a more complete personal history of your life in Kansas. It would help me fill in the blanks in my mind when I think of you, which, by the way, I do often. I'm looking forward to your return to Chicago and, when the term ends, to spending time together working on something other than a thesis.

Love,
Tom

Josie shifted uneasily in the rocker, a frown furrowing her forehead. Caught up in the swirl of emerging feelings for Mack, it had been easy to dismiss Tom from her mind. Or to think of him only in the context of her work. The ambiguous nature of their personal relationship paled beside her recent intimacy with Mack. What should she do? Was there anything to do? It was hard to read Tom's mind, and yet evidence of his interest stared her in the face. Perhaps she could write a noncommittal letter about her comings and goings and keep all other communication strictly thesis-related. She'd just have to deal with Tom when she returned to Chicago.

As she stood, a folded clipping fell to the floor. She picked it up. It was a page listing teaching vacancies from the *Chronicle of Higher Education*. Two ads were circled carefully in red. One was for an undergraduate zoology teacher at a college in Wisconsin. The other was a tenure-track entry-level position at Southern Illinois University. Scrawled in the margin in Tom's small hand were the words, "Not Chicago, but close enough for weekend commutes."

The fanged dragon of the future stared her directly in the face. In thinking about life after graduate school, Josie realized she had, so far, successfully played Scarlett O'Hara—"I'll think about it tomorrow." Now with an insistent hiss, an inner voice announced the arrival of that distant tomorrow. The reality was that, with a little more work, before Christmas she'd receive her degree and be out on the proverbial streets.

Although she'd made some preliminary inquiries at universities, with various state wildlife-management agencies, and with the departments of Agriculture and Interior, she still had few job leads. The applications she'd received were gathering dust on her desk. She should be grateful for Tom's letter, she supposed. Setting aside the personal dimension, it had at least given her the motivation to finish her thesis, complete the applications and get them in the mail.

It was just as well Mack was working the extra hours. She could buckle down and bury herself in her work. At the same time the new resolve hardened in her mind, she was aware of the void growing within her. She would not see Mack again for several days, and then only in the awkward midst of the area hunters.

MACK UNLATCHED the outdoor dog-kennel gate to release an ecstatic Stranger, torn between bounding across the yard and licking Mack to death in a frantic welcome. Jumping up and down and wagging his tail excitedly, Stranger made Mack chuckle with delight. All those field-trial dogs were exceptional, but it was great to be greeted so lovingly by your own dog. He'd arranged for Frank to come over while he was gone and feed Stranger and take him for a couple of walks. But Stranger had gotten used to more. "Come on, fella. Let's head out. You've been cooped up long enough."

Mack picked up several canvas retriever-training dummies. He tossed one several yards ahead of Stranger, who sped after it, picked it up and trotted back to Mack. "Good boy. Sit." The ritual was repeated several times as the two walked across the field.

After a while Mack abandoned the game, and Stranger roamed ahead into a grove of trees. Mack relished the sun's afternoon warmth, though the air hinted of a frosty night. He whistled aimlessly as he reviewed the weekend with Josie. He was aware he'd not felt so relaxed or so at peace in a long time. The halo of her silky red curls framing her creamy skin, highlighted by the faint sprinkling of her cute freckles and the deep mossy green of her eyes, created a face he cherished, a face transparent with the interplay of her emotions. She was so open, so natural in her responsiveness. He felt himself harden as he recalled the lushness of her breasts, her pink nipples teasing the pads of his fingers, and the length of her, fitting into him as if they were the two final pieces in some perfect jigsaw puzzle.

In the distance, he heard Stranger barking. Nearing the grove of trees, Mack saw the Lab looking skyward at a pair of circling mergansers. Instinctively his sporting blood raced. Then he thought of Josie and her stubborn resistance to hunting. Had he made a mistake inviting her to the sportsmen's-club meeting? The group could hardly be receptive to her point of view. Yet in the interests of fairness . . .

Stop it, Mack. It was more than concern for fairness that had prompted him to invite her. He'd wanted to pacify her, to forestall the distancing the issue caused between them. He leaned to pat the dog. "Time to go home, Stranger. Come." The two headed back across the field.

With a full evening ahead of him before his next shift, Mack looked around the small living room. Rather than settling at the computer, he opened the small door leading into what had once been a root cellar. Mack had installed wiring and converted it into a darkroom. He descended the wooden steps, pulled the string attached to the bare electric bulb and looked around at the photographs tacked on the walls. Soon he would have to decide which to include in the Harvest Festival exhibit. Damn Beth Ann, anyway. Maybe when he finished working overtime to cover for Pete and before he made his final selections, he'd find time to take more pictures. The autumn sky offered some amazing light effects.

He glanced at the small insurance-company calendar over the sink. Since the Harvest Festival was the Saturday after Thanksgiving, he had only two months left to get the exhibit pulled together. Extinguishing the light, he picked up an empty film canister, rolled some bulk film into it and snapped it into his camera. As he turned on the light, he was brought up short by a photograph of Sarah. Sarah—smiling at him, her flaxen hair caught in an updraft, the blue sky framing her face. His heart lurched. Sarah, everyone's sweetheart, not a mean bone in her body. Sarah, my love.

Ready to leave, he pulled the string, plunging the room once again into darkness. In the image imprinted on his retina, the blond hair changed to copper, the flawless skin began to sport freckles, and Sarah's face slowly faded as

Josie's laughing visage replaced it. Mack felt his eyelids smart, whether with regret or promise he didn't know.

JOSIE'S SHOULDERS ached and her neck felt as if it were on a rusty swivel, but the next-to-last chapter was safely consigned to the computer memory. She picked up a sheaf of papers and leaned back in her chair. There was still one elusive piece of data she knew she had somewhere. She started carefully reviewing her notes from last spring's field trip to the breeding grounds in Manitoba.

She smiled, thinking about the intelligence and fidelity of Canada geese. Although naturally wary, they had an uncanny sense of the difference between man as a threat and man as a natural part of the environment, a fact that made scientific observation easier. Josie had not been particularly interested in waterfowl until that first field trip to Canada to observe the spring migration and mating season. While other students had been fascinated by the varieties of ducks, she'd felt an instinctive kinship with the geese. Their longevity—life spans often exceeding twenty years—and the bonding with one lifelong mate enlarged their study, in her mind, from the merely scientific to the personal. The flock and family identity, communicated by repeated rituals, bordered on the human. As they lifted into the air, huge wings spanning nearly six feet, their haunting calls served to gather the strays, to mark the course and flying strategy and to broadcast to the humans far below the promise of the season. Quite simply, they not only fascinated her, they aroused a reverence.

Thankfully, these past few days she'd been able to immerse herself in her writing. She had disciplined herself so that thoughts of Mack, powerful though they were, were kept at bay. She was pleased, too, that she'd sent out several applications, including some to agencies and colleges in Kansas. Although she could have permitted herself the rationalization that the sole appeal of Kansas was home and Gramps, in all honesty it was also Mack.

With a small cry of triumph, she located the missing data and returned to the computer, searching for the place to make the necessary insertion. The phone rang insistently in the distance. "Josie, it's for you," Gramps yelled from the foot of the stairs.

She completed the insertion, pressed Save and scampered down to the kitchen.

"Hello? Oh, hi, Amy." Josie pulled the kitchen stool nearer the phone and perched on it, wrapping her feet around the legs.

"My weekend? It was nice."

"Nice?" Amy squealed with derision. "Come on, Josie. Don't hold out on me. I'm the pregnant lady wanting all the vicarious thrills, remember? I promise to hang on to your every word."

Part of Josie wanted to gush, to share the wonder of Mack with her friend; the other part wanted to savor the memory for herself for fear that broadcasting it would dilute it. "Amy, I'm almost afraid to put it into words. It was a special time, and he's a very thoughtful, fun person. But it's still early in our relationship. I'd hate to get my hopes up. After all, you told me he cared a great deal for Sarah."

"That's true enough. But time has a way of changing things. And you're a pretty special person yourself, you know."

"You've always been able to make me feel better, Amy. Thanks. But I don't think this relationship has much of a future."

"Why do you say that?"

"Well, for one thing, we have a serious difference of opinion about hunting. Is Les involved in that awful sportsmen's-club project?"

"Sure. Don't you remember I told you he and Mack have been looking all over the county for just the right site?"

"Great. Looks like I'm going up against the whole town."

"What are you talking about?" Amy was clearly mystified.

"Yours truly is appearing before the hunting enthusiasts Monday night to argue for wildlife preservation, not destruction."

Josie could sense the unusual length of Amy's hesitation. "You're not!"

"I am. And why not?"

"Josie, you're treading on dangerous, even sacred ground. Men around here don't take kindly to being crossed, especially about the issue of hunting. What does Mack think?"

"He's the one who invited me. He's trying to be fair, but I don't think I can budge even him. And, Amy, I want to. I guess the truth of the matter is, I'm very interested in him, but I don't want to set myself up to be disappointed."

Amy sighed. "There you go again, selling yourself short. Tell you what. You're going to my baby shower at Beth Ann's. If I could ride with you, you could pick me up a little early. Then I can hear more about your weekend. Remember, you promised me the graphic details."

Josie found herself blushing as the picture of Mack nuzzling her breast flashed across her mind. "I'll be happy to pick you up. The graphic details? Well, we'll wait and see. Thanks for calling."

Josie hung up, hoping against hope that the techni-
color wraparound-sound motion picture projecting in her
head, the one starring Mackenzie Scott and Josie Calhoun, wouldn't be doomed to a short run.

OCTOBER ARRIVED in all its glory—crisp frosty mornings, cloudless ocean-blue skies, hazy evenings redolent
with the scent of burning leaves. Josie had always loved
October. MJ, too, had been an autumn person. The
crunch of a crisp apple, the spicy fragrance of ginger-
bread and the promise of the jack-o'-lantern waiting to
be carved from a bulging pumpkin always brought MJ's
eager face to Josie's mind.

The longer Josie stayed at the farm, the more MJ
seemed to be there with her. The memories, once painful, now became a source of comfort and peace. It was a
special kind of immortality that brought one's presence
into a room through the snatch of a hummed tune, the
smell of homemade soup simmering on the stove or the
texture of a needlepoint pillow.

Gramps, too, seemed to settle more comfortably into
his routine. The evenings the two shared in front of the
living-room fireplace were punctuated by animated conversations ranging from shared reminiscences to the latest controversy in the news. Although he'd not intruded
by asking how her relationship with Mack was develop-
ing, every now and then, Josie would catch him peering
at her over the edge of his newspaper. She didn't mean to
shut him out, but there really wasn't anything to say yet.
Maybe there would never be.

GRAMPS DROVE HER to the Oasis Steakhouse the night of
the meeting. Assorted pickup trucks and utility vans
dwarfed the occasional motorcycles in the parking lot.

Several older men, clustered in the doorway, smoking, gave Frank a greeting, but only nodded curtly in her direction. The unmistakable odors of greasy chicken-fried steak and barbecued ribs warming under the lamps on the steam table caused Josie's stomach to somersault.

Gramps steered her by the elbow into the pseudo-Spanish private dining room, festooned with a Kiwanis Club banner and lined with the serious-faced photographs, placed at intervals around the mustard yellow walls, of the past presidents of the Maizeville Rotary Club. In stands at the front were a large American flag and the bright blue of the Kansas flag. Josie grimaced remembering the Kansas motto: *Ad astra per aspera*—To the stars through difficulty. Glancing at the tanned stoic faces of the gathered men, she appreciated fully the difficulty of her mission.

Mack rose from a table at the front where he, Les and a uniformed man whom Josie assumed was a game ranger sat. "Frank, Josie." He shook Gramps's hand. "Glad you could make it. Have a seat."

Josie sank gratefully into a chair, wilting in the closeness of the hot air blowing from the vent above her. As she nervously waited, with surprise she noticed toward one side a group of about fifteen adolescents sitting with a thin, wan gentleman nervously cleaning his glasses with a handkerchief.

At precisely seven-thirty, Les rose and called for order. First he introduced Mack and then Paul Beecham, who was, indeed, a ranger with the Kansas Department of Wildlife and Parks. Gesturing to the group of students, he announced, "Also here this evening is Wint Ferris's biology class from the high school. Wint thought this might be an educational experience for them, and the kids don't mind those extra credit points, I'll bet." Appreciative laughter greeted that remark.

As Josie turned to look at the students, she noticed the familiar smirking face and sprawled slender body of the boy who'd accompanied Mack and Les on the dove hunt.

"And, finally," Les continued, "we have with us Frank Calhoun's granddaughter, Josie." To a man, heads swiveled and Josie flushed under the scrutiny of so many masculine eyes. "She's here to educate us good ol' boys about wildlife preservation." The glances hardened from curiosity to mild hostility; then the men shifted uncomfortably in their seats as they turned to face the front again.

"Don't mind them," Gramps whispered and patted her hand. "Just speak your piece. Do what you came to do."

First, Les gave an overview of the project—finding a site where they could build blinds, provide both cover and feed for the birds, put out decoy spreads and enjoy some convivial times hunting. The idea of a hunting lodge or clubhouse drew grunts of affirmation, and one saturnine fellow in mechanic's overalls even volunteered to "whomp up some eggs and bacon of a morning" if a kitchen were installed. Next, Paul Beecham went into a technical discussion of the legalities and limitations of the project. By eight forty-five, many of the men were squirming in their seats or slumped forward, elbows on their knees, holding their chins cupped in their hands. From the adjacent kitchen, the clatter of dishes being scraped and prepared for washing punctuated the warden's remarks.

At last, Les introduced Josie, whose dry tongue was stuck to the roof of her mouth. She carefully made her way through the crowd, feeling the eyes of every person

in the place on her. As she turned to face the bored indifference of her audience, she saw the familiar blond
teenage boy lean toward his neighbor, whisper something in his ear and then guffaw behind his cupped hand.
Several men in the audience shifted miserably on the hard
chairs. Only from two or three of the girls from the biology class did she sense any support.

"I am grateful to Mack Scott for being invited tonight." She paused and cleared her throat, Amy's warning dinning in her brain. "I realize that my topic may not
be too popular, but before you proceed with this project, I would like you to consider the impact of your decision, both on wildlife and on the example you're setting
for the next generation." She nodded in the direction of
the students. The teacher sat up straighter and nodded
almost imperceptibly in approval.

"At one point in our history, game was a staple, even
a necessity, on our tables. No one could dispute the decision to provide food for a hungry family, rather than
preserve the life of a duck or deer. In those days game
was plentiful. No doubt some of your grandfathers have
told you stories of the immensity of the migrating
flocks—there was an abundance of birds, more than
enough for all."

She noted several heads nodding in agreement. "I am
here to tell you, gentlemen, that such is no longer the
case. For numerous reasons, flocks have decreased—the
use of chemicals, fertilizers and pesticides has poisoned
the food source. The building of cities with the inevitable pollution has choked out natural nesting grounds and
migratory resting places. And changes in water courses,
the construction of dams and decreasing water levels have
altered the migratory flyways. Fewer and fewer waterfowl are surviving the long trip back to their Canadian

nesting grounds. Many die of natural causes, more are
the victims of man's thoughtlessness. That thoughtlessness includes hunting. In this day and age, hunting is an
indulgence." She paused, feeling the wave of animosity
emanating from those impassive faces.

Squaring her shoulders, she continued, "You are not
hungry, you do not need feathers to stuff your beds or
pillows, and a photographic print would decorate your
walls as well as a taxidermist's handiwork. Beyond these
considerations, think of your children and grandchil-
dren. Are they to be denied the thrill of watching a flock
of ducks circling and setting down on one of your ponds
for the night? Of sensing spring is coming, not by the
warming of air or the budding of tulips, but by the high
distinctive calls of geese homing north? Like it or not,
these beautiful creatures are not ours to do with as we
please. They are certainly not ours to destroy." The biology teacher gave her a subtle thumbs-up.

She gathered her courage for the conclusion. "Gentlemen, I appreciate your invitation and implore you to
consider your options, not for my sake but for the birds
that I love and for your children whom you love."

Blushing furiously, she groped her way back to her
seat, aware of the cold faces turning away from her. Les
rose. "I reckon most of you have had enough for one
night. Is there enough interest in pursuing the idea of a
sportsmen's club to meet again?" A hearty round of ap-
plause greeted his question. "All right, then. I'll let you
know the time and place of our next get-together."

Amid the confusion of the chairs scraping back and
tired bodies standing and stretching, Josie felt Gramps's
arm around her shoulders. "I'm not convinced I want to
give up hunting, but I'm proud of you." Holding her
head up and meeting straightforwardly the gazes of any

who caught her eye, Josie made her way toward the door. A welcome gust of cool air greeted her as she stepped outside and headed for Gramps's car.

"Miss Calhoun, Miss Calhoun!" a voice called. Turning, she saw the biology teacher coming toward her. He reached out to shake her hand. "That was a tough audience in there I'm here to tell you, but you did a bang-up job."

"I doubt it'll do any good, though, but I appreciate your vote of confidence."

"We've just got to keep trying." He rubbed his nose between his thumb and forefinger. "Lord knows I'm trying with the kids. Some of them are really pretty receptive—ecology appeals to their better instincts. But in this neck of the woods, antihunting sentiments don't sell real well. They've been at it too long. It's a way of life. But I'll tell you one thing—I can use this talk as a hook to try to change a few impressionable young minds."

"I surely hope so. Thanks again for your support. I needed it."

He raised a hand to his forehead in a gesture of farewell. "Don't let the community get to you. You're dead-on. A pleasure meeting you."

"The pleasure was mine." Josie climbed into the passenger's seat, waiting for Gramps to break away from his conversation with Marvin Haggerty. She'd hoped to have a brief moment with Mack to gauge his reaction, but he'd been surrounded by men offering their ideas. What had he thought?

She sighed. Even if she'd jeopardized their relationship, convictions were convictions, and no man was going to cause her to soften on this issue.

JOSIE PULLED the knitted afghan off the back of the sofa and wrapped it over her legs as she stretched out on the sofa after dinner. Gramps was deep into a rerun of "Matlock."

It was only this past weekend that she'd seen Mack since the meeting at the Oasis. Initially she'd felt ill at ease, concerned how her impassioned speech might have altered the chemistry between them.

She needn't have worried. As soon as they'd gotten into the car, he'd put one arm around her shoulders and playfully hugged her. "It's okay, Red. You were sensational! Just because I don't see it your way doesn't mean anyone else could have explained your position any better."

She'd relaxed and enjoyed the steak dinner in Manhattan, followed by a movie. With pleasure, she recalled his laughing brown eyes, the intimacy of sitting shoulder to shoulder, hands entwined in the darkened theater. Afterward, he'd driven her high up on one of the hills surrounding the university town and pointed out the sweep of the Milky Way and the glittering constellations. Josie hugged herself with the memory of how he'd turned to her, his eyes liquid with feeling. The kiss had started tentatively, exploringly, and deepened into a wildly arousing probing. She'd returned his passion with the ardor that had been building in her all evening.

"Honey, do you want to watch the news?" Gramps asked.

Josie pulled the afghan higher as she came back to the present. "I don't think so, Gramps. I'm about ready to turn in." *And continue my shameless fantasizing....*

"Okay, I'll turn the TV off." He hoisted himself out of the recliner. "Say, you were busy at the computer after dinner and I haven't had a chance to tell you about my call this evening from Harold Parnell. You remember. My old army buddy.''

A vague memory surfaced of a man who'd visited Gramps and MJ one summer when Josie was a child. ''I think so.''

''Well, his wife passed away this last year, too. He's bought a new bass boat and wants me to join him in Texas for some fishing. I'd kind of like to go.''

Josie smiled. ''I think that's a great idea. Do it,'' she urged.

''I hate to leave you alone, though, sweetheart. I'd be gone nearly three weeks, from the end of October until right before Thanksgiving.''

''I'll manage. I might even be more productive. You go and have a good time.''

''I'm going to talk to Mack and see if he'll keep an eye on things and help feed the cattle.''

''We'll get along fine, Gramps. A vacation will do you good.''

''And my absence might give you two a chance to do a little sparking without some old geezer on the premises.'' He chortled with delight as he started up the stairs.

THE DAY of the baby shower was overcast. A gusty northwest wind howled and rattled the windowpanes.

Josie pulled a delphinium blue knit dress over her head. She hadn't been this dressed up since...since the Kansas City trip.

Although she looked forward to seeing Amy and sharing in the festivities for the baby, Josie felt apprehension lying heavy in the pit of her stomach. She couldn't put her finger on its exact source, but she was aware Beth Ann Johnson had something to do with it. Although Amy discounted Sarah's continuing influence in Mack's life, Josie wasn't so sure about Beth Ann. *Don't borrow trouble,* she told herself. Glancing in the mirror as she scooped her keys from the top of the dresser, she tried hard to see in her reflection the Josie that Mack had seen.

As Josie pulled into the driveway with fifteen minutes to spare, Amy's Kewpie-doll face peered from the picture window. She opened the front door and pulled Josie quickly inside. "Brrr. It's cold out there!"

Josie looked Amy up and down, noting the way her stomach stretched the crimson wool maternity jumper. "When exactly are you due?" she asked.

"The official date is November 5, but the way I feel, I don't see how I can last two and a half more weeks. The regular duck hunting season starts near the end of October, so Les says I better hurry up and have the baby. Heaven forbid the birth of a child should interfere with his sport." Although Amy smiled, Josie noted her sad eyes and inwardly cursed the insensitive Lester Peterson.

After the two settled on the kitchen bar stools, Amy fixed Josie with a mock-serious stare. "Okay. Tell Mother all about it. Are you in love?"

Josie was startled by the directness of the question. She'd never put it to herself that way. Was she in love? She enjoyed thinking about Mack in a dreamy sort of way, relished the titillation of recalling his embraces and expert kisses, but in love? That was serious business. That implied commitment, a future.

And what about Mack? Could he possibly be in love with her? Was he ready for anyone? If he was, a bigger question was whether he was ready for her.

She cleared her throat. "Amy, I don't know. All I can tell you is that I've never felt this way before." Amy's eyes shone with friendship as she watched Josie's struggle for honesty. "If this is love, Amy, I'm scared."

Amy covered Josie's hand with her own swollen one. "Why, Josie?"

Josie stared at the smooth almond countertop. "Because . . . I can't believe someone like Mack could choose someone like me."

Amy spun Josie around on the stool to face her. "Ever think of it the other way around? Why would a caring lovable person like you choose a sad sack deputy sheriff, handsome as he is?" Before Josie could respond, a menacing rumble of distant thunder distracted Amy. "Darn. I only have one decent pair of shoes to fit over these swollen feet. I don't want to get them wet."

"No problem, little mother. Let's get this show on the road." Josie helped Amy into her raincoat, too tight to button.

On the short drive to Beth Ann's, thunder rolled around the skies, but the rain held off. "Amy, I need you to answer a question for me." Josie kept her eyes fixed on the road.

"Shoot."

"I need to know about Sarah. What was she like?"

Amy pondered. "Okay. I'll tell you about her and you can listen, but you're not to compare yourself to her. You two are—were—very different yet particularly special." Amy frowned with the effort of picking her words carefully. "Sarah was a delight. Everyone's friend. No wonder she was Homecoming queen. Yet she didn't create envy in others. We all just accepted her honors as her due. It was no surprise to any of us that she became a nurse. She had a soothing quality that just naturally made people feel good. And I won't kid you. She had a petite kind of china-doll beauty that made everyone feel protective of her."

A streak of lightning illuminated the sky, followed by a roll of thunder. Large drops of rain fell randomly on the windshield. Josie swallowed the sour lump in her throat. "Here we are," she said, drawing up to the curb. "Let's get you into the house before you get soaked."

A shrill chorus of women's voices and high-pitched laughter assaulted Josie as she wandered in a blue-white daze into the living room. The multicolored dresses, the pink and blue balloons, the swirl of ribbons atop the piled gifts, all formed a kaleidoscope of color and movement that made her dizzy. She felt a sob scratching against the walls of her throat. *Petite. Delight. Everyone's friend.* The words rolled around in her head, magnifying the lump in her throat.

Josie found a folding chair in a far corner of the room and accepted the pad and pencil requisite for the baby-shower games. Participating halfheartedly, she used the time to remonstrate with herself. Her loneliness and insecurity were things of the past. She *was* a valuable person. She forced the litany of self-acceptance to roll in her mind.

By the time the games were over and the packages opened and passed for inspection, Josie felt calmer, more in control. She'd had little contact with the hostesses who bustled in and out of the kitchen arranging the refreshments on the dining room table. Her glimpses of Beth Ann, intent on perfection as a party-giver, were fleeting.

Directed to a buffet where delicate china plates and highly polished silver were displayed, the guests lined up and chatted animatedly as they waited their turn. Beth Ann entered from the kitchen to exchange the empty coffeepot for a full one, and an older lady with blue-tinted tight curls stopped her.

"Beth Ann, honey. Surely that wasn't your Clay with that group of ruffians having a wild party over at Jessups' last weekend." The room quieted, indrawn breaths suspended.

"Now, Lillian, Ralph and I always know where Clay is." She set down the coffeepot and drew the woman to her by the elbow. "And I can assure you Clay and his friends are as nice a group of young people as you could find anywhere." Beth Ann's smile looked set in stone. "Come on, now, everyone. Enjoy the food. There's plenty of it."

Josie was relieved when at last the gathering began to break up. Amy announced that her mother would take her home in her station wagon, since they had all the gifts to transport. Picking up some empty cups and soiled paper napkins, Josie headed for the kitchen to deposit her load and thank the hostesses before making her getaway. As she pushed against the swinging door between the dining room and kitchen, she was stopped in her tracks by a conspiratorial voice. "Beth Ann, you don't mean *that's* who Mack's been seeing." Josie froze, unable to avoid hearing the response from Beth Ann's prim mouth.

"I can't understand it, Marcia. After Sarah, small, lovely and so talented—what can he possibly see in that awkward, gangly, strawberry roan colt of a girl?"

Josie choked, set the cups down with a clatter on the buffet and fled to the master bedroom to unearth her coat. On her way back to the front hall, she met Amy coming out of the powder room. "Please give the hostesses my thanks. I couldn't find them and I'm leaving now." Josie bolted out the front door, dodging the puddles on the sidewalk.

As she drove home through the slashing icy rain, the monotonous whish-whoosh of the windshield wipers provided accompaniment to the anvil chorus in Josie's head: "Awkward, gangly, strawberry roan colt of a girl. Awkward, gangly, strawberry roan colt of a girl." How could she for one moment have thought Mack cared about her? Her? An awkward, gangly, ugly duckling.

CHAPTER SEVEN

MACK RETRACTED the ballpoint pen, snapped closed the notebook and stretched his arms over his head before standing to leave the weekly briefing. Pete Wells slapped him on the back as he passed. "Come on, Mack. No daydreaming allowed. Front and center."

Mack grinned at Pete's retreating back. A good man, Pete. As two young deputies, they had a lot in common, although Pete definitely had his sights set on a permanent career in law enforcement. Mack didn't say much at work about his writing and photography. It was important for morale that he act as committed as the rest. He'd worked in his darkroom till late last night, trying to sharpen the contrast in several photos of ice formations in the Flint Hills. A couple of them had real promise for the festival.

The festival! He fingered the note in his shirt pocket that Alice had handed him just before the briefing. He was supposed to call Beth Ann ASAP.

As he walked past Alice's desk, she looked up inquiringly. He held up the note, gave her an affirmative nod and picked up the phone on his desk.

"Beth Ann? It's Mack. What can I do for you?" He opened his desk drawer as he listened and pulled out a pack of gum.

"I'm working on it," he said after she spoke. "How many? I'd estimate about thirty." Unwrapping the foil from the stick, he frowned. Why was she checking on him already? The exhibit was still a month away. He'd told her he'd do it, and he would—in his own sweet time.

Popping the gum into his mouth, he rolled his eyes as she babbled on about the plans for the arts-and-crafts exhibit, the judges, the concessions. "Er, Beth Ann. I am calling you from headquarters. We need to cut this short."

Despite the gum, her next words caused a sour taste in his mouth. He cupped the receiver with his left hand and leaned forward, certain he couldn't be hearing what he was hearing. "Mack, I know you've been lonely since Sarah died, and maybe I've been remiss in not encouraging you to have a social life. I met the new attorney in town the other day at the golf course. Her name's Monica Austin. She's quite attractive, and I'd love to introduce you to her."

Exasperated, Mack tried to interrupt. "Now look here, Beth Ann—"

"She's really much more your type than that gawky Calhoun girl. Honestly, Mack, she's so plain, nothing like our Sarah. Not suitable for you at all, if you don't mind my saying so."

Barely containing the snarl in his voice, Mack spoke loudly into the receiver. "Beth Ann, when I need your help matchmaking, you'll be the first to know. For now, I'll handle my life myself. Furthermore, I'd appreciate it if you'd confine your social calls to my home and refrain from comments about who I am or am not seeing. Goodbye."

He slammed the receiver into its cradle. Fuming, he was unaware of the stillness in the room and Alice's discreet scrutiny. Standing, he strapped on his holster, checked his pockets to make sure he had everything and picked up his hat.

As he started to leave, he paused, then returned resolutely to his desk. Dialing quickly, he held his breath, listening to the rings. On the fourth, a breathless voice answered.

"Josie? I'm so glad I caught you." He relaxed as he savored the enthusiasm in her response and pictured her long lean body punctuated by delightful curves. "How good are you at getting up early? I mean really early?"

"Are we going worm-catching?" She giggled on the other end.

"Not exactly, although we are in search of 'early birds.'" He waited for the obligatory groan. "Remember when you asked me why I hunt? I said I'd rather show you than tell you. Well, regular duck season opens this coming Saturday. I have Friday off and I'd like to take you out before opening day to some of the ponds and reservoirs to watch the birds. I emphasize 'watch.' Maybe I can answer your question then. Can you be ready at four-thirty? I do mean a.m. And, Josie—" he lowered his voice "—I'm really looking forward to seeing you." Replacing the receiver, he strode purposefully across the room toward the door.

Alice looked up with a knowing smile. "That second phone call put the first one to shame. Ready to tell me anything yet?" She stared at him innocently, and when the only response was a cryptic grin, she resumed her keyboard work.

JOSIE PULLED the down comforter up around her shoulders, burrowed into the pillow and moved her feet in search of a warm spot. The halcyon lazy autumn days had been abruptly replaced by an Arctic cold front, and

forecasters expected the first freeze tonight. Josie loved
the feel of the soft flannel sheets and the worn percale
pillowcase. Snuggling under the covers, she willed herself to sleep. Her clothes were laid out, her alarm set for
3:45 a.m. She needed a good night's sleep.

Unfortunately, her mind was racing. The notion of
spending an entire day watching the birds felt almost like
playing hooky. And her pulse raced in anticipation of
spending hours with Mack. She visualized the familiar
body in camouflage, his strong legs striding across a
cornfield, his hands cupped to his mouth to call in a
mallard drake.

How would he see her? He'd almost made her believe
she was beautiful, but Beth Ann's words echoed in her
ears still, and the mirror tonight had reflected a strawberry roan, not a swan.

She sighed and turned on her back, her fingers worrying the satin edging of the blanket. The self-fulfilling
prophecy. She almost snorted. Self-fulfilling, all right.
Why was she so much more willing to buy Beth Ann's
image of her than Mack's? Maybe Mack was just hu-
moring her. All those junior- and senior-high classmates
couldn't have been wrong.

Amy had called her the day after the shower. Like the
good friend she was, she'd sensed Josie's pain and urgency when she'd left Beth Ann's. With much coaxing
and reassurance, Amy extracted from Josie the story of
Beth Ann's cruel remarks. She was beside herself.

"Josie Calhoun, you are the most stubborn aggravat-
ing woman I know!" Amy was wound up. "Beth Ann
Johnson'll do anything to keep Mack from getting serious about another woman. All she bases her judgment on
is whether someone plays golf, gets her nails done every
week and shops in Kansas City. She wouldn't appreciate

a natural beauty like you in a million years. Forget her. Gosh, Josie, believe in yourself.''

Amy's impassioned defense had soothed Josie. In truth, she had to admit that the most vicious self-destructive voice of all was not Beth Ann's, but the small nagging whine from within herself. If she was so likable, such a "natural" beauty, why had Cheryl been ashamed of her, embarrassed to be her mother? Why had her high school peers made her life a living hell?

Josie flopped over on her stomach, lifting her head to read the illuminated dial of the alarm clock. Almost midnight! What kind of beauty sleep did four hours give you?

The alarm brayed its wake-up call. Josie groped for the Off button. Blissful stillness returned and she lay back down. She'd been buried deep in a warm snowdrift of sleep. Just a little more.

Abruptly she sat straight up in bed. Today. The date with Mack. What if she'd fallen asleep again? She planted her feet on the cold wooden floor, grabbed her robe and dashed for the bathroom.

Dressing, she felt like a walking L.L.Bean catalog. Heavy knee-high wool socks; layers above the waist—first a long-sleeved thermal undershirt, then a forest green flannel shirt and finally a maroon pullover; and over the socks, a pair of flannel-lined khaki jeans. Carrying her hiking boots in one hand, she scooped up the gloves and parka lying across the rocker.

Downstairs, she plugged in the coffee, laced up her boots and located her field binoculars. Just as she was pouring the coffee into the thermos, she saw the headlights of the Bronco rounding the curve in the lane.

Mack rapped softly on the door. Entering the kitchen, he filled the space with the scent of wood smoke and leather. He wrapped her in a bear hug. "Mmm-mmm. You're warm." He rubbed his unshaven cheek across hers, sending sparks to the tips of her toes. "Button up. The wind's picking up." He helped her into her parka, looped the binoculars over her head and handed her the thermos. "Ready for our big adventure?"

"You bet." She turned off the kitchen light and locked the door behind them. There was something deliciously mysterious and conspiratorial about escaping into the darkness and riding in companionable silence through the deserted countryside. It was as if they and they alone inhabited this predawn world. Then Josie smiled to herself. They weren't quite alone. Stranger had bounded forward, draping his head over the front seat and pressing his moist nose into Josie's cheek. She reached up and scratched him behind his ears.

Mack pulled the Bronco off the rutted cow path and parked under the limbs of a large cottonwood, taking care that the vehicle was not visible from the air. Snapping a leash on Stranger's collar, he handed it to Josie. "Would you hold him while I get my equipment out?"

He went around to the back and gathered a big canvas bag, a flashlight and a camouflage jacket. "Here." He handed her the jacket. "Put that on over your coat. There's a camouflage hat in the pocket." Her arms swam in the man-size jacket and the hat covered her ears, but a delicious sense of being in Mack's skin enveloped her.

When he reached in the driver's side to turn off the headlights, they were plunged into darkness. "It's always darkest before the dawn," Mack whispered, coming around the Bronco and handing her the thermos. "You carry this and lead Stranger, and I'll get the rest."

He illuminated the weed-overgrown path with the flashlight and started ahead of her into the darkness.

Stranger yelped in anticipation. Half tripping through the undergrowth, Josie struggled to keep up with man and dog. From a distant tree, she heard the mournful hoot of an owl. Otherwise the silence was broken only by the thrashing of their progress toward the large farm pond. Mack stopped and shone the beam on his watch, then started off again. Josie knew it was important to be settled in the blind very early, since the birds generally flew about half an hour before dawn.

Reaching the rocky incline of the dam, Mack signaled her to pause. Slowly he inched up to the top and prostrated himself to peer over the edge. After a moment he motioned her to join him. Quietly she lay down beside him. At first, the darkness obscured the shoreline. Slowly her eyes adjusted. She followed the line of the finger he pointed. Against the north shore, rocking in time with the lapping waters, were about twenty small ducks.

Mack took her by the hand and led her back down the slope. "Let's circle around to the blind. Maybe if we stay downwind, we won't disturb them."

Once again Josie followed Mack through the undergrowth, Stranger eagerly pulling her along. About five minutes later, Mack slowed, then turned and placed his finger over his lips. Stealthily he took off through a patch of dry weeds and tall cattails. Then he doused the light, waited for her and grabbed her wrist.

They'd reached the blind, a structure of planks covered by grass and weeds. He lifted a burlap flap and motioned her inside. Stranger jumped in beside her. Hoisting the canvas bag onto the bench, Mack joined them, carefully closing the makeshift door behind them. Through a long horizontal slit in the blind, Josie could see the edge of the pond and hear the lapping of wavelets against the muddy bank. Her heart thudded in response to the unexpected intimacy of huddling together against the sharp cold.

Mack leaned over, his breath seductively warm against her ear. "I think we have time for a cup of coffee." Josie fumbled with the thermos, managing to spill only a few drops in the darkness. His cold hand closed around her gloved one as he reached for the cup of steaming coffee. Studying his profile, barely visible in the darkness, she felt cozy and secure. He handed her the cup, the sharing creating a silent communion.

Mack curled her against him, reaching his arm around her and engulfing her hand with his. They huddled in hushed anticipation, as the eastern sky lightened, gradually bringing the water and shoreline in sharp relief. The outline of scudding clouds and distant trees brought definition to the landscape. A gentle quacking aroused the floating flock, and a few teal began swimming in desultory fashion. Josie squeezed Mack's hand and nodded at the aperture as the first tentative pink-violet streaks emboldened the shades of gray on the horizon. Josie became aware that where a moment before there had been silence, now the countryside was alive with the chattering of birds, the distant crowing of cocks and lowing of cattle, and a general rustling of unknown but purposeful activity.

Mack withdrew his arm and gripped Stranger's collar, motioning him to lie down. A tangible expectancy gripped Josie. Just then a distinctive whoosh-whoosh began to grow behind them, quickly intensifying as straight over the blind about fifteen feet in the air, a flock of mallards came in for a landing. The sound and sight sent a thrill of recognition through Josie. She felt Mack's hand on her leg, clenching her thigh in excitement. Her breath came in short gasps. The brilliant orange tip of the sun protruded on the rim of the horizon pushing the scattered silver clouds to one side. Josie marveled at the phenomenon; she felt like a witness to creation.

Mack quietly began to unzip the canvas bag. Extracting his camera, he removed the lens cap and leaned forward toward the slit, taking care to keep the camera shielded until the last minute. Fixing his eye to the sight, he gently moved the focus rings. He froze.

Slowly, in a maddeningly random ballet, a drake and a hen swam nearer the blind, then feinted to one side, only to round again and paddle toward them. When they came within about twelve feet, the drake beginning to cross in front of the hen, Mack snapped the picture, quickly taking another. At the click of the camera, the other ducks raised their heads, squawked in alarm and jumped off the glittering water and ascended across the emerging copper ball of the sun. The shutter clicked in succession as Mack followed their exodus.

He turned and grinned at Josie, the planes of his face illuminated in the tremulous, dusty shafts of light penetrating the blind. "This is the only shooting I'm doing today." He replaced the lens cover and carefully laid the camera in the open bag. "It'll probably be a while before we see more. How about another cup of that coffee?"

Josie stamped her feet several times to renew her circulation. "Sounds good. That was a big drake with that hen. I hope you were able to get some clear shots."

As the sun rose, the stiff wind abated and warmth began to penetrate the blind. Josie removed the heavy parka, covering up again with Mack's jacket. After a long stretch of inactivity, Josie, her eyelids heavy, leaned drowsily against Mack, finally succumbing to the desire to snooze. Through her layers of drowsiness, she became aware of a subtle shifting, Mack pulling her down across the bench to rest her head in his lap. She sighed and turned sideways, away from him, settling her head on the arm draped across his knees.

Sometime later, she stirred. As she fought to open her eyes, she felt his hand gently kneading her shoulder. She rolled over onto her back and found him watching her pensively. What was he thinking about? Sarah?

Josie struggled to sit, but he pulled her onto his lap, crushing her in an embrace. "Now this is what I call a wonderful way to keep warm in a duck blind," and he rubbed his stubbly cheek across hers.

His brown eyes, flecked with hazel pinpoints, found hers. The moment hovered, like the sun poised on the horizon. He removed her floppy hat, exposing her unruly curls, and framed her face with his hands. "Lady, you're enough to distract any guy from the serious business of hunting." He planted a kiss on the top of her head. "What do you say we get out and stretch our legs a little?"

STANDING IN FRONT of the blind, Mack watched Josie, with Stranger at her heels, break into a jog in an effort to get warm. A large mass of clouds moving rapidly across the watery gray-blue sky threatened the early sun, and the recently dormant wind was freshening. The sight of Josie's large hat bobbing on her head creased his face in an amused smile.

As they turned to jog back toward him, Mack reached into the blind and brought out his camera. Just as Stranger leapt toward Josie's raised hand, he snapped the shutter. Oblivious to Mack, she knelt down, burying her head in Stranger's neck. Then she raised up and, nose to nose with the dog, muttered something Mack couldn't hear. He clicked the shutter again. Alerted, Josie looked up. "No fair. Stranger and I are camera shy."

They returned to the blind. Another forty-five minutes passed, punctuated by small talk and periods of easy silence. Mack drained the last of the coffee, then checked his watch. "Nine-thirty. I doubt any birds will fly for a while. What do you say we go have a big breakfast somewhere?"

Josie looked up in relief. "I thought you'd never ask. I'm ravenous." They gathered their gear, emerged from the blind and started off through the undergrowth. Suddenly Josie stopped in her tracks. "Mack," she whispered. "Quiet."

He strained but could hear nothing. Looking back, he saw her, hand shading her eyes, staring intently at the sky. Scanning the clouds, she froze and slowly raised her other hand to point high above them. Barely discernible, the tiny V formation trailed across a cloud, shifting and changing in a gracefully orchestrated movement as it approached. Then as if from nowhere, the raucous "hronk, hronk" reached them, at first muffled in the distance, then growing distinct and engulfing them as the flock, winging south, moved high over their heads. Josie, transfixed, swiveled her head to follow the flight with the binoculars.

As the last haunting cry faded, she turned to him, eyes dazzling. "My geese! Oh, Mack, aren't they wonderful?" Enthusiasm animated her whole being. His heart lurched at the joy illuminating her face.

Later, sitting over a plate of steaming flapjacks and sausage, he reached across the table to touch her hand. "Tell me about those geese you love so much."

She wiped her mouth on the edge of her napkin. "Birds have always fascinated me," she began carefully.

"Something about the mystery of how they communicate and their instinctive knowledge of habitat, seasons, flight patterns. Even as a little girl watching them build nests, I wondered how they knew what to do."

She paused. "It was natural, I suppose, for me to study birds. There's a danger, though, of becoming so clinical you lose sight of the wonder. But Canada geese have never lost their mystique for me. Their majestic size, their graceful and practical flying formations, and their wariness all intrigue me."

Her expression became almost reverent. "But what sings to me—that's the only way to put it—is their devotion to their mate. It's hard to define scientifically, but I feel a bond with the geese." Picking up her coffee cup, she eyed him over the rim. "Does that sound ridiculous?"

"Not at all. In a way, it's the same kind of identification I have with Stranger. He's more than just an animal." Mack scooped the last mouthful of flapjack onto his fork and chewed thoughtfully. "When we were in Kansas City, I promised I would show you why I hunt, remember?"

He washed the food down with a final swig of orange juice, then reached across and held both of her hands. "I hope this won't sound ridiculous, either. This morning in the blind with you, I felt a togetherness that was distinct and very special. Maybe you did, too." He noted a flush spread across her cheeks. "That experience we shared has a great deal to do with what hunting is all about."

He cleared his throat. "When I was a little boy, my grandfather, a grizzly irascible scarecrow of a man, used to take me hunting with him. He was stoic, not a man given to displays of affection. In fact, sometimes I was scared of him. On my eighth birthday, he grabbed me by the shoulders, sized me up and said, 'Boy, you'll do. You're old enough to go hunting with me.'

"Josie, I can't explain it, but something happened between him and me sitting together in a cold duck blind and trampling the cornfields for pheasant. I felt worthy. With his actions and in his few plain words, he taught me about nature and gave me a sense of belonging to the land. Above all, that old curmudgeon gave me his acceptance and love. He made me feel like a man."

Josie squeezed Mack's hands, encouraging him to continue. "Killing birds is not what my hunting is all about. Any birds I kill, I eat. It's about something instinctual and, some would say, male. Friendships of a kind that can't start many other places begin and grow on a tramp through a field or in the privacy of a duck blind. It's too easy an answer to dismiss it as simply the hunter-gatherer force in humans. There's something beyond that. Something like the mystery of your affinity for the geese. That mystery is what I tried to share with you this morning." Mack lowered his gaze, awaiting Josie's response.

She shoved her empty plate to the edge of the table. "Life is full of urges and feelings we don't fully understand. As a zoologist, I try to approach the subject of hunting rationally. The blood hunters and the careless ones who leave birds in the field to die a slow death anger me.

"I'm not stupid. I know that a clean kill is preferable to an insidious disease or maiming by a coyote. But every time I think of hunting, I see that cold triumphant sneer on Gus's face. To deliberately take up a shotgun and blast a bird is something I could never do. Even if I could understand your motivation, even the satisfaction you gain, I couldn't share in it. It seems to me that you could experience the same results with a camera as with a shot-gun."

She shrugged into her coat, then leaned across the ta-ble. "Let's compromise." She wagged her index finger in front of his face. "I'll climb down off my soapbox if you promise to leave my husband-and-wife geese alone, okay?"

"It's a deal." The light humor of her request was be-trayed by the intensity of feeling flashing in her green eyes.

AN AFTERNOON RAINSTORM, stalled over the plains in a leaden curtain, intensified Josie's fatigue. Mack, hunched over the steering wheel, looked hollow-eyed and drawn. "Red, not to seem ungentlemanly, but you look bushed."

Josie raised a weary eyebrow. "Most ladies would protest, but I plead guilty as charged. Morning came early today." The hum of the engine and the predictable rhythm of the windshield wipers drained her of energy. The idea of an afternoon nap was irresistible.

Mack peered glumly out the window. "I'd hoped to show you the wonders of the scenic Flint Hills, but they're not at their best today."

Josie chuckled. "Some friends in Chicago, who'd driven to Dallas via I-35, scoffed—actually that's too mild a word to describe their reaction—at the sign di-recting their attention to the Scenic Flint Hills."

Instead of laughing, Mack tightened his grip on the steering wheel. "What's *your* reaction to the Flint Hills?"

Mack's sudden tension puzzled Josie. "I think they're like dill pickles. You either like them or you don't."

"And?" His question hung in the air. Josie knew that for some reason her answer was important.

"And . . . I'm crazy about dill pickles and believe that my good taste in recognizing the beauty of the Flint Hills makes me more discerning than most." He nodded his head imperceptibly, but made no response. To lighten the inexplicably serious mood, she smiled and turned to him. "Did I pass the test?"

"I'm sorry it felt like a test. I owe you an explanation. When I told you writing is what I really want to do, I didn't tell you that I'm working on a book—about the Flint Hills. I've always loved their grandeur and antiquity." He picked up a strand of curly red hair escaping from her hat and rubbed it between his thumb and forefinger. "I figured a true friend would take me, Flint Hills and all. I'm glad I was right."

There was that word again—friend. Just when she'd begun to relax with him. Just when she'd gotten used to his arms around her. Just when he'd made her feel special. Friend. She'd have to settle for that, she supposed. A friend would understand about Sarah. A friend would help him over the pain.

Mack interrupted her thoughts. "It's just as well we're calling it quits. I'm on duty all day tomorrow and again Sunday night."

Josie rode along, awash in a sea of ambiguity. When she was in his arms and his hungry mouth sought hers, she felt desirable, invincible. Yet there'd been few declarations, no promises beyond friendship. Was she like some schoolgirl mooning over a crush? And what room did she have in her life right now for romance, anyway? She needed to be all business, emotionally detached. In the cold light of day, she admitted thoughts of him had sidetracked her from focusing on her future.

The rain intensified, beating a metallic tattoo on the roof of the Bronco. Mack adjusted the windshield wipers to high speed. Josie crossed her arms over her chest and huddled against the passenger door. The Flint Hills. It was hard to imagine Mack as a writer. She'd observed his poetic streak, but she'd never have guessed the Flint Hills would fuel his passion. No matter how well you thought you knew somebody, you could always be surprised, she mused.

As if in response to that idea, Mack squinted through the windshield and mumbled a question. Josie strained to hear, not believing her ears. "What did you say?"

"Has your grandfather made any decisions about the pond?"

"Decisions about the pond? What are you talking about?"

"Ooh, boy." Mack leaned forward to wipe the befogged interior of the windshield with his gloved hand. "I guess I've stepped in it big time."

"Stepped in what?" Josie's voice rose in frustration.

"Calhoun family doo-doo, that's what."

"For heaven's sake, Mack, what are you talking about?"

"The pond. The sportsmen's-club lease."

"Wait, wait." She shook her head incredulously. "You can't mean what I think you mean. *Our* pond?"

"I assumed your grandfather had mentioned it to you."

"Damn you! Mentioned what?"

"Les and the rest of our group have made your grandfather a proposal to lease the pond and adjoining pasture for fifteen years for hunting, fishing and recreation."

She punched the seat with her balled fist. "No. I can't believe it! No way!"

Mack shrugged. "Josie, I'm sorry. I thought Frank would've discussed it with you."

"I wish he had. Then we wouldn't be having this conversation. Over my dead body is this going to happen!"

"I don't suppose it'd do any good to ask you to consider it from our point of view, or at the very least from Frank's point of view."

"Frank's point of view? What, pray tell, might that be?" Her jaw ached with the effort of controlling the venom welling in her throat.

"Josie, he's lonely. Surely you can see that. And he's bored. Losing your grandmother and then leasing out most of the farm to the Haggertys has knocked the pins out from under him. And you're not going to be here forever. He needs a project, a purpose, something to occupy him."

"A project? And I suppose you think a sportsmen's club near the farmhouse is just the thing?"

"We'd hoped he could help us build blinds, plant some feed, maybe even manage the clubhouse eventually."

Josie pulled her knees up to her chest and stared defiantly out the rain-smeared windshield. They drove on for several minutes in silence before she spoke. "I don't know whether to be more furious with you for telling me all this or upset with Gramps that he's even considering such a preposterous idea." She picked at a cockleburr clinging to one sock.

She felt Mack kneading her shoulder with his right hand. Tears burned beneath her lids. Damn! She would not cry! The circular motions on her back seemed to be touching the core of her confusion. Why hadn't Gramps talked to her? Clearly her speech that night at the meeting had been a mere token appearance for everyone, even her grandfather.

And why did Mack have to be involved? It just complicated everything! Mack was becoming very important to her. Her heart did a nosedive into her stomach every time she saw him. Why couldn't life be simple? If only her principles weren't at war with her feelings. Geese. They'd probably shoot them, too. Her pond turned into a shooting gallery. Never!

Mack's gloved hand traced the curve of her cheek. "I'm sorry, Red. I never intended to upset you, but I was sure Frank would've consulted you." His hand dropped back onto the steering wheel. Josie barely managed to control her anger at her grandfather's betrayal and Mack's reasonable tone. "Looks like I failed to convince you today."

Josie straightened. "Is that what this was all about— convincing me? So your precious lease idea would fly?"

"You know better than that." He slumped visibly. "That was unfair."

The remainder of the trip home was made in silence.

CHAPTER EIGHT

WHEN THEY ARRIVED at the farm, Mack broke the silence. "May I come inside to tell your grandfather goodbye before he leaves on his trip?"

With elaborate politeness, Josie answered, "Of course you may."

As he held open the storm door, she was careful not to brush against him. She was coiled to explode—barely controlled fury at her grandfather's failure to inform her and arguments against the lease proposal vied for control of her tongue. Before she could launch her diatribe, Gramps's touchingly enthusiastic and elaborate preparations for his fishing trip dispelled any thought of confronting him just then. The first sight that greeted her was the living room carpet littered with fish hooks, plastic worms, lures of all sizes and shapes, sinkers, bobbers and assorted other gear. Gramps looked up with a mischievous grin, like a small boy caught in the act.

"Just cleaning out my tackle box. Careful where you walk."

Her grandfather gave her little time to question him or to ponder a fish's chances against such a formidable array, so busy was he repeating last-minute instructions for everything from emergency numbers where he could be reached to contingency plans if the sink clogged. Several times Josie reminded him she was over twenty-one and endowed with reasonable intelligence. Mack, too, was

given his marching orders, primarily having to do with
feeding the cattle and keeping an eye on Josie.

Only after dinner, her mood somewhat lightened, did
she find the opportunity to raise the issue of the pond
lease. Gramps dismissed her concern. "Don't you worry
about that. I'm just thinking it over."

"Gramps, you can't seriously be considering turning
our pond into a shooting gallery."

"So long as I own this farm, this is my business. I don't
want you to worry your pretty little head about it."

"But—" Josie sputtered.

"Enough! Let's not spoil our last night together. I'll
mull the idea over on my trip. Nothing's been decided.
And there's certainly no hurry." He put one arm around
her shoulder and hugged her. "Now, where did I put my
rod case?"

He left her standing impotently with unanswered
questions and barely stifled accusations. *Don't worry
your pretty little head?* Damn! The "keep 'em barefoot
and pregnant" syndrome was alive and well in north
central Kansas. But she didn't want to ruin his departure; he hadn't seemed so pleased and excited since before MJ died. And as he reminded her, the decision was
not imminent. Suddenly her shoulders drooped with the
exhaustion of the long day and the tension that had
knotted her stomach since early afternoon.

"BYE, GRAMPS. Have a good trip." Josie waved from the
kitchen door the next morning as the maroon Chevy
started down the lane.

The house seemed suddenly bereft of life, the quiet
hanging like a canopy over the empty rooms. As if to remind her that she wasn't completely alone, James Cagney rubbed against her leg. Scooping him up in her arms,

Josie hugged the big tiger cat to her chest. "We'll be fine, won't we, fella?" With him in her arms she headed up to her makeshift study.

Josie relished the quiet, free from interruptions. With all but a couple of chapters in the revision stage, Josie could see the light at the end of the thesis tunnel. She pulled the fifth chapter up on the screen and carefully began editing.

Absorbed in her work, she jumped when the phone rang. As she dashed downstairs to answer, she was surprised to see that it was already nearly noon. "Hello?"

"Josie, thank God you're home," Mack's worried voice betrayed relief.

"What's the matter? Is it Gramps?" Her heart thudded.

"No, it's Amy. Can you get to the hospital right away?"

"Mack, oh, God, what is it?"

"It's okay. Calm down. Amy was in a fender bender this morning and she's gone into labor. She's all right, but we can't locate Les. He's out duck-hunting somewhere, and her folks have gone to the college football game. She's all by herself. Can you come?"

"Of course. I'll be there right away."

"I'm still on duty until three, but I've alerted those on patrol to keep an eye out for Les, and the Kansas State campus police will try to get the message to Amy's mother and dad. Some of Les's favorite hunting spots are in my territory, so maybe I can locate him quickly. As soon as we get any word, I'll call you at the hospital."

Josie raced upstairs, turned off the computer and grabbed her coat and purse. As if to echo her murderous thoughts about Les, a shotgun blast reverberated from the direction of the pond.

When Josie entered the birthing room half an hour later, Amy's eyes widened with relief. "Josie, I'm so glad you're here. It's all so overwhelming."

Amy sat propped up in the hospital bed like a stuffed Buddha, a framed print of Mary Cassatt's *Maternal Caress* hanging on the wall behind her. She was connected to an IV drip, and a mechanical finger etched erratic lines on the graph of the fetal monitor.

Josie leaned over and hugged her, capturing Amy's hand in her own as she sat down on the edge of the bed. "You had an accident? Are you all right? How are you feeling?"

"I think I'm okay. I had one or two contractions this morning, but no big deal. I needed some last-minute baby stuff from the store—shampoo, Q-tips, that sort of thing. Just as I was backing out of the driveway, I had another contraction and crashed into a car parked across the street. When I got out of the car to look at the damage, my neighbor came out and we called the police."

Amy stopped. "I think another one's coming." She gripped Josie's hand as the contraction deepened. Josie sat quietly till the moment passed. "Where was I?"

"You called the police. . . ."

"While I was talking with the patrolman, I had two more contractions and he insisted I come here."

A motherly-looking nurse bustled into the room. "How are you doing? I need to take your vitals and check the monitor."

Josie stood to one side, observing the counterfeit normalcy of the room in which every cabinet and drawer hid esoteric obstetrical paraphernalia. The county hospital prided itself on its cozy labor rooms—"next best thing to being at home," their ads read. Usually, though, a home came furnished with a husband, Josie thought derisively. Where was that fool Les? Some priorities—out shooting birds while his wife was in labor!

The nurse leaned over Amy. "Now, remember, breathing is the key. Just breathe through the contractions." She raised an inquisitive eyebrow in Josie's direction. "Will you be staying with her until her husband comes?" Josie nodded, locking knowing eyes with the nurse. "I'll be checking on her often. Press the call button when you need me."

Josie pulled a chair near the bedside and sat quietly, stroking Amy's arm. Amy's lips quivered and her eyes swam with tears. "Josie, why doesn't Les come?" A tear trickled down her pale cheek. "I've been here over two hours. Can't they find him?"

Josie suppressed the vitriolic words that rose to her lips. Standing, she brushed Amy's tears away and smoothed her hair back from her forehead. "They'll find him soon, Amy. There can't be that many ponds and lakes in the area. Meanwhile, you try to relax and think about the baby."

"Relax? I don't think so," and Amy clamped her hand on Josie's forearm as another contraction transported her into a wave of pain.

The doctor arrived, and Josie went out to the waiting room while he did his examination, promising Amy she'd return the minute he was finished. The clock on the waiting-room wall seemed stuck on three. Josie paced to the window overlooking the parking lot, searching in vain for some sign of Les or Amy's parents.

Turning her back to the window, Josie noted the cardboard Halloween witches and loose-jointed skeletons hanging from the nurse's station, a grim counterpoint to Josie's concern and anger at Les. From the other end of the hallway, Josie could hear the staccato laughter of visitors trying to cheer a loved one and the metallic rumble of a heavy meal cart being trundled toward the elevator. Dear sweet domestic Amy. Without her husband, what a cheerless experience this must be for her. Josie sat and began leafing idly through an ancient copy of a parenting magazine.

"Miss Calhoun, you can go back in now." The nurse smiled encouragement. "The doctor's finished his examination. That should trigger some heavier contractions. Any word from her husband?"

"I'm afraid not."

"The main thing for you to do is encourage her and help her remember her breathing. You'll need to stay calm."

"I'll do my best," Josie promised, inwardly wondering how prepared she really was to help with a birth, but recognizing that she was the only available stand-in for Les.

At four, there was a tap on the door. Amy turned her head hopefully. The door opened and a nurse's aide beckoned to Josie. In the waiting room, Mack stood slumped against the wall, rubbing his fingers through his hair. "Mack, any sign of Les?"

He shook his head. "I've looked everywhere, Josie. One farmer saw him earlier this morning but didn't notice which direction he was headed. The Kansas State police finally found Amy's parents at halftime, so at least they're on their way. How's Amy doing?"

"She's being a trooper, all things considered. I don't think it'll be much longer. Will you stay?"

Mack pulled her to him, massaging her tired shoulders with his comforting hands. "Sure thing. Good luck in there." He brushed his lips over her forehead and propelled her toward the room.

By four-thirty, the bustle in the birthing room had escalated, and it was clear to Josie that Baby Peterson's arrival was imminent. A nurse handed her a hospital gown and motioned to her to put it on. Amy's breath came in pants, punctuated by moans. Josie took a dampened washcloth and wiped the perspiration from Amy's brow.

"Just a little while longer. Hang in there." Amy mouthed appreciation and hiccuped a sob. Her breathing changed rhythm and she arched in anticipation of a contraction, fingers digging into Josie's hand. Although Josie hardly knew what she was saying, she kept up a constant murmur of encouragement. "Atta girl. It won't be long now. Good."

The door opened brusquely, and the green-clad doctor pulled out a stool as the nurses efficiently transformed the labor room into a high-tech surgical arena. "It's time, Amy. You're going to have that baby ready or not." From the end of the bed, the doctor's eyes signaled encouragement. "Amy, don't push until I tell you."

The next minutes telescoped into a seamless ballet of cooperation—Amy bearing down, the doctor gently cradling the tiny dark head, the nurses giving Amy instructions. "Once more. Now!"

The doctor grinned in triumph. "Amy, looks like you have a fullback here." A lusty cry emerged from the infant. Those in the room laughed with relief and exhilaration.

"A boy? A boy! Is he all right?" Amy reared her head as the nurses placed the infant on her stomach. "Josie, look. Isn't he wonderful?"

Josie, in awe, absorbed the miracle of mother and child. Tears streamed down her face. "Amy, he *is* wonderful. And you did great."

The nurses took the baby to weigh him and check him over. Amy reached for Josie's hand, and only then did the shadow of hurt and disappointment cloud her face. "Where is he, Josie?"

MACK HELD Josie's hands in his as she told him about the baby, her eyes shining with wonder. Something visceral stirred in Mack as he listened to her tell the age-old story. God, she was lovely. Her face, alive with joy, tilted to his, and he longed to explore the yielding softness of those smiling lips. She'd be a beautiful mother herself, Mack thought.

He was jolted by the realization that it was *his* baby he pictured in her arms.

A tall stoop-shouldered man accompanied by a frantic gray-haired woman stopped at the desk. "Amy Peterson? Is she all right?"

Josie jumped to her feet, intercepted the couple and embraced Amy's mother. "Everything's fine. Amy just had an eight-pound eight-ounce baby boy." Josie took the woman by the hand. "Her room's this way. I know you both want to see her. Go on in."

When Josie returned, Mack picked up his hat. "I'm going to head home and get out of this uniform. Les'll surely show up soon. He can't hunt after sundown. Want to walk me to the car, catch a breath of fresh air?" He tucked Josie's arm in his, noting the circles of strain under her eyes.

Just as they reached the small lobby, Les staggered through the automatic doors. Mack, grasping him by the shoulder, recoiled from the sour blast of whiskey breath.

"Let go of me, damn it!" Les's loud slurred voice attracted the attention of the receptionist. "I gotta see my wife.'' He reeled against a magazine rack. "I'm gonna have a baby, y'know."

Mack jerked him by both shoulders and drew his face within inches of his own. "Shape up, Les. You're in no condition to see Amy, much less your baby."

"Baby?" Les twisted in Mack's grasp to face an imaginary audience. "Hey, everybody," he shouted. "I got a baby!"

"Cool it, Les. Let's get you sobered up." Mack felt an eruption building within him. Out of the corner of his eye he saw Josie's face contorted with disgust. "Sit down, Les.''

"Get your damn-fool hands off me!" Les whirled away and with a wildly flailing arm swiped at Mack. "I'll do whatever I damn well please, pretty-boy cop. I'm gonna see my wife." Les lurched toward the elevator.

A red-hot mass of raw emotion blinded Mack. He grabbed Les from the back by both arms, pulled him around and slammed him into the wall, rattling the framed pictures of the hospital board members. Leaning toward him, imprisoning him with the flat of one hand on his chest, Mack coiled his other fist in front of Les's face, noting through the mist of his rage the bubble of saliva drooling from Les's slack jaw.

"Listen to me, you son of a bitch. You're not fit to be in the same room with Amy. You're drunk, you smell bad, and you're not going into that room like this."

"Sez who?" Les tilted his chin in drunken defiance.

"Sez me, you ungrateful bastard. If I had a wife like Amy, I'd be on my knees in gratitude, not groveling around like the town drunk." Mack slammed him into the wall again for emphasis. "My Sarah never got to be a wife. She never got to be a mother. But I'll tell you one thing, by God. If she had, I'd have loved and cherished her every day of my life."

Mack's eyes stung with angry tears. With a gesture of futility, he released Les and stood, hands hanging at his sides, as Les slid down the wall to the floor.

Mack turned away. Raising his head, he saw Josie, fist crammed tight against her mouth, eyes widened with shock. "Sorry," he mumbled, sinking into a chair. She hurried to his side, saying nothing, laying one hand on his shoulder. After a few moments, he looked up and sighed. "You go on upstairs and tell Amy I'll be here with Les in forty minutes or so. I'll take him home and stand him in the shower, get him cleaned up."

"Okay. Then I'll head home. It's been a long upsetting day. For both of us. After you get cleaned up, why don't you come on over to the house? I'll warm up some vegetable soup and make some cornbread. After all, we do have to eat."

He nodded gratefully. "I'd like that."

JOSIE PUT the soup on to simmer, laid out the cornbread ingredients and popped into the shower. She relished the needles of hot water penetrating her aching shoulders as she shampooed her hair.

It was incredible that so much had happened in so few hours. It seemed days ago that she'd been working on her thesis, not just this morning. Refreshed, she dried her hair and fastened it with a ribbon into a loose ponytail. Her purple velour jogging suit caressed her skin. Spraying a dash of Chloe on her neck, she began to feel human again.

Downstairs, she straightened the living room and ignited the logs Gramps had laid in the fireplace. James Cagney had clearly appropriated Gramps's recliner in his absence. The tawny cat posed like a sphinx, daring anyone to dislodge him from his throne.

Waiting for Mack, Josie let her mind drift over the day's events. Being part of the delivery had been an almost spiritual experience—so elemental, yet so incredibly beautiful. She'd heard women say that any pain associated with labor dims with the joy and wonder of birth. Only now did she begin to understand. Amy, though vulnerable and scared, had shown courage. Josie couldn't help but wonder, however, if Amy's memory of the event would forever be blighted by the knowledge of Les's absence.

Josie poked the fire, seeing in the licking flames the heat of Mack's rage. In his anger, Josie had sensed a primal instinctive force that was both powerful and disturbing. Usually so controlled, Mack was obviously capable of unbridled emotion. Josie, both hands on the mantel, leaned over the fire, lost in the shifting dance of the flames.

Sarah. There it was. No use pretending to herself any longer that she and Mack were anything but friends. His reaction to Les had sprung from the well of his grief. At the deepest level of his being, it was Sarah who possessed him, Sarah who inspired his actions, Sarah who lived in him.

Straightening, Josie wiped the corner of her eye. *Make peace with it, girl. Mack is a fine human being, a good friend, but that's it.* Soon she'd be back in Chicago, involved with the job hunt, exploring a relationship with Tom. What might happen about the sportsmen's-club lease would be out of her hands. Mack would simply be a pleasant but dim memory. Her good friend who lived in Kansas. Tonight what he needed was sanctuary, not demands or recriminations. Just a friend.

From the direction of the barn, Josie heard the pickup engine cough into life. The cattle! Good grief, she'd forgotten, but at least Mack had remembered. She walked toward the kitchen to mix the cornbread.

MACK THREW another log on the fire, stretched his arms over his head and settled on the floor, his back against the sofa. "Great dinner, Josie. Just what the doctor ordered." He turned and smiled up at her.

Perched in the corner of the sofa, legs curled beneath her, Josie basked in the compliment. "It's been quite a day, Mack."

He reached up and grabbed a loose sofa pillow. "Come on down here beside me." He put the pillow against the sofa skirt and patted the place on the carpet next to him.

The invitation was too tempting to resist. She uncoiled and settled contentedly into the spot, wrapping her arms around her bent knees. His nearness was unraveling all her resolution. His legs, crossed at the ankles, stretched out in firmly molded denim perfection, his hard-muscled thighs alive under the fabric. She stared intently at the fire as if watching every spark would somehow sublimate her own growing desire.

Mack moved his arm around her and pulled her against him. "Josie, we need to talk."

Oh, Lord, here it comes. Josie's throat constricted. So long as they hadn't talked any more about Sarah, she had entertained some hope. But the moment of truth had arrived. Summoning her courage, she turned and looked at him, her heart pounding. The warm, eddying depth of his brown eyes caught her unawares.

"I want to apologize for this afternoon," he said. "I completely lost control. I'm not a violent person, Josie, and I'm sorry you had to witness that scene." Contrition shadowed his face.

"Les had it coming, Mack. If I'd been a man, I'd have knocked his block off. You only did what I spent all afternoon thinking about doing."

"That doesn't excuse me. I'm supposed to be trained to let reason and expediency rule emotion. But his attitude made me mad as hell."

"Mack, it was an understandable reaction. All's well that ends well. Thanks to you, Les didn't barge into Amy's room drunk and upset her any more than she already was. You got him cleaned up and sober enough to make a presentable appearance. It's over now, anyway."

"Not quite." He took her hand in his free one. "I do remember what I said." The long pause was filled by the spasmodic crackling of the logs. "I can't explain what happened. I only know that Les's callous treatment of Amy finally really got to me. How would he feel if suddenly he didn't have her?"

Josie lowered her gaze and sat still as a prisoner at the block, awaiting the fall of the ax. She was aware of Mack tensing beside her, struggling for the next words. She stared at her lap, willing him to remain silent.

"Oh, God." He pulled Josie close again. "Oh, God, I still miss her, Josie." He buried his face in her hair. She could feel the tremors shaking his body. Gasping for control, he whispered, "I'm sorry, I'm sorry. It's just...just she will never hold a baby, never celebrate an anniversary, never..."

Josie cradled his head against her shoulder, murmuring in his ear, "Shh, shh. Let it go. Let it go, Mack."

Relinquishing the last rein on his emotion, he succumbed to racking sobs, as she rocked him in her embrace, crooning soft words of comfort. "There, there."

As if standing outside and above herself observing, she was aware of the picture they made, entwined in a classic pose of the griever and comforter. If only she *could* be the observer, the comforter; but in that very moment of objectivity, she felt herself sucked into an undertow of emotion primitive and potent. She leaned on one elbow, protecting his head with her other hand, and eased them to the floor. She wrapped one arm around his heaving shoulders and, coiling her fingers in his hair, pulled his head into the curve between her neck and breast.

Although aware of the warmth of his powerful body pressed alongside her, it was compassion that moved her to rub her hand in light soothing circles over his back. Gradually his shaking subsided and she could feel more regular exhalations stirring the skin beneath her throat.

After a while he stirred and rolled over onto his back, shielding his eyes with his forearm. Josie leaned on one elbow to watch him. Finally he uncovered his eyes and propped himself up to face her, moving one hand up and down her arm as he spoke.

"Josie, I could apologize, but I'm not going to. Sarah was very important to me, and I guess in some ways she always will be. It wouldn't be fair to her memory to apologize for grieving."

The ax had fallen. Surprisingly, Josie wasn't as devastated as she'd expected. There was something heroic about a man who could love so deeply and enduringly, even if the person he loved wasn't her.

He reached for her and pulled her against him, nestling her into his shoulder. "I hadn't been able to cry until now," he said. "Even though I'm embarrassed as hell, I want to thank you for that."

She blinked into the soft material of his shirt, only now permitting the weight of disappointment and loss to sur-

face in her consciousness. Lord, she wanted him.
Fiercely, she wanted him.

So consumed by her emotions was she that she only
half heard his next words, " . . . you, too." What had he
said? Had he said she was important to him, too? Before
she could ask him to repeat, he lifted her chin with his
thumb and forefinger, and with sweet thirsty lips dried
her tears, one by one, sucking each droplet with feathery
nips.

Then he lowered his mouth to hers, convulsively cupping her buttocks as he pulled her on top of him. Withdrawing, he covered her forehead, her eyelids, the soft
skin of her neck with kisses, drowning her in a pool of
warmth, exciting deep currents of sensation from places
she barely knew existed. She could feel the heavy throb
of his heart beating against the soft willing flesh of her
breast.

Gently he turned her over onto her back. Her arms
moved instinctively to pull his head close as she buried
her fingers in his hair. His tongue traced tiny flicking
circles beginning at the base of her throat and moving
tantalizingly toward her ear. She was dimly aware of a
delicious moistness between her thighs and a palpitation
defining the route from abdomen to breast. He moved to
place his left leg between hers as his tongue inscribed tiny
dots, dashes and circles on the fleshy part of her ear and
then probed the orifice in seductive simulation. She
arched into him, panting hoarsely with inchoate desire.
"Mack, oh, Mack!"

She felt his shaking hands fumbling with the zipper of
her velour top as his mouth reversed its route, now trav-
eling from her ear, past her throat, onto the warm flesh
just above her bra. She was aware of the silent com-

mand screaming in her head as she ached for him to release her breasts. As if reading her mind, he moved his fingers from the completed task of the zipper to the fastener at the front of her bra. His mouth moved lower when at last her breasts fell free of constraint.

As if electrified by the voltage generated by his hungry mouth engaging her swollen nipple, her body again arched in involuntary response. He raised his head, filling her field of vision with his handsome face, backlit with desire. He cradled her gently, slowly removing each arm from the sleeves of her top. She reached up and began undoing the buttons of his shirt, one by one. He pulled the shirt from his jeans and stripped it off, throwing it to one side, then lowered himself on top of her again, the soft hair of his chest tracing a path of warmth on her bare breasts. She couldn't get enough of the feel of him, flesh to flesh. If only her nipples and breasts could burn her brand of possession into his warm wood-scented skin.

Locked in a kiss, they rolled in abandon, exploring one another. Josie felt his hand slip beneath the elastic waistband of her slacks, coming into quick contact with the lacy bikini. Trailing his fingers back up to her navel and around toward her back, he snaked her slacks and panties down over her hips and legs. She kicked off her moccasins in a sudden yearning to lie before him, naked in the darting light and shadows of the fire.

He drew one tentative finger down from the hollow of her throat, over her erect nipple, feathered past the small crater of her navel and traced the smooth alabaster flesh of her abdomen before entangling his fingers in the flame red nest below.

"Don't ever doubt it, Josie. You are one beautiful woman," he murmured into her ear. This time "beautiful" pealed in Josie's head with all the joy of bells on Easter morning.

"Mack, keep this up, and I'll start to believe you," she gasped. She reached for the top button of his jeans, moving beneath him to exert leverage on the metal button. The buttons stubbornly refused to yield the hard flesh swelling beneath her frantic fingers.

"Believe it, Red." He reached to help her with the difficult fasteners. Then he stood and quickly stepped out of the jeans, looming over her in molded perfection. He reached down and pulled her to her feet, only the thin cotton of his jockey shorts between them as he ran his fingers slowly down her back and over her buttocks, then up over her hips to her breasts.

Leaning down and lifting one swollen nipple to his mouth, he flicked the other lightly with his fingers, until she felt her knees weakening in a spasm of desire. They eased back to the floor, hands and mouths advancing, retreating, seeking, withholding. The sudden memory of Mack emerging from the pond, manly and natural in the summer twilight, caused a violent shudder deep within her.

"Please, Mack. There." She twisted into him. He buried his lips in the warm crevice between her breasts. His hand sought her moist triangle of coppery curls.

"Sarah, Sarah...."

His moan, though muffled, was distinct. Josie felt the volcano within her implode, heavy boulders crashing down into the pit of her stomach, black lava cooling and freezing the hollow in her heart. He went on caressing her, seemingly oblivious to what he'd just said. As much as she wished to deny it, the name he'd moaned so passionately and clearly was Sarah.

Again, Josie found herself flying above the scene, looking down with detachment. What irony! In the moment she knew she loved him, had allowed herself to believe he cared for her, the truth, unbidden and instinctive, had risen to his lips. The twin, hovering dispassionately over her body, mocked her. *What did you expect?* Josie felt sudden embarrassment at her nakedness; like Eve, she longed for a fig leaf.

Mack, at last sensing the change in her, stilled his wandering hand. "Josie, I wouldn't hurt you. But maybe we're not quite ready for this."

Josie laughed inwardly. He was worried about her virginity. Not quite ready. She sighed. No, not quite ready. Maybe never ready. "It's okay." She sat up. "Really. I'm fine." Liar, liar, pants on fire—the old schoolyard taunt, never more accurate, echoed in her brain.

He put his arms around her from behind, pulling her near, resting his chin on her head. "It's better this way. I was pretty emotional tonight. It wouldn't be fair to make love to you and have you think I did it out of grief. When I make love to you the first time, I want it to be right. I want you to feel cherished, special."

The "when I make love to you the first time" played softly in her head, floating pianissimo in her blood, battered and ultimately subdued by the two-beat kettle-drum din, "Sarah, Sarah...."

The awkwardness of the moment was as hushed with expectancy as the barely glowing embers of the fire. James Cagney eyed them warily from his Olympian perch on the recliner. "Let's get our clothes on and have a cup of coffee," Mack suggested.

Relief surged through Josie as she realized the embarrassment of standing up was going to be salvaged by a minor miracle. "We'll have to get up."

Josie giggled semihysterically as, rising to her feet, she pulled from the fleshy pad of her buttock a tiny metal fishhook.

CHAPTER NINE

MACK LIFTED the print from the enlarger and examined it thoughtfully. The figures were silhouetted nicely against scudding clouds, rays of light crossing the background from right to left. Stranger's cocked ears and the tilt of his head were matched by the delighted spontaneous smile of the woman, her hands holding the dog's head as if to say, "Aren't we having fun together?" Josie's kneeling figure, at a diagonal to Stranger's classic sitting pose, gave the photo strong composition.

Mack smiled with pleasure at the way the print had turned out. He didn't know if he would use it for the festival exhibit, but the close-up shot of the mallards taken that same day had printed up beautifully, and he penciled a notation on his list of tentative choices. Next week was the opening of goose season, and he needed to get some shots of the Canada geese to complete the waterfowl portion of his display.

So far he'd selected fifteen photographs. The process was complicated by the fact that he didn't want to use too many of those he planned to include in his book. He felt frustrated by the demands of this darned exhibit; they limited his opportunities to work on the text for the book. Whether it was the snap of cold weather or simply the passage of time, he felt energized and itched to get back to his writing.

He was also frustrated by the time he spent as a deputy sheriff. Removing the last print from the enlarger, he pondered, not for the first time lately, how much longer he could go on with the job. He didn't mind it; in fact there were days he felt genuinely helpful and valuable. But there was no escaping the reality that it was keeping him from realizing his dreams and ambitions.

As he tacked a sheet of contact prints to the cork wall, he found himself at eye level with Sarah. Sarah, eyes shining sweetly, gentle smile dimpling her porcelain complexion. Just when he'd thought he was healing, the nightmares had started again, her haunting eyes agape in horror, her mouth drawn against her teeth in a shattering scream that brought him abruptly from sleep into panicked wakefulness.

The scene with Les. Perhaps that had triggered the recurrence. When Mack had taken Les home that evening to get him sobered up, Les, somewhat abashed, asked Mack why he'd gotten so angry.

"I have learned, Les," he'd said, "that you cannot take someone you love for granted. Life is short and tenuous, and we have so little time with those who are important to us."

"So I suppose you think I'm a jerk?"

"That about says it. You seem to have Les Peterson and his desires at the top of your priority list."

"Who's gonna look after me if I don't?" Les had asked defiantly.

"Getting plastered is your idea of looking after yourself?" Mack had shrugged in disgust. "And who's going to look after Amy and the baby if you don't? Answer me that. Look. You have a chance I'm never going to have with Sarah. Don't blow it, buddy." Mack had

handed Les a sweater and retreated to the living room to
wait for him.

Now Mack faced the picture again. He couldn't keep
Sarah buried. Maybe he shouldn't even try. He reached
over and picked up the print of Josie and Stranger. And
what about Josie? How did she fit in?

Two such different women. Sarah with her sunny dis-
position, Sarah who had never met a stranger, Sarah
whose perfection had made him want to carry her around
in cotton batting. And Josie. Funny, freckled, tomboy
Josie. Bright and spunky, loving and compassionate.
Unsure and vulnerable. Obviously interested in him. Was
he being fair to her?

*Don't skirt the issue, Mack. The big question is how do
you feel?* Sure, he enjoyed Josie's company. Yes, he
found her warm and sexy and fun. So...? So...he just
didn't know if he was ready for commitment to anyone.
And he sure as hell wasn't ready for more pain. Well,
he'd better start getting it figured out. She'd be leaving
for Chicago in early December.

Mack stood, snapping off the darkroom light, and
stomped impatiently up the stairs. He'd try to cool it for
a while. Problems. He didn't need any more problems.

SHE WOULD NOT, repeat not, panic. So what if it was
nearly November 15 and all editing needed to be completed by the twenty-first? So what if Tom had just returned three chapters and two more were to be put in the
mail today? So what if his last letter had outlined some
points to consider in preparing for her oral defense of the
thesis?

She eyeballed James Cagney, draped over the desk-
top, tail hanging off the edge. "Kitty, you know what?
This whole project is for the birds!" She smiled in sour

satisfaction at the trite pun and removed the draft from its envelope.

And why was she in such a state? She couldn't weasel out of it. She knew it was because she'd been mooning over Mack. The vision of Mack, his body moving against hers, his hands roaming intimately over her, filled her mind and caused a thickening in her throat.

She glanced at the first set of notations in Tom's small hand. "Try not to wax rhapsodic about the mating. This is science, not poetry." Easy for him to say, she thought. Rhapsody, poetry. That was what mating for life was, that, plus commitment.

Mating. There it was again. That word. How close she and Mack had come! The memory of her abandon both titillated and alarmed her. She'd come *that* close to giving up her virginity, and for what? Those awful discordant words—"Sarah, Sarah." If it wouldn't be profaning the dead, she felt like shaking the tiny perfect paragon of Maizeville! "Everybody's friend" Amy had said. "Petite, china doll."

And you, Josie? You, the great galloping giraffe, the strawberry roan colt of a girl. Wonderful. Where had her head been?

Oh, sure, she didn't doubt Mack liked her. After all, she was his good friend, and good friends sometimes help each other get their physical needs met. Forget the happily-ever-after. It was pretty clear Mack was mated for life, all right. Mated to Sarah. Then what was that hot scene in front of the fire all about? Was she just the handiest substitute? Damn, she was confused.

There were many reasons to forget him. She mentally ticked them off: he thought hunting birds was manly sport; he was cooking up a cockamamie plan to turn Gramps's land into a hunting club; he didn't mind using

her all-too-willing body; worst of all, he was still wrapped
up with Sarah. So what was she doing? Making a fool of
herself, obviously.

Josie swiped her arm at James Cagney to dislodge him
from her work area and bent over the computer with a
scowl.

FROWNING, MACK stared at the stack of paperwork lying on his desk. As he bent glumly over his task, the
crackle of the dispatcher's radio, the irritating blinking
of the faulty fluorescent light above his head, and his own
distracting thoughts made it hard to concentrate. Something had shifted in his relationship with Josie since their
lovemaking. On the surface, everything seemed normal,
but they were both backing away. In his case, it was pure
self-preservation. But because of his obligation to keep
an eye on things for Frank, he still saw her frequently.

He checked with her every few days to set up the
schedule for feeding the cattle. If he was on patrol assignment, he'd make sure the bales were loaded in the
pickup ahead of time. He didn't want Josie repeating her
swan dive onto the hard floor of the barn. Some evenings she'd invite him in for chili or pot roast, but he
would excuse himself early, careful to avoid situations
where he'd be tempted to forget common sense and
plunge into intimacy.

It wasn't that easy to cool it. He didn't want to lead her
on, so until he was sure of his feelings and his future, it
seemed prudent to avoid temptation. Josie, too, seemed
wary, although friendly. He couldn't put his finger on it.
Things weren't exactly strained, but the ease they'd found
during their trip to Kansas City and their morning in the
duck blind was lacking.

LAURA ABBOT 163

Maybe part of it was that lease business. They *had* avoided talking about it. He figured it was a subject best left to Frank. In any event, his involvement in the sportsmen's club represented an obstacle to their relationship. And maybe, too, he had frightened her the other night with the intensity of his emotions. Had he come on too strong? These past few days it was as if they were circling each other, aware of the chemistry between them, but studiously avoiding letting it draw them into a repeat of that night.

He looked up from the traffic reports he was filling out. Alice eyed him with concern. "That bad, huh?" she asked.

He was nonplussed. "What?"

"I assume the reports. You were frowning so much your eyebrows were about to collide."

"I've just got a lot on my mind, Alice."

She raised her own eyebrows knowingly. "Probably not all patrol business, I'd wager. But, as Ann Landers says, MYOB." She turned back to the mail piled on her desk.

No, not all patrol business, he thought wearily. He couldn't deny the attraction he felt for Josie. He loved to watch her face light up when something excited or moved her. Her unaffected demeanor, her easy feminine athleticism, even her stubbornness . . . hell, she was becoming very important to him.

Admit it, Mack. You're falling in love with her. If only he could lay Sarah's ghost to rest once and for all, then maybe he could move on. Until then, he had to be careful of Josie's feelings, and of his own, which were like a runaway train when he was near her.

The pen he'd been rolling between his fingers clattered to the surface of his desk, arousing him into a determined resumption of his paperwork.

JOSIE WATCHED Mack's short-cropped head, bent over the Scrabble board. His strong fingers toyed with the tiles as he searched for the best combination. Triumphantly he placed the *H* and *W* on either side of an *E*. He leaned back, smiling with satisfaction. "There." He'd spelled HEW.

Before he could savor the moment, she quickly planted a *C* at the beginning and tacked *ING* onto the end. He drew his body up, set his elbows on the table, chin cradled in his hands. "Hmm. This presents an interesting challenge."

"I certainly hope so." She smiled with smug assurance. She already had her next move figured out, one using an *X*. If only he didn't work in a *Y.*

As he pondered his next move, his lowered lashes and furrowed brow caused a quickening of her breathing. *Control yourself, Josie.* She was trying very hard to keep her emotions in check, to permit him the distance he needed and to protect herself from further disillusion.

But how could he have kissed and caressed her so intimately and then go about his business as if nothing had happened? By way of reinforcement, she reviewed the list of reasons she should avoid him like the plague. It was hard to concentrate on them when he was so close. Still, because she was powerfully attracted to him didn't mean she was going to make a fool of herself again.

She'd looked in the mirror. She was a realist. And she was no Sarah. Not now. Not ever. She would yield to the anger building inside her rather than ever come across as pathetic!

Joining the *O* at the end of RADIO to the *L* at the end of GIRL, Mack rubbed his palms with relish as he formed DOLL.

Doll. How appropriate, Josie thought sardonically. Just when she was thinking about Sarah, he spells DOLL on the Scrabble board. Great. If she had the letters she'd put CHINA in front of it. She could feel the tension coiling in her stomach, and her fingers tightened on the table edge. *Face it, Josie. Just face it. You're who you are. And it's not enough.*

In her distracted state she forgot how to spell. She put her *E* and *D* at the end of FRY. Immediately Mack smacked the table with his fingers. "Ha! Challenge. That's not how you spell 'fried.'"

She felt tears of frustration smarting behind her lids. "You're right. I concede." Concession. That about described her life right now, especially the part of it revolving around Mack. At least she wasn't going to give him the satisfaction of seeing her hurt—or of conceding the pond-lease issue.

Totaling the score, Josie was not surprised to find she'd lost the game. It figured. "Would you like some more coffee?" she asked halfheartedly.

"No, thanks." He scraped his chair back, carried his mug to the sink and shrugged into his goose-down jacket. "I'm on duty early tomorrow." He leaned on the kitchen counter and found her eyes. "Josie..." He paused uncomfortably. "I sense we're both somewhat on edge with each other." She lowered her eyes. "But I want to tell you I appreciate the space you're giving me. I need it."

And what about what I need? And how much space is enough? In a tight voice, she replied, "It seemed the best thing to do."

He rounded the end of the counter and laid an awkward hand over hers. She withdrew her hand, shifted away and looked at him neutrally. "Do you want me to feed the cattle tomorrow?"

"No, I'll do it. That's about the time I'll be getting home." He opened the door, then turned back to her. "By the way, just so you'll be prepared, goose season opens day after tomorrow. Good night."

He left the house. She stared intently at the door, aware of a nameless frustration and incipient fury muddying her thoughts.

THE NEXT DAY, unseasonably warm for November, offered a brief reprieve from the cold northern winds. Although most of the leaves had blown off the trees, a few brilliant stragglers clung to the skeletal black limbs as a reminder of autumn glory.

Josie was enjoying her run after a day of hard work on the thesis. The late-afternoon sun struggled to hold its own against the onset of night. She slowed her pace as she neared the house, grateful that exercise had banished some of the cobwebs in her head. She windmilled her arms, then flung them high, stretching on her tiptoes and inhaling the fresh cool air. Glancing beyond the house, she saw the upper pasture; succumbing to an impulse, she jogged slowly upward toward the old wall overlooking the pond. With her departure for Chicago looming ever closer, this might be the last time the weather would permit her to visit her special place.

Although the ground was cold, she sat, legs bent, elbows resting on her knees, drinking in the panorama of land closing in on itself and stripped for dormancy. Rather than dryness and emptiness, the hibernation signaled a time of gathering resources for renewal. She reflected that she, too, was in need of a change, of a new direction.

She cocked her head, suddenly picking up in the distance a familiar sound. Silhouetted against the western sky, the black forms of two geese made their descent, accompanied by clearly discernible honking. Putting one hand up to her eyes to shield the sun, she followed their glide toward the pond, amber in the reflected light of the sun's rays. A pair, searching for a haven for the night.

Just then, to her stunned horror, she saw two figures stand up on the far bank, shotguns shouldered. Before she could shout or rise to her feet, loud blasts echoed in the still air. For one second, the pair of geese soared on. But then, with a sickening loss of altitude, one of them plummeted toward the north bank of the pond, the other hronking its terrified forlorn outcry.

Josie stood, screaming, "Stop! Stop!" She thrashed down the hill in blind pursuit of the camouflaged figures. "Stop where you are!" The two hunters took off at a run toward the road.

Josie felt the brambles catching on her clothing but, heedless, she ran on, hurdling rocks and stumbling on the uneven ground. My God, it wasn't even goose-hunting season yet, she thought. Who the hell were these two? If she had to expire trying, she'd catch them. Gasping and holding the stitch in her side, she reached the south edge of the pond where she picked up the worn path to the road.

Ahead of her, she could see the two hunters, one smaller than the other, frantically climbing through the barbed-wire fence. In the distance, she saw a late-model blue pickup parked along the edge of the road. As soon as the pair cleared the fence, they took off on a dead run toward the truck, the one flinging open the door and

starting the engine before the other one had reached the
truck. She raced the last few yards to the fence and arrived just as the second hunter vaulted into the passenger side. Panting, she clung to the fence post, her vision
clearing just in time to read the license plate as the truck
pulled away in a cloud of dust. BLUEROK.

She hit the post with her fist. Damn! Somehow she'd
find them, and when she did . . . !

She stood for a moment catching her breath and then
started resignedly toward the spot where she'd seen the
goose go down. High above, she could faintly make out
the mournful cry of the surviving mate. She felt overwhelmed by anger and sadness.

When she reached the north shore, it took only a few
minutes to locate the resting place of the bird. She carefully parted the dried weeds and stared at the lifeless
Canada goose, head and neck elongated at a grotesque
angle from the body, blood trickling from the neat round
hole in its breast.

Gently Josie reached under the bird, laying its neck and
head over one forearm as she stood and lifted it, cradling it to her chest. Her cold fingers, buried in the
feathers, were warmed by the body heat still radiating
from the goose. She hugged it to her. "Poor bird. It
shouldn't have happened, it shouldn't have happened,"
she crooned.

She carried the goose toward the road; it was easier to
walk that way than to go back up the hill. She'd have to
get a shovel from the barn and bury the majestic creature. As she walked, her anger mounted. What in hell
were those hunters doing here at all, much less before the
damned season even opened?

As she trudged up the lane between the mailbox and
the house, she heard a vehicle approaching. It was

Mack's Bronco. The cattle. He was coming to feed the cattle. Well, she had a surprise for him first—no way was he going to ignore her and the damning evidence in her arms. Determined not to budge, she stood, feet planted resolutely, facing the slowing Bronco. The vehicle stopped and Mack climbed out.

Josie lifted up her arms, offering, like a sacrificial lamb, her lifeless burden. "See," she accused. "See, *this* is what comes of your sport!"

"Josie, for Pete's sake, what happened?"

She thrust the goose at him. "This is what happened. Your damned hunters shot her. Just picked up their guns and blew her out of the sky. My God, it's not even hunting season! Is nothing sacred?"

He reached out and gently took the goose from her. "Who did it, Josie? There's no excuse for hunting out of season."

"There's no excuse for hunting at all. Just look at her!"

Mack walked to the rear of the Bronco, opened the door and carefully laid the limp body inside. "I'll take care of it." He closed the door and took her by the shoulders. "Josie, what happened?"

As she told him, her teeth began chattering and she shook in delayed reaction. Mack brushed her hair back out her eyes and waited until she could again control her breathing. "Take your time."

She took a deep breath and finished, "I couldn't catch them. One was bigger than the other. The little one was thinner. They ran to their truck and drove away."

"The truck, Josie, can you describe it?"

"It was a fairly new blue pickup, one of the bigger models. Maybe a GMC or a Dodge. It had a personalized license plate. B-L-U-E-R-O-K. Bluerok."

"Do you want to pursue this? Press charges?"

She nodded emphatically. "You're damn right I do."

"I can use my mobile phone to trace the license, if you're sure."

"Do it."

He opened the driver's-side door and slid into the seat, reaching for the receiver.

"Alice, Mack here. Need you to trace a vehicle registration for me...."

Josie paced, her fists clenching and unclenching at her sides. Finally she saw Mack replace the receiver. She watched as he hit the steering wheel with the flat of his palm and slumped back on the seat. "Damn!"

"Well, don't just sit there," Josie said. "Whose truck is it?"

He stepped back out of the truck and stood facing her. "The truck is registered to Beth Ann Johnson." He looked defeated. "'Bluerock' is another name for a clay pigeon. I'm afraid one of your hunters was Beth Ann's son, Clay."

CHAPTER TEN

FURIOUS, JOSIE GRABBED Mack by his upper arms. "Let me get this straight. You're 'afraid' Clay Johnson is involved?" She shoved him away in a gesture of disgust. "What difference does it make who it is? What he did was wrong!"

"Easy, Josie. He's just a kid. You remember him. He was out here that day with Les and me."

"Well, then, Mr. Macho Hunter, he sure as hell should have known the rules, shouldn't he? Hunting with the deputy sheriff and all."

Mack stood, one arm draped over the car door, staring incredulously at her. "Josie, he's a minor. There ought to be some reasonable way to resolve this."

"A minor? Does that make him less guilty?" Her jaw jutted. "Or are you interested in protecting him because he's Sarah's nephew?"

"I'm not suggesting letting him off the hook. What he did was wrong, but there's no need to crucify him. You could consider giving him a break."

"Give him a break? Give *me* a break! You don't give a damn about my feelings about the geese—you're too wrapped up in your precious Sarah! Sarah, the perfect one. Sarah, your long-lost love!"

Her mind caught up with her mouth. She covered her lips with one shaking hand.

He stared at her, the planes of his face rigid in the effort to control himself. "Josie, I warn you. Leave Sarah out of this."

Something snapped. All of the pent-up uncertainty and frustration of the past few days mixed with her current outrage to fuel her invective. "How can I leave Sarah out of this? That's the big question mark between us, isn't it? The saintly Sarah and her blameless family. Mack, I can't fight a ghost. You really don't give a damn about my feelings. So much for friendship and trust."

Her mouth was in high gear, hurtling her toward the brink of some irrevocable cataclysm. "Obviously if you can be so cavalier about my feelings about the geese, you're probably also cavalier about our lovemaking." Her amphibian-green eyes, muddied with hurt and anger, shot holes in him. "Not to mention using me to get Gramps to agree to the lease idea."

Heedless of the bands of dread cramping her stomach, she catapulted on. "And you—I thought your job was to uphold the law. So do it. I want justice."

Deliberately, almost in slow motion, he reached into the Bronco and extracted a notebook and pen. "Okay, Miss Calhoun. We'll do it your way." His voice was cold and steady. "Let's get this down for the record. You saw two male suspects of indeterminate age trespassing on your grandfather's land. You heard firing, observed shooting and saw a goose subsequently fall from the sky. The perpetrators fled by foot and then drove off in a late-model blue pickup truck." He stopped writing and asked sarcastically, "Have I got it right so far?"

She nodded. As he continued writing, he muttered between pen strokes, "I'll take this report to the wildlife conservation people. They'll handle it. They'll be in touch and you may have to sign a complaint."

"Fine, officer. I'll be more than happy to comply."

"Cut the high-and-mighty act, Josie. After all, I didn't kill a goose. And it was only one. There'll be plenty more shot tomorrow."

Her temples throbbed and a furious crimson flushed her face as her body tensed. "And that makes it all okay? I suppose you'll be right in the thick of it tomorrow, shooting geese to your heart's content!" Her voice rose to a hysterical pitch.

"You've got it, lady. Not you or anybody else is going to tell me what I can or can't do. In season I'll shoot a goose or any other bird any time I want and in whatever way I choose."

He climbed onto the driver's seat, slammed the door and started the engine. Pausing, his expression frozen in fury, he rolled down the window and leaned out, his eyes level with Josie's flashing ones. "I don't know why, Josie, you're so hell-bent to prove to yourself that you're unlovable, but you did a damn good job of it just now."

His resolute features were tinged with regret. As he rolled up the window, he said, "I'll feed the cattle tomorrow," and then drove up the lane.

Josie stood rooted, a chill wind chafing her face, oblivious to the starless darkening sky.

MACK, REMEMBERING yesterday's angry confrontation, kicked the rotten hedge apple into the weeds with such savage intent that Stranger scuttled off into the brush bordering the tire-tracked path. The strap of Mack's camera bag bit into his shoulder, and he paused momentarily to set down the tripod and adjust the load.

"Damn her," he muttered, reshouldering the bag. He'd had no intention then or now of killing any geese. He didn't take lightly the feelings of others, particularly those he cared for. She didn't know him very well if she thought he was that insensitive to her love of the geese. And hadn't she noticed that morning they'd gone into the field that all he'd taken aim with was a camera? Okay, okay, so it hadn't been hunting season. But using her to get the lease? Preposterous. It was pretty damn clear she held a low opinion of him if she could think that!

The worst, though, was that blow about Sarah. What the hell was he supposed to do? Pretend that Sarah had never happened? That he'd never loved her?

His boot caught on a half-buried vine and he nearly fell. Cursing, he readjusted his grip on the tripod and trudged on toward the fence enclosing the cornfield. Women! Josie had her nerve. And he sure as hell didn't need too many doses of that temper of hers. She was right; she *was* no Sarah. Not at all. She was a feisty impetuous unreasonable whirlwind. Who needs it?

As he reached the tall cover at the edge of the field, he carefully parted some of the weeds to make a place for his equipment, taking care to keep as much concealed as possible. Who needs it? In the call of the distant dove, he heard the disturbing answer: "You doooo, you doooo."

With unnecessary force, he extended the legs of the tripod, positioning it so that the camera lens wouldn't be obscured by the brittle yellow stalks brushing against him.

"Like hell, I do," he muttered as he screwed the camera down tightly on the platform of the tripod. With care, he pulled the zoom lens out of its soft pocket in the camera bag and attached it over the aperture. Okay, okay. It wasn't that easy to forget her. But she had no right, no right at all to question his feelings or his motives. And definitely no right to attack Sarah.

And as for Clay, the kid certainly needed to face the music, but he didn't need to be pilloried. As he'd promised Josie, Mack had called Paul Beecham, the conservation officer, who, with a little persuasion from Mack, had agreed to meet with Beth Ann, Ralph, Clay and him before interviewing Josie. With any luck, maybe a compromise could be achieved, but that depended on Josie's being reasonable. Right now, he wouldn't put much stock in that possibility! And he resented the hell out of being squarely in the middle of this mess, trapped between Josie, the law and the Johnsons.

Mack sighted through the lens, focusing on the distant windmill in the corner of the field. Stranger circled the immediate area, sniffing in exploration, then returned to Mack. "Sit. Stay. Time to be quiet." His palm flattened just above the dog's nose to reinforce his words.

As Mack waited, scanning the horizon, he rubbed his hands together to keep the circulation going and then plunged them into the warm flannel-lined pockets of his parka. He had to keep his hands gloveless to fine-tune the focus. After a few minutes, he stamped in place and blew on his hands.

What's your problem, Mack? his inner voice asked. He sighed. Well, nothing was going right. First Sarah's death, then abandoning the writing and photography, now Josie and the damnable confusion he felt. Despite the compelling message of his inner voice, damn it, he didn't need it—all this indecision over his job, his love life, his future. Instead, he decided to listen to the voice of Thoreau whispering his siren song—"Simplify, simplify." Okay, he would. That was exactly what he'd do. Disentangle himself. Set priorities. Get on with his life. Without women.

Stranger bristled, cocking an ear. "What is it, boy?"
Then Mack saw, too. A distant pencil-thin line wavered
above the horizon, widening, then narrowing, expand-
ing and contracting in subtle orchestrated strings. Nearing, the geese filled the cold air with their unearthly
clamor. Mack tensed in anticipation, his breath coming
in shallow gasps, his fingers feathering the focus ring. He
made a swift sure adjustment of the tripod tilt. Then, as
the flock glided between the morning sky and the waiting field, he clicked off several shots, then turned the
camera quickly to zoom in on a majestic pair of honkers
coming in to land among the broken cornstalks. Another pair strutted toward him on a diagonal just as the
sun appeared on the horizon, backlighting their black-
and-white heads and feathered gray-brown bodies.

Mack closed his finger on the shutter button. He felt
his stomach muscles relaxing as he watched them. They
were magnificent. Speaking a language all their own, they
had sighted this field and, with unerring accuracy and
grace, made their descent.

Josie would've loved being here. The thought came
spontaneously. Josie and her geese. Call her irrational
and sentimental, but she was right about one thing. The
birds *were* wonderful. Her effusiveness about them was
infectious. The picture of her in her camouflage outfit,
scraggly locks of red-orange hair spilling from the oversize hunting cap, came unbidden. So did the grin that had
illuminated her when she'd first spotted the geese. *Stop
it, Mack. Stop it. You're getting on with your life, remember?* Stranger stood up and licked his hand.
"Thanks, pal. At least you don't ask anything in return.
Uncomplicated. Simple. That's us, buddy, from now
on."

"BETH ANN, Ralph, I'd like you to meet Paul Beecham. He's with the Kansas Department of Wildlife and Parks, Law Enforcement Division." Ralph and the uniformed Beecham exchanged handshakes, while Beth Ann grimly motioned them into the picture-book family room.

"Have a seat, Mr. Beecham, Mack." She studiously avoided catching Mack's eye. The deep freeze was definitely on.

Ralph stood uncomfortably by the hearth, elbow on the mantel, fingers laced. "Clay will be down in a minute. I've told him you're here."

Ramrod straight, Beth Ann circled the room with a tray of coffee mugs. "Sugar, cream, anyone? Well, then, I'll just set the tray down. Help yourselves if you need more." Then, she sat, hands clasped in her lap like a dutiful schoolgirl.

In the uncomfortable silence that followed, Ralph crossed the room, muttering, "Where is that kid?" He paused at the bottom of the stairs. "Clay, we're ready. Hang up *now*."

Mack took a sip of the scalding coffee and caught Paul's eye. This wasn't going to be easy for anybody. He himself felt caught in a moral dilemma—Josie expected justice and he *was* an officer of the law; Beth Ann would expect his loyalty to the family even if it meant compromising his duty. And then there was Clay. He'd spoken with Paul about the possible consequences of Clay's actions; the alternatives were not appealing. In the present atmosphere, he was not optimistic about the likelihood of striking a compromise that would both allow Clay to experience the consequences of his actions and satisfy Josie.

Muffled footsteps on the stairs announced Clay's arrival. He stood in the doorway, shoulders hunched defensively.

"Son, shake hands with Paul Beecham, the conservation officer for this district." Avoiding eye contact with Beecham, Clay stuck out his hand.

"Hello, Clay. Why don't you have a seat? I know you're anxious to get on with this meeting."

"You got that right," Clay muttered as he sat down in the empty wing chair, balancing one ankle over the other knee.

Mack stood up, holding his coffee mug in both hands. "Clay, why don't you start by telling us what happened the other day out at Calhouns' pond?"

"It wasn't my fault, Mack. Jeez, Jeff and I were just doing a little target shooting and scouting ponds for the opening day of goose season." He ran his fingers through his lank blond hair. "When we saw that pair coming in, it was too good to pass up. Heck, it was only a few hours before the season. We didn't think anyone'd care."

Mack pressed. "So you were aware the season hadn't started?"

"Well, yeah, but—"

"Which of you shot the goose?"

Clay leaned back. "How am I supposed to know?"

With mild reproof Mack quietly asked, "You were there, weren't you?"

"Yes. I guess we both shot at them. I don't know whose shot hit it. Does it make any difference?"

Mack sighed. "It could. It won't be necessary to charge you both if only one of you is guilty."

"You mean you're going to drag Jeff through this, too?"

Paul Beecham interjected. "We'll have to unless we ascertain which of you is involved."

"Jeez, are you gonna do ballistics tests or something?" Clay asked.

"Not if we don't have to," Beecham responded. "Do you have anything else to say?"

Clay uncrossed his legs and sat forward. "What if I say I did it?"

"Did you?" Ralph asked.

"I guess so. I don't want Jeff dragged into this."

Mack sat down and Beecham leaned forward, elbows on his knees, hands dangling between his legs. "Clay, here's the story. If you were sixteen, in Kansas you could be facing a Class C misdemeanor charge and as much as a month in jail."

"For one stupid goose?" Clay was incredulous.

Calmly, Beecham continued, "As a juvenile, however, you will not face those penalties, nor will you be turned over to the U.S. Fish and Wildlife Service, where the fine for an adult who kills a goose out of season is $325."

Beth Ann leaned forward hopefully. "Are you saying, then, there's no penalty for juveniles?"

"No, I'm not saying that, ma'am. If a complaint is signed by Miss Calhoun, the matter will be turned over to the juvenile court."

"Why, that's outrageous!" Beth Ann exclaimed. "Surely you can understand this was a harmless mistake. After all, Clay's not even sixteen."

Suddenly Ralph Johnson stood up straight and looked first at his son and then at his wife. "It's time Clay learned that choices have consequences. If he's old enough to drive that truck you gave him, if he's old enough to shoot a gun, then he is, by God, old enough to atone for his actions."

Beth Ann's mouth fell into an O of disbelief, while Clay squirmed in his chair.

Mack spoke into the hostile silence. "Clay, we've had some good times hunting together. I know you know the regulations because I've taught them to you. A man faces up to his mistakes."

Clay had the grace to hang his head. "I guess so."

"Because Miss Calhoun wants to file a complaint, by law I've had to call in Mr. Beecham. However, if Miss Calhoun is amenable, there's a compromise I'd like to suggest. It's a long shot, but I'd like you to hear me out.

"One likely action the juvenile court would take is to require some kind of related community service. If Miss Calhoun would agree not to file the complaint, you and your parents would have to agree to the following stipulations. One, you would not be permitted to hunt again during this waterfowl or game season." Clay winced. "Two, you would undertake a service project related to wildlife preservation under my direction and with the guidance of Mr. Ferris, your biology teacher, who has kindly consented to be involved. It would be up to Officer Beecham to determine if your project is acceptable."

Beth Ann rose in protest. "Mack, don't you think that's a bit much?"

Ralph strode across the room to stand in front of Clay. "Son, the truth. Did you shoot the goose?"

Clay stood, looked into his father's eyes and said quietly, "Yeah, Dad, I did. We both aimed, but I'm the only one who fired."

"Well?"

Clay turned to Mack. "I agree."

Mack clapped a hand on Clay's shoulder. "Atta boy."

Beth Ann's mouth turned down in distaste. "But what about Josie Calhoun? From what I know about her, I can't believe she'll just let this pass."

"Ma'am, Mack and I will discuss the matter with her." Paul Beecham turned to Clay, "You'll be hearing from me, son. Good night."

Ralph escorted the two men to the door. "You've been more than fair. I just hope Clay deserves this chance."

JOSIE ROCKED the baby to and fro in her arms, cooing at him, awestruck by the miracle of his tiny fists, his heart-shaped mouth, his downy head. Amy watched her friend with her son, smiling in contentment. "Is he always this good?" Josie asked.

"Try being here about four in the morning." Amy chuckled, reaching over to tuck the flap of the blue receiving blanket over the infant's feet. "Bring Troy over here to the rocker." Amy gestured to the antique wooden chair.

Gingerly Josie lowered herself with her precious bundle into the seat. "Will we wake him with our chatting?"

"When he's asleep, he's just like Les. Out like a light." Amy curled up in the corner of the overstuffed sofa.

"How are you and Les adjusting to the baby?"

"Okay, I think. No doubt about it, Troy's changed our lives. Les even missed the opening day of goose season to stay home and help me. And he rarely mentions the sportsmen's-club lease idea. Can you believe it?"

"Miracles do happen." Josie struggled to keep her expression impassive. "To what do you attribute this unusual behavior?"

Amy grinned. "First to the fact that he's busy admiring his newest potential linebacker, golf partner and hunting buddy." She added more seriously, "And to something Les said Mack helped him figure out. He won't say any more. Josie, do you know what he's talking about?"

Josie considered. "Sounds like it's something between Les and Mack. If Les wants to tell you, he will."

"Speaking of Mack, what goes?"

Josie lowered her eyes and fussed with the baby blanket. "Oh, Amy, you and I were having such a good time." With a face she hoped was composed, Josie looked at her friend. "I'm going back to Chicago soon, and I don't need any complications in my life."

Amy leaned forward. "Mackenzie Scott is hardly a complication. What gives?"

Josie struggled with her emotions. "Amy, I really don't want to dramatize anything. We had some good times, but discovered we had a few incompatible ideas and unresolvable differences. Can we leave it at that?"

Amy shrugged. "We can if that's what you want, but wouldn't it help to talk about it?" She gestured to the sleeping baby. "Let me put Troy in his crib and then we'll chat." She rose and gently removed the sleeping baby from Josie's arms.

Josie stared woodenly at the stuffed mallard mounted above the fireplace. Mack. Why had it come to this? She'd lain awake several nights replaying that awful scene where, in her anger at the boys, she'd not only made Mack her punching bag, but she'd jeopardized all hope of reviving any possible romance. Her impetuous ultimatum had forced him to choose. And what could she expect? What right did she have to ask him to share her convictions about hunting? In fairness, she supposed geese and hunting clubs were no big deal to most people. But he *knew* how she felt about them! How could he?

That romp in front of the fire? She was a big girl. In this age of casual sex, why had she supposed that implied any sort of commitment? Anyway, what had possessed her to think there might be a future with him? He couldn't stop thinking about the beloved Sarah.

What if he *was* only using her? In her heart of hearts, she knew Mack wasn't capable of that kind of deceit. Maybe she *had* been out of line with that cheap shot about Sarah. But it was truly how she felt. Competing with a ghost was bad enough, but competing with a saint was out of her league.

Just as well. Chicago, the thesis defense, Tom, her future—plenty to think about without the complication of Mackenzie Scott in her life. Mackenzie Scott with his engaging grin, his strong hands, his solid body... *Stop it!* It was over, whatever *it* was.

"He's down now." Amy settled back on the sofa. "You may think you have a poker face, but I can tell you're upset." She waited.

"Okay, okay." Josie held up her hands in surrender. "The truth is I was growing very fond of Mack. I even thought maybe I was falling in love with him."

"But?"

"Just lots of things. First of all, there's the memory of Sarah."

Amy harrumphed. "You're making too much of that, Josie. It's been a year and a half. He has to go on."

"Well, beyond that, we are at absolute cross-purposes about the proposed sportsmen's club. At the meeting at the Oasis, I couldn't even convince my own grandfather, much less Mack or anyone else, that preservation is more important than wanton destruction."

"Josie, you must've known that viewpoint would be a hard sell around here. For ages, boys in this area have grown up on tenterhooks of excitement waiting for their first hunting season. They look forward to doing what their daddies and granddaddies do—not only the hunting itself but the male bonding, too."

"But do I have to accept 'the way it's always been'?"

"Of course not, but don't delude yourself that you'll change much of anything. Frankly, you've not been the most popular person in town since that meeting, at least among the men."

"As if I give a damn!" Josie stood up abruptly and began pacing. "I suppose I better tell you about my latest true-life adventure, guaranteed to endear me further to the populace."

"Yes, I guess you had." Amy's eyes followed Josie's furious route from one end of the room to the other.

"Yours truly caught two hunters shooting out at Gramps's pond the day before the goose season. When they just happened to kill a goose, I went ballistic and asked Mack to press charges."

"So?"

"So, it turned out that the illegal hunter was none other than Beth Ann Johnson's precious Clay!"

Amy rose. "Oh, Josie. You don't need her for an enemy." Her tone said it all.

Josie stopped. "So now I'm persona non grata in town, the object of Beth Ann's eternal displeasure, and I've put Mack smack-dab in the middle of it."

"What's going to happen?"

Josie, staring at the floor, resumed a more deliberate pacing. "Mack and Paul Beecham, the conservation officer, came to see me yesterday. They presented a proposal enabling Clay to avoid juvenile court. Although it seemed a fairly light punishment, after much argument, discussion and explanation, they finally convinced me.

I've agreed not to press charges if Clay is prevented from hunting any more this season and if he completes a wild-life-preservation project, which Mack and Wint Ferris will oversee."

"Are you satisfied with that?" Amy looked intently at Josie, who once more stopped pacing.

"The boy *is* only a minor, and I struggled to keep my feelings about Sarah or Beth Ann from influencing me. Maybe he'll learn more this way. I may be unpopular, but I'm not vindictive."

Amy rose and turned Josie around so she could reach up to massage the tense muscles in Josie's shoulders. "Of course you're not. And you're not fooling me. You *do* give a damn about the people in this town. It's your home. And you especially give a damn about Mack Scott."

"But he knows how I feel about birds, the geese in particular."

Amy led her to the flowered sofa. "You're going to throw over a chance with one of the best men around because of the issue of hunting?"

Josie threw up her hands. "See, that's just what I mean. It's not a big deal to anyone but me. But if it's a big deal to me and he knows it and cares about me at all, he should respect my feelings."

Amy eyed her intently. "And what about Mack's feelings?" Josie stared at her lap. "I can understand your disappointment that Mack doesn't see eye to eye with you, but he's hardly a cold-blooded killer. In that way, he's no different from most of the other men around here. In another way, he's a lot different." Josie looked up slowly. "He's a fine, decent man, Josie. He reached out to Les and helped him when nobody else could. Don't be so quick to condemn him for being who he is. He deserves better. And Josie? I've seen the way he looks at you. He's crazy about you."

Josie stiffened. "In that case, he sure has a funny way of showing it. Even if there was a chance for us, I've blown it now, and no way am I setting myself up for any more rejection. Enough said, okay?"

"For now. Please note I am tactfully changing the subject. When does your grandfather get back?"

Josie's wan grin reflected relief. "Right before Thanksgiving. He called the other night, crowing like a rooster over the fish he's caught. All, he claimed, 'that long.'" Josie held up her palms about two feet apart.

"It was probably good for him to take a vacation."

"I agree. He's just getting over the worst of his grief. I'm worried about Thanksgiving, though. MJ always made Thanksgiving a special occasion. This will be our first without her, and I'm going to do my darnedest to keep up the tradition. We'll get through it somehow, I guess."

"Well, speaking of Thanksgiving, let me recruit you for the Harvest Festival. Since I just had the baby, I can't help much, but I did volunteer to get the bake-sale items lined up. Now, what can I put you down for?"

Josie groaned. Thesis revisions, preparing for the oral defense, getting her stuff organized to pack, Thanksgiving... She needed the Harvest Festival like a hole in the head. "What's easiest?"

"Probably cookies or pumpkin pies."

"Okay, pumpkin pies it is. I'll make four."

DRIVING HOME LATER in the afternoon, Josie remembered that Mack was on duty. It was her turn to feed the cattle. Ever since the day of their confrontation, they had politely but aloofly checked with each other about the cattle. When Mack came, he went directly to the barn and left immediately after putting the truck away.

One rainy evening, she had almost called to him to come up to the house to dry off and have a cup of coffee. She caught herself just in time. If he came, what was there to say? She certainly was not about to eat crow! Any invitation would only complicate matters. She didn't need any more conversations like the one in the lane. Let him go on home. Forget him.

After finishing the cattle-feeding chore, Josie warmed a tin of vegetable-beef soup and complemented it with half a dozen stale crackers before settling again in front of her computer. So intent was she on the screen that only when James Cagney jumped up on the windowsill and pressed his nose to the pane did she look up.

"What's happening, kitty?" She crossed to the window, pulling back the unbleached-muslin curtain. The bare branches of the elm trees were scratching at the darkening sky as the wind tossed the lighter limbs. As she watched, a distant flash of lightning illuminated the dark horizon. Thunder rattled the hills, the rumbling followed by another jagged chain of light in the northwest. The computer. She'd better turn it off.

She quickly saved her latest corrections, exited the program and unplugged the machine. No sense taking any chances with her thesis. The electricity flickered, went out, but came back on.

She straightened the pile of papers on her desk, scooped James Cagney into her arms and went around the house checking and resetting the clocks. Still carrying the cat, she sank into Gramps's recliner. She picked up the mystery novel she'd checked out of the library. James Cagney nestled in her lap as she began to read.

The wind howled down the chimney and the bushes rasped against the living room windows as the furor intensified. Josie became aware of a sudden furious pelting against the dining room windows. Just as she set the book aside to go look, the house was plunged into darkness. The refrigerator hum ceased, the yard light went out, and the rain and wind clawed at the house.

She moved to the dining room windows and peered out into the darkness, almost palpable in its denseness. Only when lightning streaked could she make out the barn, the cattle gate, the lilac bushes. She hugged herself. MJ had loved storms, even waking Josie sometimes to come view the spectacle with her. She'd called them "God's fireworks," and Josie couldn't help but remember how cozy and secure she'd felt wrapped in MJ's arms watching the powerful tumult outside.

After ten minutes or so, the storm showed no sign of abating. Josie decided she might as well grope her way upstairs and go to bed.

She had just pulled on her flowered flannel granny gown and started to brush her hair when a loud banging on the back door startled her so much the hairbrush clattered to the wooden floor. With a pounding heart, she found her way to the window overlooking the stoop. There, hat pulled low over his head, stood a man with a flashlight aimed at the ground. As lightning briefly lit up the yard, Josie could see Mack's Bronco. The knock came again, insistently.

She found the banister and counted the stairs until she arrived safely at the bottom. With shaking fingers she unbolted the door. Mack entered on a blast of cold wet air, his dark rain suit running with water, which puddled at his feet. He pulled off his hat, shaking drops from the brim. Some of them splattered onto her bare feet, chilling her.

He brought the flashlight up to illuminate the two of them in a circle of light. "Are you all right?"

"I guess so. What are you doing here?"

"I told your grandfather I'd keep an eye on you. That's what I'm doing here," he answered frostily.

"Why wouldn't I be all right? I'm a big girl, you know." Something about him made her feel defensive, even though a part of her instinctively wanted to reach out to dry him off.

"Yes, but you're a city girl. Where are your candles?" He shone the flashlight in the corners of the kitchen.

"Candles? What for?"

"For light, woman. Most people keep candles around and light them in just such an emergency."

"Oh. I guess I didn't think about it. They might be in the buffet in the dining room."

She followed the beam of the flashlight and his broad back into the dining room, suddenly and powerfully aware of her body naked beneath the soft flannel of her gown. He pulled open a drawer, searched it, closed it and opened another. Caught in the beam, several candles lay near the back. He reached for two.

"Here. Hold them while I get out the matches I brought."

As he struck the match, his amber eyes were caught in the light, his face becoming softly illuminated as each wick caught and spread a halo of light upward. Her stomach clenched and she nearly gasped at the potency of her physical reaction to him. The smell of wet wool and a hint of cedar were doing her in.

He took one of the candles, his warm skin grazing her hand. She looked up, feeling her anger dissolving in a spasm of desire. His pupils, adjusting to the light, narrowed. His eyes hardened and his voice was coldly indifferent as he asked, "Do you have an auxiliary generator?"

Her heart plummeted. "A generator? I don't know. What for?"

"For your well." He started toward the basement steps. She followed tentatively, holding one palm under the candle to catch the dripping wax. She waited at the top of the stairs while he examined the basement. "No such luck." He lumbered back up the steps. "See if you can locate a couple of candle holders."

She returned to the living room where two brass candlesticks had been pressed into duty as book ends. "Here," she called.

He found her setting one candle into a holder. She reached out for his and found him staring at her, a quizzical expression on his face. "So what's the big deal about the generator?" she asked, taking his candle and fitting it into the candlestick.

"Nothing. Unless you need water." A half grin flitted across his face, immediately replaced by a neutral expression. She checked the impulse to caress his face, to tease the smile back to the surface.

"You mean I can't wash my face?"

"That's right. There are certain other amenities provided in a bathroom that are also unavailable to you."

She could feel the strain of withheld laughter growing in him. She stood suspended between hurling herself into his arms and the comfort of his broad chest, and protecting herself from damaged pride and further rejection.

Pride won. "I'll manage just fine on my own, thank you. My plumbing may be more complicated than yours, but my brain works perfectly."

The humor in his eyes died as he glared at her. "So I see. It's clear my services are no longer needed here." He smacked his hat onto his head. The ray of the flashlight did a 180-degree turn as he stalked toward the kitchen door.

Holding one of the candles in front of her, she gathered her gown in her free hand and followed him. "I do appreciate your checking on me, Mack. Thanks for coming."

He turned at the door and said formally, "I promised your grandfather. Sorry to have bothered you." Another cold wet gust filled the room as he opened the door, pulling it shut behind him with a metallic click.

The frigid air blew out the candle and sent shivers through her. The room was dark again and empty— emptier than it had ever been. The warmth had been sucked outside along with him. "My services are no longer needed here," he'd said. Reluctantly she admitted to herself that it was true. As much as his protective presence had tempted her to throw herself into his arms, things had changed. His services were no longer needed here.

GRAMPS ARRIVED HOME late the Monday afternoon before Thanksgiving. His wrinkled face was tanned and the worry lines around his eyes had relaxed. He told Josie the highlights of the trip before his increasingly frequent yawns sent him shuffling off toward the comfortable haven of his own bed.

He'd looked so relaxed that she'd postponed bringing up the subject of his decision about the pond lease, but just as he mounted the first step, he turned and said, "Honey, in case you're still worrying, I haven't made up my mind yet about Les's proposal. I need some more information."

Josie crossed to the stairs, gripping the newel post tightly. "It's your farm, Gramps. But I just can't stand the thought of turning the place into a commercial hunting venture."

"Your feelings matter to me, honey. I love the birds, too. But I've hunted all my life—enjoyed it a lot. There are two sides to every question. I wish you could see that."

"It would be easier if I could, but I can't. Oh, Gramps, let's not argue. I've no right to insinuate my opinions into your business."

"Honey, you've every right. After all, this place will be yours one day." He smiled wearily. "I won't make any rash decisions." He started up the stairs.

"Gramps, wait a minute." She placed a restraining hand on his arm. "Something happened while you were gone, something you need to know." She told him about the trespassing hunters, the killing of the goose and the agreed-upon arrangement for Clay Johnson to make restitution.

Gramps listened thoughtfully. "You did the right thing by agreeing to the stipulations. Better for Clay to learn something from his mistake than simply be punished." He patted her hand and began climbing the stairs.

"Good night. See you in the morning." Josie relaxed her grip on the newel post and caught her breath. She hadn't realized just how important the pond-lease issue was to her. Just how much she wanted to preserve the place exactly as it had been when MJ was alive.

ON TUESDAY Josie spent part of the day rearranging the freezer to accommodate the packages of bass, catfish and crappie Gramps had brought back. From that point on, she was consumed by Thanksgiving preparations—grocery shopping, thawing the turkey, assembling the vegetable casseroles, jelling the strawberry-sour-cream salad and finding the right combination of wheat shocks, striped gourds and colorful Indian corn to fill the cornucopia centerpiece that had always graced MJ's harvest table.

Wednesday evening, snow flurries spit on the sidewalks and frosted the tree limbs, dried grass and weeds with a thin layer of rime. Gramps came huffing into the kitchen, stamping his feet and pulling off his gloves. "Cold as a well-digger's you know what." He hung his lumberjacket on the peg, hooking his John Deere cap over it.

"Think it'll snow?" Josie looked up from the bowl of cornbread dressing she was stirring.

"No. Mother Nature is just giving us a preview." He leaned back against the kitchen counter, watching her. "I saw Mack in town today."

"Oh?" She kept stirring.

"You two get along all right while I was gone?" He turned and reached into the cookie jar, then faced her again, a gingersnap in hand.

"The cattle didn't miss a meal." She avoided looking at him.

"I wasn't worried about the cattle." He took a bite from the cookie. "Mmm, good cookies. I was just wondering. I invited Mack to join us tomorrow for Thanksgiving dinner."

Josie's spoon nearly bored a hole in the mixing bowl. "What did he say?"

"Funny thing. In the past he's been mighty partial to a home-cooked meal. This time he mumbled about having things to do before the festival."

"Oh, darn! The festival. Don't let me forget to bake the pumpkin pies Friday."

"You're so busy cooking—have you had any time for your thesis?"

"I put in long hours the last few days before you got home. I'm finished except for the bibliography." She sighed.

"Big sigh, honey."

She put the spoon down and gave him a hug. "I know. I can't help thinking about MJ and about how soon I have to leave."

His callused hands caught on the back of her sweater as he patted her. "I miss her, too. And I'll miss you when you leave. But, honey, life has to go on."

She snuffled into his flannel shirt, then drew back and gave him a teary smile. "I'm trying, Gramps."

He held her in so long a gaze she finally had to look away from the mingled concern and love she read in his eyes.

THANKSGIVING DAY broke sunny and cold, fluffy white clouds driven across the heavens by a brisk wind. Josie pulled on a red fleece jogging suit and her running shoes. A quick run before starting on the Thanksgiving dinner would justify the feasting she knew lay ahead.

She started slowly down the lane, pumping her arms in rhythm, taking deep breaths of the clear frosty air. She gained speed, turned onto the road and ran to the bridge where she turned and headed for home. Just as she approached the lane, she saw Mack, clad in a maroon-and-black sweat suit, jogging toward her. Damn, double damn. She didn't want to see him, but there was no place to hide. Anyway, Stranger was bounding straight at her, tail wagging in excited greeting.

"Hello, boy." She bent over the dog, busying herself in an exaggerated petting display. She could hear the thud of Mack's feet approaching. Finally he stood behind Stranger. She looked up.

"Happy Thanksgiving, Josie." His face betrayed no emotion.

"Happy Thanksgiving to you, too." She moved her feet in place. "All set for your dinner?"

"I guess so."

"I suppose you're having goose?" Damn again. What had possessed her?

"I shot so many I hardly know how to cook them all." He looked as if he'd just swallowed a jigger of vinegar. "Tell Frank Happy Thanksgiving for me." He lifted one finger in farewell and jogged into the sun.

Josie sprinted up the lane, cheeks flushed with effort and self-reproach. She had enough to do without letting Mackenzie Scott ruin her day. Reaching the back stoop, she leaned over, hands on her knees, and filled her lungs with air drawn in deep pants. Straightening, she squared her shoulders, promising herself she would do everything in her power to make this day happy for Gramps.

GRAMPS PULLED OUT the dining-room chair to seat Josie. The turkey, savory and brown, surrounded by pickled peaches and cinnamon-spiced apple slices, stood waiting to be carved; the mashed potatoes were still steaming; the jellied salad quivered on lettuce beds on the salad plates; the green bean casserole was piping hot; and the dressing bowl stood empty, ready to receive the moist oniony stuffing. The gleaming silverware and delicate bone-china pieces were displayed to advantage on the ivory linen tablecloth. Josie smiled in satisfaction.

Gramps scraped his own chair back and sat down. He surveyed the table, a wistful smile playing across his face. Turning to Josie, he held out his hand. She placed her soft hand in his work-worn palm. He bowed his head.

"Heavenly Father," he began, "we give you thanks this day for the bounty of the land and this food on our table, so lovingly prepared. As we offer our gratitude for your many blessings, let us also remember those less fortunate than we are. Bless them and keep them near to you." He paused. "And, Father, we commend those missing from our table to your love and care." He squeezed Josie's hand. "Give us courage, Lord, to discern and follow your plan for us and to love one another as you have loved us. Amen."

"Amen!" Josie echoed. "That was lovely, Gramps. I'd been kind of dreading this moment, you know, without MJ. But your prayer was perfect, soothing. Thank you."

After a playful exhibition of carving, Gramps began passing the serving dishes, and the feast was under way. Even though MJ's accustomed place was empty, her presence filled the room, causing both Josie and Gramps to trade happy reminiscences until, by the dessert course, they had laughed so much their sides ached.

As they lingered over their coffee, Josie relaxed in her chair and allowed herself another moment of quiet satisfaction. It *was* a good dinner.

The phone rang. Frank moved to the kitchen to answer it. Josie stretched her legs and pressed the back of her fork into the few remaining pie-crust crumbs.

"Honey, it's for you." Gramps resumed his seat, sitting more rigidly than before.

"Who is it?"

"It's your mother, calling from Europe."

Josie's face sagged. "The ritual holiday call." She walked into the kitchen and picked up the receiver. "Hello, Cheryl.... Yes, Happy Thanksgiving to you, too." Her mother's voice was bright and chipper.

"Can you hear me, darling?"

"Yes, I can hear you just fine. Where are you?"

"Gus and I are in Salzburg. We're taking a little trip through Austria and Switzerland. You'll just love the Christmas present I found for you in Vienna."

Josie rolled her eyes. "I'm sure I will. Where will you be for Christmas?"

"Actually, we'd given some thought to coming to see you, but there's a wonderful festival in the Pyrenees then, and Gus doesn't want to miss it."

Yes, I'm sure, Josie thought. "Well, Cheryl, maybe another year."

"Oh, I hope so, darling. It's been so long since I've seen my little girl."

"I'm hardly a little girl any longer." With great effort, Josie kept the resentment out of her voice. "In fact, I'll soon be the full-fledged recipient of a master's degree."

"That's wonderful, darling! Gus and I are proud of you. How is the work on your big paper coming, you know, the one about the, er, swans, isn't it?"

Josie bit her lip as she felt the familiar stinging behind her lids. "No, Mother, it's geese. You know, like Mother Goose." The sarcasm spewed out.

"Of course, how silly of me. You keep in touch, now, sweetie. We love you and hope to see you this spring sometime."

"I'll count the days."

"Well, Happy Thanksgiving again. Bye now."

Josie stood holding the phone, staring at it with enmity. Nothing like a little maternal attention to make a girl feel really good about herself. She shrugged and laid the receiver in its cradle. Slowly she made her way back to the dining room.

Gramps glanced at her. "Honey, why don't you bring us in some more coffee?"

She realized with a rush of affection that he was trying to buy her time. Bless his heart, he didn't miss much. She returned, freshened their cups and set the coffeepot on a trivet.

Frank studied her. "How does Cheryl's call make you feel?"

She toyed with the cup. "The truth?" She glanced up. "Lousy."

"How so?"

"Most of the time I don't even think about her. Calls like this are almost an intrusion because they remind me of all the things she wanted me to be that I could never be. And she reminds me that I didn't have the kind of mother most children have. You know, the kind who bakes cookies, tucks you in bed at night and sews your prom dress. I don't really hate her, but I don't love her. I'm indifferent, I guess. And part of me feels guilty about that." Josie lifted the steaming brew to her lips.

"Josie, who are you blaming?"

"I try not to blame Cheryl, but it's hard not to."

"Who else?"

Josie picked up her wrinkled napkin and twisted it between her fingers. "I just wasn't good enough or pretty enough or smart enough."

"For what?"

"For what she wanted me to be."

"Are you sure she was the one who wanted all those things?" Gramps's eyes caught hers and seemed to bore into her soul.

Josie lowered her eyes. "I've wanted those things, too, Gramps." She carefully folded the napkin.

"From where I sit, I think you're way too hard on yourself. You've taken too much blame for what you see as a failed relationship. It's as if you think if only you'd done this, that or the other thing, you'd have had a regular mother."

"Yes, I do feel some of that."

"Honey, *you* weren't the failure. Cheryl was. You need to understand she was always flighty and self-centered. And when your father was killed, whatever unselfish impulses she had went out the window. She's lived first and foremost for herself. If, in the process, she could benefit you, that was fine. But make no mistake, you are not to blame for her deficiencies as a mother. Your feelings of anger toward her are natural and justified. But MJ would want you to think about forgiving her... and yourself."

Josie pinched the edge of the tablecloth between her thumb and index finger. "But I always *felt* so unlovable."

He reached over and covered her hand with his. "Honey, you were never unlovable and you aren't unlovable. Don't let her shallowness and her inability to love poison you. You have so much to give. The failure was hers, not yours. Love yourself, honey. Love yourself in that very best way, the way that frees you to love others. The reason your grandmother was beloved by so many was that she was comfortable with herself. She liked herself, and that enabled her to reach out, to love others. You're very like her, if you just give yourself a chance."

He drained his coffee cup. "So no more long faces. I've got a surprise in store for you. Your old granddad is going to help you with the dishes."

THAT EVENING, as she unloaded the dishwasher, Josie pondered Gramps's words, rolling them over and over in her mind.

Mack, too, had challenged her about acting unlovable. Why *was* she so determined to think of herself in that way? Was she bitter? Had she, in fact, let her fear of inadequacy and failure paralyze her? Did she withhold herself in relationships because of fear of rejection? Could she lay her girlhood to rest? Forgive Cheryl? Move on? Such heavy questions at the end of a long day exhausted her.

She finished her chore and flipped off the overhead light, the room now eerily illuminated by the yard light filtering through the elm branches and dappling the kitchen floor. The phone jangled on the wall. Now what? It was nearly eleven!

"Hello?"

"Josie? Thank heavens I reached you." Tom's voice had none of its characteristic lilt.

"Tom, it's nice of you to call. Happy Thanksgiving."

"I hope you've had a good day so far, Josie, but I'm afraid I'm about to ruin your Thanksgiving."

Josie clutched the phone. "What's wrong?"

"We have to reschedule your thesis defense. Dr. Gonzalez was diagnosed yesterday with cancer. His surgery is scheduled for a week from tomorrow."

"Oh, Tom. I'm so sorry. What do I need to do?"

"If possible, you need to plan your thesis defense for this coming Wednesday. Since he's on your committee, we either have to finish it before his surgery or wait until next semester. If we wait until next semester, you won't get your degree until June."

Josie's head whirled. The bibliography, packing and, damn, the stupid Harvest Festival pies. "I'm still working on the bibliography. I'd have to leave here Sunday or Monday. I don't know, Tom."

"Dr. Henry and I can review the bib later, if necessary. We know this puts you at a disadvantage, but we don't see any other alternative. I'd have called you earlier, but Dr. Henry, Dr. Gonzalez and I spent most of today figuring out how to cover the end of the semester. If you want to, think it over and call me tomorrow."

Josie made a quick mental review. "Tom, I'm too close to that degree to sit around for five or six more months. I think I can leave here early Monday. I can drive it in one day and try to put my act together on Tuesday." Gramps materialized in the doorway, hands braced on the frame. "Go ahead and schedule the oral defense for Wednesday."

"Good girl. You're a trooper, among other things." His voice lowered seductively.

"Thanks for the call, Tom. Please give Dr. Gonzalez my best. I'll phone you Tuesday morning." She glanced at Gramps, remembering their dinner-table conversation. "Oh, and Tom? You didn't ruin my Thanksgiving. Goodbye."

She turned slowly from hanging up the receiver. "I have to leave Monday, Gramps."

"We've had a good visit, honey. I guess it's time for you to fly." He held out his arms. "But you'll be back.

From time to time, you'll be back.'' He wrapped her in a protective hug.

I'm not ready, she thought, as she burrowed against him. And with painful searing clarity, she knew why. *Mack! Oh, Mack, I don't want to leave.*

CHAPTER ELEVEN

THANK HEAVENS for Libby's. Josie emptied another can of pumpkin into the huge mixing bowl. And for Pet milk. The big can of pumpkin made two pies, so she only had to repeat the process once. Sprinkling the cinnamon, ginger and nutmeg into the deep orange mixture, she found the spicy aroma transporting her to a day when she was about ten. A day she and MJ had been making pumpkin pies.

They had gotten the giggles about the stout county fair blue-ribbon pie baker who'd insisted on making pumpkin pie from scratch. Josie could still hear her grandmother's lilting laugh as she said, "No way am I going to spend hours scooping strings and seeds and pulp out of a pumpkin when Libby's'll do it for me. It can't taste *that* much better!" Not only was Josie using canned pumpkin, she was also using frozen pie shells. Desperate times called for desperate measures, she thought.

With everything else going on, Amy had understood that Josie would have to bring her pies Saturday afternoon, instead of early in the morning. "Actually," Amy had said, "we may be running short and need pumpkin reinforcements by then." The last load of wash was in the dryer, and Josie calculated that if she got home early after the festival chili supper, she could get her preliminary packing done, leaving her most of Sunday to attempt to wind up the bibliography. Maybe it was better to be in such a rush. It meant she hadn't the leisure to deal with the conflicting feelings coursing through her.

Why was everything happening at once? Friday's mail had brought a response to her job inquiry from the Kansas Department of Wildlife and Parks. They were interested in her credentials and would have an opening in the spring. Her application would be filed for review in March. Earlier she'd received an encouraging response from Southern Illinois University. No doubt about it, the future loomed.

The oven timer went off just as she finished brushing her hair. She ran down the stairs to remove the second pair of pies from the oven. As she did so, Gramps came blowing in from outside.

"Smells good. Suppose the old man could buy a pie before we get to the bake sale?"

"Aren't you tired of pumpkin? Let's dump these and buy a huge fattening coconut-cream."

"Mmm. Sounds good, too. Let me wash up and change my shirt and we can be on our way."

Scrubbed and resplendent, he reappeared in his best red-checkered cowboy shirt and string tie. "I'm all duded up and ready to go. You look pretty good yourself, kiddo." He smiled approvingly at the teal corduroy slacks, topped by a matching teal-and-rust striped turtleneck. "The orange in the sweater matches your hair."

"Not orange, Gramps. Bittersweet. That's what the lady in the store called it. Bittersweet."

Another darned omen. Bittersweet. That aptly described her life right now. Damn!

THE GOLD-TINSELED Christmas trees attached to the tops of the streetlights danced in the wind as Gramps maneuvered his car into the armory parking lot. Large silver letters attached to the wall above the entrance spelled out Season's Greetings. Two painted wooden snowmen guarded the door. Just inside the foyer a cloth banner streamed across the far wall—Welcome to the Twentieth Annual Maizeville Harvest Festival. As a result of the hard work of Maizeville residents, visitors seeking Christmas-gift bargains, annually thronged to the festival.

In the background, "Jingle Bells" blared from the loudspeaker. Crowds jostled past. Those entering milled unsurely while those leaving gloated over the finds burdening their arms—papier-mâché angels, grapevine Christmas wreaths, stick horses and quilted table runners. Gramps put his hand under Josie's elbow. "Which way?"

Josie held the large box protectively, hoping to preserve the pies long enough to reach the bake-sale booth. "Amy said it's near the side exit."

Gramps steered her to the left. "Okay, I see it. Follow me." He ran interference for the pies, which she gratefully set down on the card table. A woman, dark hair pulled back in a bun, smiled and wiped her hands on her calico apron. "Let me check you off. There. Calhoun. Thanks."

Looking around, Josie was amazed at the variety of booths—food displays ranging from caramel-covered apples to elaborate fruitcakes; artisans hawking everything from blown-glass Christmas-tree ornaments to cornhusk dolls; and even a dunking booth sponsored by the Pep Club, where an uncomfortable-looking man perched suspended over a cattle tank full of water.

Gramps leaned over to explain. "That's George Hamlin, the principal. What some people'll do for kids!" He shook his head, chuckling. "The crafts and food sales are in this building. The art exhibit is next door in the high-school gym, and the chili supper will be in the school cafeteria. If you don't mind, I'm going over to visit a spell with Jake Pfitzer at the Lions' Club booth while you mosey around a little. Let's meet at five-thirty for the chili supper.'' He waved and was swallowed up by the crowd.

She stood, wondering what she was going to do for one full hour. She'd already bought Gramps's Christmas present. Who else was there? Maybe Tom. But what could she find here for him? A small boy ran past her, smearing her slacks with the ice-cream bar in his hand. Lovely! She dabbed at the spot with a Kleenex. Several people, vaguely familiar from her school days here, brushed past, with smiles and hellos. A thin man she recognized from the sportsmen's meeting met her eyes and deliberately snubbed her.

She couldn't just stand there. She started wandering from booth to booth, fingering a set of woven place mats here, cuddling a stuffed rabbit there. She paused momentarily at a booth of leather-tooled items. Maybe Tom would like a belt. She ran the length of one through her fingers. What size? She replaced the belt on its hook. A billfold? Not very original. Would he even give her a Christmas gift? One more bridge to be crossed. The Tom bridge. She set down the billfold and turned back into the flow of the crowd.

By five-ten, she'd scrutinized every possible ware offered in the armory. Twenty minutes would be just about right for the art exhibit. She slipped out the side door and crossed the gravel parking lot to the gym doors. As she opened them, the smell of stale popcorn, sweat, floor cleaner and old sneakers evoked a memory of her eighth-grade PE class.

The bleachers had been shoved back to allow more room for the art displays. The number and variety of exhibits took her by surprise. Maybe twenty minutes wouldn't be long enough to see it all. She began in one corner, admiring some watercolor landscapes of the Kansas State campus. Moving more quickly past a metal-sculpture booth, she stopped to examine some glazed pottery.

As she rounded the far end of the gym, she halted dead in her tracks.

About halfway down the center aisle was the back of a display partition. Hanging facing her was a haunting black-and-white photographic enlargement of a pair of Canada geese, heads held proudly, feet planted in the rich loam of a cornfield. One was slightly taller than the other and seemed to be protecting the smaller one. Whoever had taken the picture obviously had captured what she loved about the devotion of the mates.

Ah, that was it. She could buy Tom a framed print. Not too personal a gift, yet wonderfully appropriate. Josie bustled toward the photograph, which drew her like a magnet.

When she reached the booth, she examined the other prints hanging alongside the geese. One was of a meadowlark poised on a stone fence post, another highlighted a flight of ducks soaring across a sunset, or was it a sunrise? A close-up of a wren emerging from her house also intrigued her.

She returned to stand in front of the pair of geese. The light dappled the earth in subtle variations. She liked it. She really did. She wanted to meet the photographer.

She stepped around the partition and found herself face-to-face with a print of a familiar-looking mallard drake and hen, swimming head-to-head through the silvery water. Where had she seen them? Then she noticed the festival signage for the booth: Booth 19. Photography by Mackenzie Scott.

Her feet grew leaden roots into the hardwood of the basketball court, the voices around her buzzed in delirious cacophony, her hands felt as if they were enshrouded in boxing gloves, and her heart hammered against her ribs. Mack! All these photographs? She swiveled her head. All about her were black-and-white and color photographs of birds, of flowers, of Kansas pastures stretching to the limits of the sky.

She forced herself to move, setting one foot deliberately in front of the other, back around the partition. There they were again. Her geese!

Her cheeks, crimson with surprise, held the breath she was too paralyzed to expel. The mallards. She knew now where she'd seen them before. With Mack that day in the duck blind. He'd taken his camera and gotten several shots of them. Shots! The cymbals in her brain crashed. What had he said that afternoon? "I will shoot a goose anytime I want and in whatever way I choose."

Josie's mouth went dry. She could hardly swallow. Could he possibly have meant his way was with his camera? Tears of regret moistened her lashes. Furtively she rubbed her fist across her eyes. All those words she'd vomited about the hunting and the lease and, oh, God, about Sarah. She stifled a sob at the thought of what her impetuosity had cost her this time.

Struggling for composure, she looked around the noisy gym for Mack. At the very least she owed him an apology. She'd made such a jackass of herself. What must he think of her?

Just then, she saw him, cola in hand, working his way through the people clustered at the adjacent booth. He stopped, the straw to his lips, when he saw her. Then he approached, setting the drink carefully down on the table. "Hello, Josie." His voice was expressionless.

"Mack, I...the photographs are wonderful. I..." She couldn't stop stammering. "Mack, I didn't know."

"Know what?" He wasn't going to make this easy for her.

"That you're a photographer." She stood motionless, staring at her feet. After a moment, she gestured helplessly toward the waterfowl photographs.

"Yes, I am. And I know more than one way to shoot a goose. These were taken opening day."

She looked into his forthright brown eyes and laid a tentative hand on his sleeve. "Mack, I misjudged you. I'm sorry."

"I'm sorry, too."

"The photographs are beautiful, professional. You're very talented."

"I don't know how good they are, but I enjoy *shooting* them." The hint of a twinkle flashed in his eye, whether one of genuine humor or sardonic mirth she couldn't tell.

"Mack, I know there's no way we can go back. For whatever it's worth, though, if I could cut my tongue out, I would."

"That's a bit too much for you to sacrifice, I think." Maybe it *was* amusement she saw in his eyes.

She glanced at her watch. "I need to go meet Gramps for supper, but I want you to know how sincerely I apologize. Also, I won't be seeing you again, because—"

Before she could finish, she felt a clawlike hand dig into the flesh of her upper arm. "Josie? Josie Calhoun? Why, I haven't seen you since Amy's baby shower." Beth Ann's grasp on her arm intensified. In an icy voice, she continued. "Although I don't see why you had to make a mountain out of a molehill, I suppose I really should thank you for not pressing charges against Clay."

Finally releasing Josie, she insinuated herself between Josie and Mack, laying a proprietary palm against Mack's shirtfront. "Mack, I know Josie won't mind—" she whirled to flash a quick dismissive glance at Josie "—but there's someone I want you to meet." Mack's face betrayed bewilderment. "Come on now, Mack."

Mack permitted himself to be maneuvered through a group of chattering women, past a bored man yawning discreetly and finally up to a tall woman, her back turned to them.

"Monica?" Beth Ann trilled as the stunningly attractive, casually but elegantly groomed woman turned to face them.

Josie could not avert her eyes. She was witnessing Armageddon. Her life going down the tubes. She felt as if she'd been kicked by an angry mule. Chili. Oh, Lord. The mere thought caused her stomach to revolt. Nevertheless if her only escape was by means of the chili supper, so be it.

MACK FOUND HIMSELF staring into the black eyes of a dark-skinned exotic-looking young woman. Her self-assurance was evident in her straightforward gaze and businesslike hand clasp.

Beth Ann made the introductions. "Monica Austin, meet Mack Scott."

"Mack, I'm delighted to meet you at last." She nodded in Beth Ann's direction. "I've heard a lot of nice things about you."

"Monica's the new attorney in town I told you about."

"Welcome to Maizeville." Mack dropped her hand, irritated by Beth Ann's peremptory manner. Mack sensed Monica's expectation, felt Beth Ann's gentle poke in the ribs. "Are you enjoying your job?" Inane question.

"Very much. It's taking some getting used to, though. I passed the bar in Colorado, so I'm having to bone up on Kansas law." Her voice, deep and carefully modulated, displayed her command of the situation. No giddy gushing from this female.

"You and Monica have something in common, then," Beth Ann simpered. "After all, you spent quite a bit of time in Colorado yourself."

"Not all that much. Anyway, I hardly think operating ski lifts puts me in the same category as a law student."

He couldn't keep the edge out of his voice. What was Beth Ann trying to do, anyway? And where was Josie? He craned his neck, hoping to catch sight of her. What had she said about not seeing him again? What had she meant?

Monica's velvety laugh drew his attention back to her. "Mack, after three years of debates with chauvinistic male law students, a ski-lift operator looks pretty good. I understand you're working with the Sheriff's Department here."

"At least for now." He felt trapped, certain that Beth Ann was getting ready to set him up. She'd stepped back, watching their exchange with all the pride and pleasure of an accomplished matchmaker. Damn it, anyway. He didn't need this.

"Look," he said, "it's been nice meeting you." He noted Beth Ann's eyes narrowing. "Hope to see you around the courthouse." He took Beth Ann's elbow in his. "And now, if you will excuse us, Monica, Beth Ann and I have some business to discuss."

He felt the rigidity of Beth Ann's body as he propelled her past the amateur art connoisseurs and down the narrow dark hallway leading to the locker rooms.

"Mack, you're hurting my arm."

He stopped, released her arm and loomed over her, blocking her escape. "Beth Ann, we need to talk and it might as well be now."

She thrust her chin out, folding her arms defiantly across her chest. "Well, you don't have to manhandle me to do it. And you don't have to be rude to my friends, either. I was just trying to do you a favor. Introducing you to an attractive female in town."

"That's just it, Beth Ann. I don't need any favors. My welfare cannot be your personal pet project. And I certainly don't need to meet every attractive new woman in town."

"No? I think you do. You certainly can't call that Calhoun girl attractive." Her eyes, cold with disdain, met his.

Mack felt the anger boil within him. How dared she judge Josie, or anyone else for that matter! "Not that it's any of your business, but I find her very attractive. But that's not the point. The point is, why are you trying to direct my life?"

She placed a conciliatory hand on his shoulder. "Mack, I certainly don't mean to 'direct your life.'"

"I hope not. I'm a grown man, in case that's escaped your notice."

She wilted in feminine defeat, whether by artifice or genuine capitulation he couldn't tell. "Mack, Mack. I don't want to argue with you. I just want what's best for you."

He wouldn't let her off the hook that easily. "You certainly have an odd way of showing it. I'd hope you'd respect me enough to let me be the judge of what's best for me."

"Mack, you need someone, I know that. For a long time, I wouldn't even let myself think of you with anyone besides Sarah. Ralph's been trying to help me see that I've been smothering you." She twisted her wedding band.

Mack felt the breath rush from him like a deflating tire. "Yes, Beth Ann. I have felt smothered." Before she could interrupt, he went on, "I know you mean well. And I know you feel somehow closer to Sarah when you cling to me. But it's time, Beth Ann. It's time to move on."

He felt her sag against him. He put one arm around her back, feeling her sharp pointed shoulders heaving under the assault of her sobs. "Can you just be my friend, not my keeper?" He forced her to look at him by gently lifting her chin with one hand.

"Mack, I don't mean to try to run your life. Sometimes I can't help myself." She reached into her skirt pocket and withdrew a tissue to wipe her nose. "Ralph says I haven't been myself since Sarah's death. He says I'm brittle and manipulative and judgmental. Am I?"

Mack diplomatically sidestepped the question. "Beth Ann, it's only natural that your grief would affect you. But it's been long enough. Sarah wouldn't want you to feel like this. And she sure as hell wouldn't want you to give Ralph the short end of the stick. He's a good man who deserves the best you can give. Promise me something?"

"I guess."

"You worry about taking care of yourself and making a loving home for Ralph and Clay, and I'll take care of Mackenzie Scott. Deal?"

She gave him a fleeting hug of surrender. "Deal."

As they walked arm in arm back into the gymnasium, he felt as if a weight had been lifted from him. Scanning the people milling around the exhibits, he experienced a thud of disappointment at not finding Josie's flame-colored head. Even though he had spent the past few days determinedly putting her out of his mind, seeing her again had aroused strong feelings, feelings he now realized would not stay buried.

DRIVING HOME after the chili supper, Gramps prattled to Josie about the Lions' Club, their local scholarship efforts, their pancake supper. Josie, holding the calorie-laden coconut-cream pie in her lap, remained silent, grateful she didn't have to make small talk.

Was Gramps oblivious to her anguish or was he helping her cover up? His cryptic final remark as they drew up to the house gave no hint of his motivation. As he shut off the engine, he stared straight ahead, and his words hit her with the force of nails being pounded into a coffin. "Mack really did some fine shooting of the geese, didn't he?"

CHAPTER TWELVE

JOSIE TURNED EAST onto Highway 24, headed for Topeka. She deliberately avoided looking left, knowing the gaunt bare branches of the Pioneer Oak would serve as a stark reminder of the pain in her heart.

Leaving Gramps and the farm had been tougher than she'd imagined. Although he'd tried to hide his disappointment, she'd noticed with alarm the slump to his shoulders and the hangdog look on his face. He'd aged almost overnight. The past few days he'd spent more and more time in front of the television, often falling into a light doze. What did he do all day? What would he do in the future? Maybe Mack hadn't been too far off base in suggesting Gramps needed a project. But a sportsmen's club on Calhoun land? Maybe she'd have to consider it if it gave Gramps a purpose. Josie sighed.

She was worn-out, too. Worn-out from the past few weeks of putting the finishing touches on her thesis and worn-out by the frantic last-minute rush to get her things packed and loaded for the trip. She was getting away just ahead of the first snowstorm forecast for Kansas. The harsh northwest wind occasionally caught the little gray Honda, and she clenched the wheel tightly. She hurtled down the road, miles passing in a blur of oblivion, only to jolt into awareness at the sight of a familiar landmark.

At Topeka, she got on the turnpike. She put the Honda on cruise control and dialed in a Kansas City radio station. Christmas carols! Indulging herself in sentimentality, she turned up the volume and let the tears course down her cheeks. "White Christmas" taunted her with its haunting refrain. Christmas. Her apartment lease wasn't up until March and she wouldn't be able to afford another trip home. Where would she be? By herself in her third-floor walk-up apartment? With Tom? Doing what? And Gramps, alone his first Christmas without MJ...

"White Christmas" segued into "I'll Be Home for Christmas." Were the diabolical gods of radio deliberately trying to upset her? Home for Christmas? And where was home? As of this moment, she had no home, not even an identifiable future beyond Wednesday.

She was driving away from the only home she knew. As if in accompaniment to the music, a flock of birds just above the horizon ebbed and flowed in rhythmic flight, their wings beating in time as they headed south, driven by some ancient nameless instinct.

A sob caught in her throat. The geese! She envied them the certainty of their destination, the encircling protection of the flock, the devotion of the mate. From the speaker, "Break Forth, O Heavenly Beauteous Light" swelled triumphantly to escort the geese south. And Josie, she knew not where.

DR. HENRY LEANED forward, clasping his hands on the seminar table. "Now, Josie, remember, take your time with your answers. This is not an inquisition but a gathering of scholars, you included."

"Dr. Henry, if I may?" Dr. Gonzalez interjected, turning to Josie.

Her Adam's apple suddenly felt as large as a basketball, and under the table she surreptitiously rubbed her sweaty palms on her skirt.

"I appreciate your willingness, Josie," he said, "to advance the date of your thesis defense, and we want you to know that we realize this places you at some disadvantage. However, my knowledge of your work in the past suggests you will rise to the occasion." Tom caught her eye, and she thought she discerned a fleeting wink. "With that said, I'd like to ask what your data suggests about the frequency with which males who have become widowers—" he smiled at his word choice "—select another mate."

After three hours spent in a blur of questions, explanations, citation of statistics and anecdotal references from the field, Josie's head was throbbing and her throat was raw from the effort of acquitting herself creditably. She felt as if her brain had been through a threshing machine.

Finally Dr. Henry scooped his notes into a neat pile, capped his pen and sat back in his chair. With raised eyebrows, he glanced at his colleagues, soliciting further questions. When none was forthcoming, he rose and extended his hand across the table to Josie. "Very interesting thesis. You've obviously put in a great deal of effort. As you know, the committee will be meeting to evaluate your work. We'll be in touch."

"Thank you, sir. I appreciate your consideration." She turned and added, "Dr. Gonzalez, I hope your surgery goes well."

Dr. Henry and Dr. Gonzalez left the room quickly. Tom removed his steel-rimmed glasses and rubbed the bridge of his nose with thumb and forefinger. When he looked up, he was smiling in quiet satisfaction. "You realize I can't comment on your defense. That would be unethical." He circled the end of the table and came to stand beside her, his arm around her waist. "But now that it's over, may I take you out for a celebration dinner?"

She turned in his grasp. "Thank you, Tom. After an aspirin or two, I think I'll live. I'd like to celebrate."

He rubbed both hands up her arms, resting his palms on her shoulders and fixing her in a solemn gaze. "I've missed you, Josie."

Her temples throbbed. She felt the tickle of his mustache brush her forehead. Her empty stomach caved in on itself. "I'll pick you up about seven," he said. "We've got a lot to talk about."

Why did she feel like a parakeet in a cage? "That'll be fine, Tom. Thanks for everything." She put her copy of the thesis back in her briefcase, fumbling with the clasps. " 'Bye, now." She fled into the hall.

THE LETTER officially informing her of the successful completion of the requirements for her master's degree arrived in the mail on December tenth. An abbreviated graduation ceremony was to be held on the eighteenth. It seemed anticlimactic to pay for the cap-and-gown rental and march with a group composed mostly of strangers. Yet she *had* worked hard, and Gramps would be disappointed not to have a picture of her complete with master's hood. He had wanted to come for the commencement. However, because of his very real fear of

flying—a result of the manner of his son's death—and
the uncertain weather he might encounter driving, Josie
had convinced him to stay home.

Time weighed heavy on her hands after the thesis defense. Aside from sending out more job queries and
cleaning her tiny apartment, there was little to occupy
her. The throngs of college students exhilarated by the
approach of the holiday break underlined the contrast
between their seasonal gaiety and her melancholy.
Spending the holidays in Chicago watching the mailbox
for responses to her job inquiries was hardly her idea of
a festive yuletide.

In an effort to dispel her "Bah, humbug" mood, she
bought a miniature tree that she set on top of a sheet-
draped suitcase in one corner of the apartment. Trimmed
with cranberry-and-popcorn strings, it brightened the
room, but not her mood. Instead, it served as a reminder of happier Christmases on the farm when she and
MJ had spent days making the tree decorations.

She was delighted, therefore, when Dr. Henry called to
offer her a temporary job helping research a book he was
writing. Although she didn't know how long the assignment would take, it would engage her mind and provide
a stipend. She hated draining her small savings, which
had to bridge the gap until she secured employment.

Besides worrying about her career, there was Tom to
think about. She wished she could get a handle on her
feelings for him. He was very busy with the end of the
semester, but they'd been out twice since the evening of
her thesis defense. He was always charming, considerate
and solicitous of her. But there was an uncomfortable
innuendo she couldn't put her finger on, as if he thought
their relationship was already settled.

Coming home from the Bulls' game in the taxi the next night, Tom, in a deliberately offhand manner, brought up the subject of her future.

"Josie, I hope you're planning to send follow-up letters to Southern Illinois and the other places you've applied."

"They're in the mail, Tom." She felt a prick of irritation.

"Assertiveness is what it takes in this difficult job market." His tight smile was meant to reassure her.

"I'm still not certain I even want to consider college teaching."

He patted her hand, which lay next to him on the frayed seat of the cab. "You know it would make it more convenient if we were doing the same thing."

More convenient? Make what more convenient? She held her breath, refusing to ask the obvious question. "I think I'm more the outdoor type."

"There'd be plenty of field trips. Academia has a lot going for it, especially once you get tenure."

"That's a big 'if.' "

"True. But you're a very talented young woman. And being a woman has its political advantages these days." He pulled her hand into his lap, smothering it with both of his. "And you're a very special young woman, at least to me." He squeezed her hand.

Why did she feel like a tongue-tied adolescent out with a friend of her father's? She stared straight ahead, feeling constricted.

"You're awfully quiet tonight," he continued.

"I guess I'm just missing my grandfather."

"From what you've told me, he sounds like a fine gentleman. I'm looking forward to meeting him before too long."

Meeting him? Josie, you dummy, don't you see where this is going? Tom assumes the two of you are a couple. Oh, Lord. It was one thing while she was in Kansas and Tom was a shadowy substance safely in Chicago. But now... She had to face the music. She had to decide how she felt. She couldn't keep holding Tom at arm's length.

"Yes, he is a fine gentleman." She swallowed hard.

"He must be very proud of you. I'm sure you wish he could be here for the ceremony, but I'll be sure to take many pictures of you. After all, I have a proprietary interest in your success."

"That will be nice." She felt like Eliza Doolittle, finally achieving Professor Higgins's long *a*. "The rain in Spain..."

At her door, he held her face in his cold hands, his eyes level with hers. "Even though I know you miss the farm, you're making this old professor very happy." His glasses bumped her forehead as he planted a dry kiss on her lips. "Don't forget the departmental holiday party at Dr. Winchester's the evening of the eighteenth. Maybe we'll have some news to announce." He pecked her again on the cheek and departed.

News to announce? Her job? His promotion? Not... surely not... Did he think their relationship had progressed that far?

Damn it all, every time he embraced her or kissed her, she couldn't avoid contrasting him with Mack, Mack whose strength and passion blended with his tenderness. Couldn't avoid the recognition that Tom's touch failed to set her afire the way Mack's had. Rats! Why did she always screw up? Couldn't she get anything right?

THE CEREMONY was just about what she'd expected. Proud families craning their necks for a better view of their particular graduate, a speaker who droned on in predictable generalities, and the graduates themselves giddy with accomplishment and eager to dispense with the formalities.

Josie posed for the obligatory pictures and accepted the congratulations of several of her peers and professors before heading for her apartment to bathe and dress for the departmental party.

Just as she stepped out of the shower, her phone rang. "Gramps, oh, Gramps, it's so good to hear your voice. I wish you could've been here, too."

His call helped make up for the fact that he couldn't be with her on her special day. There was little news from Maizeville—the Harvest Festival had been the most successful ever, the Lions' Club party for the grade school had gone well, he'd seen Amy and little Troy at the grocery store. Wint Ferris had called to ask if his biology class could take a field trip to visit the Calhoun pond. Gramps said nothing about Mack. It was all Josie could do to keep from asking.

As she pulled on her panty hose, she forced herself to list all of Tom's appealing qualities. Scholarly, urbane, considerate, witty, stable. Why, any woman in her right mind would consider him a catch. She liked him, she really did. Certainly she admired his intellect. Could they be happy together? She tried to visualize a life with him. Tudor house with a wood-paneled library, Oriental rugs, maybe an Irish setter. Tom sitting in a leather armchair, his glasses perched on his nose, reading *The American Scholar.*

And what of her? Dressed for the Faculty Wives' Bridge Club? The image blurred and shattered. She couldn't see herself in the picture at all. What was missing? As if by way of an answer, she heard Gramps's words from last summer. "Sparks, Josie. Wait for the sparks."

Straightening, she twisted to look at the back of her legs. Damn! Why did hose always run when you were in a hurry?

THE STATELY REDBRICK Georgian home was ablaze with lights as Tom escorted Josie up the curved sidewalk.

"With Dr. Winchester's retirement at the end of the year," he said, "I have high hopes of being named department chairman. One thing about these faculty parties—they're as political as they are social."

Josie clutched her purse under her arm. Was this his way of warning her to be on her best behavior?

Before Tom could ring the doorbell, the door swung open, letting loose on the night air the babble of male and female voices rising and falling in animated chatter. Dr. Winchester himself, sporting a Christmas-red blazer, held his hand out to Tom.

"Welcome, Tom. And Miss—don't tell me, now—Calhoun, isn't it? From my seminar Elements of Field Research?"

"Yes, sir. Merry Christmas."

He gestured them into the marble foyer, taking their coats and handing them to a tuxedoed college student. "The hors d'oeuvres and drinks are in the dining room. Help yourselves."

Josie felt horribly self-conscious. The men, clustered in groups of two and three, engaged in earnest pedantic conversation. The women—some sophisticated and graceful, others dowdy and plain—bobbed and clucked like dutiful hens to their husbands' roosters.

She glanced at Tom, only to find he was threading his way toward the bar in one corner of the large dining room. She was stranded on an island of awkwardness. A drab young woman dressed in a homespun creation that betrayed the outline of her unrestricted pendulous breasts introduced herself.

"Hi. I'm Summer Ashcroft." She flipped back her long straight, dishwater-blond hair. Her eyes were like gray agates.

"I'm Josie Calhoun. I'm here with Dr. Tom Hatcher." Was this how it would be? She'd define herself in terms of Tom?

"We know Dr. Hatcher. My husband, Josh Ashcroft, is an instructor. New this year."

"How do you like it here?" *Brilliant repartee, Josie.*

"It's hard getting used to the winters after living in Arizona." She appraised Josie and asked bluntly, "Are you and Tom an item?"

"An item? I guess I don't know how to answer that."

"Well, all I know is he hasn't been seen all semester with a woman and now you show up." She shifted her feet clumsily. "Probably wouldn't hurt Tom's chances for department chair if he had a wife."

Josie's jaw gaped. "I beg your pardon?"

"If I've learned one thing since we've been here at the university, it's this. The little woman is part of the big picture, and you'd better play your assigned role."

A firm hand materialized on Josie's elbow, and Tom pulled her away, smiling an apology over his shoulder to Summer Ashcroft.

"Here's a glass of sherry." He leaned over and whispered in her ear, "Don't waste your time on Summer. She's not exactly the prototype of faculty spouse."

Josie flushed. What was going on here? Was she some kind of window dressing? "Is there someone in particular I'm supposed to impress?" A slight edge crept into her voice.

As Tom hugged her to him, she nearly sloshed the wine down her front. "No, no. You impress everyone just being who you are. Besides, you know most of the members of the department. But we do need to mingle." He steered her over to a tall cadaverous man with a balding, high forehead and protruding ears.

"Carl, I'd like you to meet Josie Calhoun. Josie, this is Dr. Carl Schmidtberger, a former colleague of Dr. Winchester's. Carl's from Indiana University. He'll be a visiting professor this coming semester."

And so it went. The two hours seemed an eternity of mindless small talk punctuated by moments when she distinctly felt something was expected of her, like a bit player suddenly thrust into the spotlight. Summer Ashcroft's comment about Tom's possible expectations niggled. Would he expect a mate to be self-effacing, dedicated to advancing his career? Josie couldn't picture herself as either an adoring hostess or a politically savvy professional asset. It was with great relief that she bade their host farewell. She was relieved, also, that the only "announcement" that had been made concerned her recent acquisition of a master's degree.

When they arrived at her apartment door, it was only a quarter to ten. "Would you like to come in for a cup of coffee?" Tired though she was from the full day, it seemed polite to extend the invitation.

"I thought you'd never ask." He grinned acquiescence.

Tom settled on the worn sofa, unbuttoning his suit jacket and loosening his maroon-and-blue tie. Josie carried the mugs from the tiny alcove kitchen, handed him his and sat across from him in the ancient barrel chair she'd found in a secondhand store. As they reviewed the cast of characters at the party, she found herself laughing at his incisive comments and genuinely funny anecdotes.

Draining his mug, he placed it decisively on the wooden coffee table, stood up and crossed to her, removing her mug from her hand and setting it on the top shelf of the adjacent bookshelf. Pulling her to her feet, he wrapped his arms around her, gave her a warm hug, then cupped her face in his hands. "Josie, you look lovely tonight. I was so proud of you." There was no mistaking the adoration in his eyes. "I think it's time we did some serious talking." He led her back to the sofa and keeping one arm around her, pulled her down onto the cushions next to him.

Her heart palpitated as he removed his glasses and set them carefully on the table. One arm still around her, he tipped her chin, turning her face so it was only inches from his own.

"Josie, I've been patient. I'm too set in my ways to rush into things. But seeing you again has simplified my decision. We have a great deal in common and my feelings for you are deep. Josie, dearest, I'd like to spend the rest of my life with you.''

Dear Lord, how could she have allowed things to get to this point? She'd known he cared for her, but she'd thought she'd have time, lots of it, to sort out her feelings. He released her chin and she glanced down, struggling for words.

Looking up again, she hesitated. "Tom, I...I appreciate you, and I appreciate those kind feelings..."

He lifted her hand to his mouth, brushing his lips across her fingers, prickling her skin ever so lightly with the bristles of his mustache. "But?" His eyes flickered with hurt.

"But...I don't know how I feel, Tom. I have to be honest with you. Maybe I need more time. My life is full of too many question marks now."

"That's just what I want to change, dear. I want to give you stability, a home. *My home.*"

She sagged against his chest in an effort to buy time to weigh her next words. He ran his fingers gently through her hair, waiting quietly for her response.

She sat back, capturing both of his hands in her own. "Tom, you have honored me with your proposal. You deserve a woman who will love you wholeheartedly in return. I am touched, too, that you know me well enough to see how much a home would mean to me." She gathered her courage. "To be honest, I'm not quite certain how I feel. I'm just now shifting gears from thinking of you as my teacher and friend. When I give you an answer, I want there to be no doubts."

Disappointment sat in his eyes. He shrugged and wrapped her in another hug. "It was worth a try. And if you need more time, sweetheart, you take all the time you need. I've been a bachelor for so long now, a few more weeks can't hurt."

They sat, arms entwined, for what seemed several minutes. "You're tired," he said at last. "Would you like me to go?"

She stirred, then stood. "If you don't mind. I *am* tired, and you've given me a great deal to think about."

They walked hand in hand to the door of her apartment. He pulled her to him, crushing her lips against his thin mouth. "Don't keep me waiting too long, though."

When she closed the door behind him, her heart was pounding. Sparks? No, panic! Life wasn't waiting for her to take charge of it.

THE DAYS LEADING UP to Christmas were filled with long hours in the library catacombs. Dr. Henry needed a great deal done if he was to meet his publisher's February deadline. She was grateful to lose herself in the research.

But it was the nights that were the worst. She tossed and turned, trying to sort out her priorities. How important was her career? What kind of compromise would career and marriage require? Could the warm feelings she had for Tom turn to love? With time, she'd heard, you can grow into love.

Just as she would start to drift off to sleep, rationalizations neatly in place, she would feel an emptiness deep within her. And like a spirit that refuses to stay entombed, Mack's face would rise before her, his brown eyes alive with laughter. Her body would surge in response to the remembered vision of his broad bare chest, matted with brown hair, tawny in the flickering light of the fire. The image of his sculpted body emerging from the blue-brown water of the farm pond would swim before her. And then, damn it, she'd see all six foot one inches of him naked in the late-summer twilight.

She would flop over on her stomach, covering her head with the pillow. But even in that burrow, the memory of how he made her flesh tingle and her blood pound would intrude. Try as she might, Mackenzie Scott could not be exorcised.

Meanwhile, she saw Tom almost every evening. He was true to his word. Patient, undemanding, although she could read the longing in his eyes. Three days before Christmas they took a cab downtown and spent a delightful late afternoon walking through the stores along Michigan Avenue. As the dusk deepened, the Christmas lights flickered on, illuminating the boulevard in a riot of seasonal color. Tom swung her hand in his, humming "Silver Bells" in a pleasant true baritone.

It should have been a magical time. But the harder Josie tried to create romance, the more pedestrian everything seemed. What was the matter with her?

They planned to celebrate their Christmas on Christmas Eve. Tom was driving to Madison on the twenty-fifth to spend the week with his parents. He'd invited her to accompany him, but she'd demurred, using the research for Dr. Henry as her excuse. She was not yet ready to "go home to meet Mother."

She spent Christmas Eve afternoon preparing a gourmet dinner—Cornish game hens in orange sauce, mushroom-and-wild-rice casserole, a green salad with Balsamic-vinegar dressing, homemade crescent rolls and cherry torte. She covered the Formica table with a red paper cloth and laid the poinsettia-patterned napkins beside the forks. A large green candle surrounded by plastic poinsettia blooms served as the centerpiece.

At precisely six o'clock, Tom knocked on the door. Josie took off the apron, smoothed her hair and let him in.

"Wow!" he said. "I don't know which to comment on first—the beautiful creature in front of me or the delectable aroma coming from the kitchen." He set down a tall paper bag. "A lovely lady must always come first." He pulled her to him, lowering his mouth over hers. After a long kiss, he released her. "Merry Christmas, Josie."

"Merry Christmas, Tom."

He stripped the bag from a bottle of champagne. "Got room in the fridge to chill this?"

She took the bottle from him and wedged it between the eggs and the mixed greens. He followed her to the refrigerator and pulled her into his arms again. "I liked the sample." The refrigerator door slammed shut behind them. He smothered her lips once more. Holding her at arm's length, he surveyed her from head to toe. "You look like Christmas walking. Beautiful red hair, bright sparkling green eyes and a gorgeous green dress that fits you like a dream. It's hard to keep my hands off you, so I don't think I'll try." He crushed her to him, kissing her until she was breathless.

"Tom—" she struggled away "—the game hens. They need to come out of the oven."

"Saved by the oven bell, huh? Very well. Why don't I fix us a cocktail? The champagne's for later." He pulled two glasses from her cramped cupboard and filled them with ice and retrieved the bottle of Chivas he'd left under her sink on his last visit.

He handed her her drink. "Cheers." He knocked his glass against hers. "I'll just sit here and keep you company, dear." He sipped from his drink. Turning the glass in his hands, he seemed to be considering his next words. "This is one of the best Christmases I've ever had." He looked up at her. "You're like the angel on top of my Christmas tree."

Josie turned back to the stove, hiding her trembling fingers. She didn't want to be anyone's angel on a Christmas tree. Why was she so shaky? What was she afraid of? Here was a nice man who clearly adored her giving her a wonderful compliment.

Somehow she got the dinner on the table, and Tom was genuinely effusive about her culinary efforts. She dawdled over the torte and coffee, dread building in her as Tom bathed her in affectionate glances.

Finally there was no more postponing the inevitable. He pushed back his chair, came over to hers and leaned over to kiss her cheek. "Delicious dinner, dear. The first of many Christmas dinners, I hope." He patted her shoulder. "Now, just leave the dishes. I'll do them later. It's time for presents."

He ushered her to the sofa, setting her down, making sure she had a pillow behind her back. He sat next to her, draping one arm around her. "Shall I go first?" he asked.

She grasped at a straw. "No, you wait. I'd like to give you my present first." She leaned over and picked up a small package lying on the shelf beneath the coffee table. "Here, Tom. Merry Christmas."

She cringed as he carefully untied the ribbon and unsealed the tape. Folding the silver-foil wrapping, he laid it aside and examined the small box. He held it up to his ear and shook it. "Shall I guess?"

"Why don't you just open it?" She'd settled on a bill-fold, after all. Not very original, not very personal, but she'd been desperate.

He lifted the lid and parted the tissue. "Josie, it's just what I needed." He pulled the brown pigskin wallet out, admiring the monogram stamped on the cover. "Thank you, sweetheart." He leaned over and kissed her. "Now it's your turn."

Grinning, he reached into the inside pocket of his jacket and extracted a long thin box wrapped in shiny red paper and tied with a satiny white ribbon. "I hope you like it."

She took the box, feeling none of the usual Christmas curiosity and anticipation. The ribbon was smooth under her fingers. She turned the box over and split the ribbon with her index fingernail. The paper slid off easily. She opened the box, removing the layer of thin cotton to reveal a delicate gold chain at the end of which was a lovely filigree heart. She lifted the chain, allowing the heart to lie in the palm of her hand.

"Tom, I don't know what to say." The lacy heart suddenly weighed a pound. She looked up. "It's beautiful."

His eyes melted into eddies of gray. "You're the beautiful one. And that heart? It's mine. I'm giving you my heart, love."

The metal burned in her palm as the blood rushed to her face. Before she could say anything, he took the necklace from her and led her to the full-length oval mirror mounted by the door. "Let me see how it looks."

He stood behind her, working patiently with the clasp until it finally engaged. The heart lay just above the cleavage of her breasts, bordered by the V-neck of her dress. He put his arms around her, pulling her back into him.

Finally she raised her eyes to the mirror. His lips ruffled her hair as he whispered, "You're so beautiful."

Tears welled as she observed the reflection. Her memory warred with the image in the mirror. Another night, another man, another mirror. A time when she couldn't believe she was hearing the word "beautiful." Now she was hearing it again. But somehow it didn't matter whether she believed it or not. For her heart was knocking against her ribs with an insistence that found its source in her groin. Mack, Mack, Mack. Oh, God. What was she doing here? Who was this man with his arms around her now?

Desire drained from her, replaced by a shuddering indifference. Tom. Not Mack. She realized with awful clarity that she had not been thinking of Tom as Tom, just as not-Mack.

She felt Tom's hand drawing her hair to one side, his lips nibbling the soft skin at the nape of her neck. For a moment she felt an insane desire to laugh. It was as if she were watching herself on film attempting to play out some love scene. She desperately wanted someone to yell, "Cut." She trembled involuntarily.

"What's the matter?" His eyes in the mirror betrayed concern.

She shook loose of his embrace. "Nothing you've done. I'm just feeling overwhelmed, I guess. Let's start on the dishes."

"Nothing doing, young lady. I promised. You just sit over there and relax."

As he began clearing the table and rinsing the dishes, she felt her breathing return to normal. She kicked off her pumps and stretched her legs out on the sofa. Lost in thought, she was only occasionally aware of the clink of silverware in the sink. She turned ideas over and over in her mind, examining them from every possible angle. Each pro, each con, was balanced against her memories. If she was honest with herself, there was only one thing to do. Before any more time elapsed. Before she hurt Tom any more than she probably already had. As she heard him scrubbing the sink, she reached up and slowly, tenderly, unclasped the heart necklace.

She was still holding it in her hand when she heard a loud pop from the tiny kitchen. A moment later, Tom emerged, smiling, two glasses of fizzing champagne in his hands. "Ready for a toast to Father Christmas?"

"Tom, I don't think I'm quite in the mood. I have something to say to you."

He set the champagne glasses down, his face falling as he eyed the gold heart cupped in her palm.

FIFTEEN MINUTES LATER he was gone. Fifteen of the most painful minutes of her life. She'd hurt him. There'd been no way to avoid it.

But she'd have hurt him even more if she'd tried to love him and been unsuccessful. She'd wanted to love him. It would have been so tidy, all her problems solved. A future as a wife and mother, perhaps as a teacher. Security.

But what was security without love? Without—*say it, Josie*—sparks?

Tom had been a gentleman. No recriminations. Just hurt. Rejection had that effect. She knew all too well. She'd have given anything not to inflict that kind of pain on him. He was a good decent man who deserved better.

But to carry on with him would have been a lie. So long as Mack lived within her, she knew there could never be another.

She picked up the glasses of untouched champagne and poured them into the sink. Some celebration. Merry Christmas to all and to all a good night.

She gathered up her shoes and carried them to the closet. In the tiny bathroom, she put the stopper in the sink before removing her hammered-gold earrings. As she caught her reflection in the mirror, she stopped, startled. She stood up straight and looked again. She should see a sad ugly duckling there. Instead, a clear-eyed relaxed young woman stared back at her. An attractive woman, maybe even beautiful.

A tiny smile tickled one corner of her mouth. Honesty felt good. She was growing up. Maybe even approaching swanhood. A lovely smile wavered in the mirror as she heard a familiar deep voice echoing from her subconscious. *When you look in a mirror, always see yourself as I see you.*

JOSIE SQUINTED, forcing her eyes open. Sunlight! Streaming in the dormer window. She pushed the covers back, sat up and buried her feet in the warmth of her sheepskin-lined slippers. Pulling on her old flannel robe, she went to the window, looking out upon a pristine shimmering white cover of snow. Why was it so undisturbed?

Then it struck her. Christmas! It was Christmas, and a white one at that. Remembering the scene with Tom, she sagged momentarily against the dormer wall. But it was impossible to keep the joy from surfacing. She felt as if a great burden had been lifted. She straightened and pressed her nose against the cold pane. She knew how Ebenezer Scrooge had felt, liberated from the past, flinging open his window on Christmas morning and shouting, "It's Christmas! God bless us all!"

The Christmas Day she'd dreaded was, instead, one of decisions, new directions—and a chance to get better acquainted with Josie Calhoun. As she treated herself to a homemade cinnamon roll and specially ground amaretto coffee, she laid out her options, carefully considering each one. By the time she'd savored the last drop of the spicy-sweet coffee, she knew what she needed to do.

After indulging in a long hot shower, she tucked her unruly curls into a bun and pulled on her navy blue sweat suit. She turned on the tiny clock radio, flipping through the stations until she located one playing continuous Christmas music. She did a little jig as "Here Comes Santa Claus" bounced off the walls. She giggled. He'd certainly come to her, no doubt about it.

In the corner of her bedroom were the presents mailed from Europe and Kansas. She piled them up and carried them in to the kitchen table. Fluttering to the floor was a yellow slip from the mail carrier. A package too big for delivery needed to be picked up at the post office, but she hadn't returned home in time yesterday. Oh, well, she'd just have a two-day Christmas, instead.

She opened the package from Cheryl and Gus first. They'd probably be calling soon. The box was large and had the imprint of a store in Vienna. She opened it carefully. Inside was a beautiful boiled-wool peacock-blue Tyrolean jacket, embroidered at the lapels and cuffs with stylized Alpine flowers. Holding it up against herself, she could see the color was perfect. What had Gramps said? Could she forgive her mother? It was a day for looking to the future, not dwelling on the past. She carefully re-folded the elegant jacket and laid it back in the box. Maybe Cheryl *had* been the best she could be, and maybe that was enough.

Next she opened a small box from Amy, Les and baby Troy. It was a three-ounce bottle of Elizabeth Taylor's Passion cologne. She grinned as she read the intent of Amy's selection. Amy just wouldn't give up on her, would she?

She'd saved Gramps's present for last. Bless his heart, he'd wrapped it himself. She remembered the crumpled green-and-gold pinecone paper from seeing it stuffed in the back of the linen closet. The ends were secured with enough tape to baffle a safecracker.

She smiled as she fought the tape, finally ripping the paper from the box. She wrestled off the lid, also encumbered by inches and inches of tape. Her breath caught as she pulled back the tissue.

Lying in the box was a beautiful quilt worked mainly in soft blues, daisy yellows and pinks on a white background. Josie stood up and gently unfolded the quilt, draping it over the sofa. The wedding-ring pattern. Josie had loved hearing MJ's stories about the different quilt designs, had loved leaning her elbows on the edge of the table, watching as her grandmother worked her needle in precise, intricate motions. Still lying in the box was a note in Gramps's familiar scrawl. Through a mist of tears, she unfolded it. His words brought his presence to her with great immediacy:

Dearest Josie,
Your grandmother was working on this when she died. She intended it for your hope chest. I took the

liberty of asking Mrs. Haggerty to finish it for you. No matter where you go or what you do, always remember how much MJ loved you and what dreams she had for you. I share in that love, dear girl. Merry Christmas!

A tiny tear fell, blurring the signature. Josie ran her hand gently over the quilt, tracing several of the rings with one finger. Even the faint camphor odor emanating from the folds reminded her of MJ. It was a lovely once-in-a-lifetime gift, one to be cherished and handed down to the next generation. Leaving it draped across the sofa to be enjoyed for a while, Josie picked up the loose wrapping paper and ribbons, crushing them into the kitchen wastebasket. Rubbing the flat of her hands over her thighs, she took a deep breath and dialed the familiar Maizeville number.

Gramps answered on the fifth ring. "Hello?"

"Merry Christmas, Gramps, it's me."

"Josie, honey, merry Christmas to you, too. I've been thinking about you all morning. You just caught me. I was already out the door on my way to have Christmas dinner with the Haggertys when I heard the phone ring."

"Gramps—" her voice thickened "—I don't know how to tell you how much the quilt means to me. It was the best Christmas present ever!"

"I'm glad you like it. It's a special gift for a special young lady." He cleared his throat noisily. "The bathrobe fit perfectly. I guess you thought it was high time I threw away that old green plaid one."

"You mean the one that came over on the *Mayflower?*" She giggled. "Yes, I thought it was time. Anyway, you'll look terribly distinguished in your new paisley number.''

"If I don't watch out, next thing I know, you'll have me wearing one of those dang-fool Ascot ties."

"I promise I won't go that far, Gramps."

"Honey, I hope you're not having to spend Christmas by yourself." There was a question in his voice.

She hesitated, knowing he was fishing for information about Tom. Time to bite the bullet. "Gramps, I have a big favor to ask."

"Ask away, honey."

"When I finish my work for Dr. Henry, I'd like to come home for a while."

His voice conveyed the huge grin she imagined was breaking across his face. "That's wonderful. You know you're always welcome, honey, for as long as you want to be here. This is your home."

"I'm not sure how long I'll stay, but I've made a decision. I'm not cut out for college teaching. What I really want is to work for a wildlife agency of some sort in a job where at least part of the time I can be outdoors. I'd like to come back to Kansas while I work on finding that type of position."

"That's just about the best news you could give your old grandfather at Christmas." He paused, his next words articulated with care. "But what about your obligations...in Chicago? Your work there?"

"My work here will be finished sometime in February. As soon as it is, I'll pack up and head for the Land of Oz. And, Gramps, my other obligations? Let's just say I've tied up all my loose ends here."

"You sound chipper and determined. I'm glad. Jimmy Cagney and I will count the days, sweetheart."

"I'll be in touch. Wish the Haggertys Merry Christmas for me. And, Gramps, thanks for everything."

She hung up the phone, her eyes dancing with anticipation.

BY THE NEXT DAY, the snow was trampled and blackened with soot and the splat of mud and cinders from passing vehicles. Josie dodged icy piles of hardened gray snow and puddles of frigid water as she traversed the obstacle course of the post-office parking lot.

After fifteen minutes in the line, shuffling forward a few inches at a time, Josie reached the counter, handing the postal agent her crumpled yellow notice. He disappeared into the back room, returning in a few moments with an oversize flat box about two feet by three feet. She grasped it carefully under one arm and retraced her steps through the busy parking lot to her Honda.

Back in her apartment, she laid the parcel on the kitchen table and slit the knotted strings. She didn't recognize the block print writing on the brown paper. Removing the outer wrapping, she encountered thick corrugated cardboard wrapped around something slightly smaller. Inside was a black picture frame, the glass covered with protective masking tape. Gently she peeled the adhesive from the glass.

Her breath came in short stabbing gasps, and her pulse went into high gear as, strip by strip, she gradually revealed a magnificent black-and-white photograph of a pair of Canada geese standing in the dark brown dirt of a windswept Kansas cornfield. In the righthand bottom corner, tiny letters of the same block print read Mackenzie Scott.

She gripped the sides of the frame as her chest heaved, tears of relief spilling down her freckled face. Regaining some semblance of control, she turned the frame over. In broad decisive strokes was a message inscribed on the brown paper backing: "May your splendid geese be shot only in this way. Merry Christmas, Red."

CHAPTER THIRTEEN

UNSEASONABLY MILD, the early-February day was the kind that motivates children to play hooky and grown men to leave work early to head for the golf course or garden.

Mack rolled down the window of the patrol car, relishing the stream of crystal-clear air, which, in its pungent moist earthiness, carried the promise of spring. He was making his routine pass through the northwest quadrant of his territory, exploring the side roads and keeping an eye out for any signs of break-ins. The adjacent county had experienced a recent rash of vandalism and petty thievery.

As he drove along, he kept alert for photo possibilities. He needed several more good pictures for the spring section of his Flint Hills book. By late March or early April, maybe he could get shots of the massed redbuds blooming along a creek bed, a close-up of a newborn calf in the tall prairie grass, and perhaps one of a cowboy riding the fence line, a spring thunderhead roiling in the background.

Mack slowed, pulled into the rutted driveway of a weather-beaten abandoned barn and reversed his direction. Everything seemed pretty calm. As he did often lately, while he drove he speculated about his future. The more he worked on the book and some other writing and photography projects, the clearer it became that as soon as he could make a living at it, free-lance writing was what he really wanted to pursue.

The Changing Faces of the Flint Hills should be ready for submission to publishers by June, and he already had several articles under consideration by editors. More and more often now he found himself resenting the time his deputy-sheriff work took. He wanted to be writing. He'd built up a sizable nest egg. Living at the Britton place was cheap, and he certainly didn't spend much on his social life. His one date with Monica Austin, though it satisfied Beth Ann, had ended in a mutual decision to keep their relationship platonic. With Josie gone, romance was not a priority.

The thought of Josie caused a knot in his chest. Damn, he wasn't over her, not by a long shot, but he was determined to put the past behind him. Their differences were clearly etched in his brain. She would never yield on the hunting issue and her behavior was a clear example of her stubbornness. Her overreaction about Clay and her cold insistence on justice had revealed implacability. And worst of all, her childish jealousy about poor dead Sarah hardly suggested the maturity necessary for a lasting relationship. That didn't mean, though, he could entirely forget her laughing shamrock eyes, her voluptuous breasts rising from that slim waist or her refreshing natural warmth and zest for adventure.

He had debated long and hard about sending her the photograph at Christmas. Her cheap shots and lack of trust in him had hurt, but she *had* tried to apologize. Her abrupt departure from Maizeville had left no opportunity to hear her out. He'd finally decided that by sending her the framed print of the geese, she would know that things between them were settled. That he had, in fact, understood about her geese. That gesture and her sincere but noncommittal thank-you note had brought their relationship to closure as far as he was concerned.

At least he'd thought so until he ran into Frank Calhoun one morning the week before at the Main Street Café. Frank had motioned him over to the booth where he sat, the *Kansas City Star* spread across the table, a cup of coffee cooling in his rough wrinkled hands.

"Mack, care to join me?"

"Sure, Frank. It's good to see you." Mack signaled the waitress and ordered coffee and a cinnamon roll. The last time he'd seen Frank, he'd looked older, more stoop-shouldered. Now, however, he appeared jaunty, and the old twinkle was back in his blue eyes. "You're looking mighty chipper today, Frank."

"I've got good cause, young feller." Frank raised the steaming cup to his lips, sipping noisily. "Hot." He put the cup back down and fixed his penetrating gaze on Mack. "Good news. Josie's coming home next week."

Mack's stomach had done a flip-flop. "For a visit?"

"Maybe, maybe not. Her business is finished in Chicago. She's going to keep me company while she looks for a job. She's decided not to consider college teaching. Wants to be outdoors, working directly with wildlife."

It figured, Mack had thought. The idea of all that spontaneous energy being cooped up in a classroom was laughable. "Good for her. She needs to follow her dream."

Frank eyed him over the rim of his cup. "We all do, son. We all do."

The waitress set down Mack's coffee and bun, lathered with gooey white icing. "I'm coming to understand that more each day, Frank. I remember clearly what you said about MJ's philosophy. We only go around once, so we need to discover what's important and make each day count."

"Couldn't have said it better myself." Frank blew on his coffee. "I know Josie'd like to see you. Feel free to drop by anytime."

Mack had noted the laugh lines at the corner of Frank's mouth and the warm gleam in his eyes. The old man seemed to be harboring some pleasant secret, the kind of secret the old know intuitively but the young have to discover through trial and error.

Cupping his hands around his own steaming coffee cup, Mack had changed the subject. "What do you think of the latest sportsmen's-club proposal for the use of your land and pond?"

"Sounds like a fine idea. In fact, I'm downright enthusiastic about it. As soon as you fellers have the paperwork put together, I'm ready to sign my John Hancock."

Mack set down his cup and extended his hand to Frank. "That's great news. You've got yourself a deal." Mack had shaken Frank's hand to seal the bargain. "We'll get on it right away!"

"And tell that young Johnson lad that I'm right proud of him," Frank had added.

A school bus stopped ahead of Mack's patrol car to discharge several laughing children, bringing him back to the present. Kids! They reminded him how gratified he was by the changes in Clay. As they'd worked together through the winter on the mandated wildlife project, Mack had observed the sloughing off of belligerence as, despite himself, Clay became absorbed by—even enthu-

siastic about—his newly gained knowledge. Wint Ferris
had done a superb job of involving the biology class and
spearheading the project. Even Les was starting to get
excited about what the kids had come up with. Despite
her challenge concerning local hunting traditions, Josie
had sparked some rethinking among many, including
himself.

While Mack waited for the last of the straggling children to cross in front of the bus, he thought about the
inevitability of seeing Josie again. He tried to project his
feelings. In honesty, he couldn't say how he felt. He
didn't know whether to take the easier path and let
sleeping dogs lie or to explore the ashes of their relationship to see if there was anything worth rekindling. Did he
really want that kind of complication in the course he'd
determined for his future?

The bus driver retracted the Stop sign, turned off the
flashing red lights and drove on down the country road
to the intersection with the highway. Where Mack sat
now, his patrol car was partially obscured from the
highway by a tattered old signboard, flanked by several
tall cedars. He might as well stay put a few minutes and
see if he could apprehend any speeders. He turned on his
radar.

An elderly couple crept by at thirty miles an hour, followed by a semi, nosing out to pass. Several pickups going between fifty and sixty whizzed by. In the distance,
the radar picked up a vehicle doing sixty-two. Stoppa-
ble, but hardly excessive. As the vehicle crossed Mack's
plane of vision, he sat up straight. It was a gray Honda.
With a redheaded female driver.

He grinned. Should he? It was against departmental
regulations to stop a vehicle for personal reasons. But,

hey, sixty-two. A definite violation. He battled with himself only momentarily. The grin spread. It was too good a chance to pass up.

He activated his flashing light and turned right onto the highway. The Honda continued to speed on down the road, and as Mack caught up to it, the Honda slowed and rolled to a stop just before the Pioneer Oak. This time, Mack was actually chuckling, instead of reliving a nightmare. He picked up his ticket book, slammed his hat on his head, adjusted his sunglasses and stepped purposefully from the car.

The driver had rolled down her window and was looking up questioningly with apprehensive green eyes. "Will you step out of the car, please, ma'am?" A gentle, springlike breeze caught at the tendrils of copper hair as she did as she was bid. Mack drew in his breath sharply. The azure blue mohair sweater fell loosely from her shoulders, molding her generous breasts. Faded jeans showed off long shapely legs to perfection. He struggled not to smile—yet.

"Mack, I...was I really speeding?" She looked up imploringly, the dusting of freckles setting off her patrician nose and generous mouth.

"May I see your driver's license, miss?" *Keep it all business, Mack. Don't let your fool hand shake when she gives it to you.* He took the laminated card from her and glanced at the picture. Damn cute for a photo ID. "Are you aware you were going sixty-two in a fifty-five-mile-an-hour zone?"

"Was I, officer?" Did she bat her eyes at him? He could have sworn she had. "Heavens, I guess I'm just in such a hurry to get home."

"Like a horse going to the barn?" He took off his sunglasses and drank her in.

"Like a horse going to the barn," she admitted, a mirthful glint in her eyes.

He tilted back his hat and glanced over at the huge oak. "Well, ma'am, I reckon that old tree is doing more than whispering this time. It must be shouting to you."

She laughed, the warm rich sound floating through the air. "You're right."

He handed her license back, unable to stop the grin that split his face from ear to ear. "Welcome home, Josie."

"What about my ticket?"

"Consider this a warning." He held the door open for her as she sat back down and turned on the ignition. "And a personal welcome from an old friend." He closed the door and strode back to the patrol car, humming under his breath.

JOSIE COULDN'T GET OVER how Troy had grown. He smiled and blew airy saliva bubbles, gooed and cooed, and even tightened one fist on a hank of Josie's hair and held on for dear life. His downy baby hair was almost gone, replaced by the beginnings of new darker hair. He already weighed sixteen pounds. Les might get his linebacker yet. Amy, too, had changed. She seemed more relaxed, almost serene. Josie asked her how motherhood was treating her.

"Josie, I can't tell you how happy I am. Troy demands a lot of time and attention, but he's worth every minute of it. I knew I wanted to be a mother, but I had no idea how much he would add to our lives."

"Les adapting, too?" Josie held her breath.

"I really think so." A shadow passed over Amy's face. "I didn't tell you just how worried I was before I had the baby. Worried about Les and whether a baby was too much responsibility for him. And then when he wasn't there for the delivery..."

"But things are better now?"

"Much. Les and I have been going to a parenting class at the church. It's really helping. And you'll never guess what I'm doing!" She grinned, her eyes alive with mischief.

"If I'll never guess, I give up. What?"

"I'm taking golf lessons! I'm not excited about hunting or fishing, but golf is something Les and I can do together. To tell you the truth, I'd become almost too much of a homebody."

Josie clapped her hands delightedly. "That's great, Amy. I'm proud of you."

"Josie..." Amy paused, her expression becoming more serious. "One thing that's helped Les is that Mack has been spending lots of time with him. They go target shooting together and seem really excited about their plans for the sportsmen's club. Mack seems to get through to Les in ways hardly anyone else can. I'm so grateful to him."

Josie found her mouth going dry as she waited for Amy to continue.

"Josie, have you seen Mack yet?"

"Only briefly when I first drove into town."

"How do you feel about him?" Amy met Josie's eyes unwaveringly.

"He's part of the reason I came back, Amy. I'm going to find out how I feel. I wrote you that I realized Tom wasn't right for me, nor I for him. I can't say that yet about Mack. But I'm sure as hell going to find out.''

Amy jumped out of her chair and gave Josie a high five. ''Good for you! I knew you wouldn't give up without a fight!''

THE FIRE CRACKLED in the fireplace and James Cagney purred in her lap as Josie, curled up on the sofa, sewed missing buttons on several of Gramps's old work shirts. Gramps, absorbed in the Sunday crossword, occasionally tapped the tip of his pencil against his chin before writing in letters. His efforts were accompanied by a mumbled monologue. ''That can't be right . . . five letter word for willow, starting with *O* . . . ha!''

Josie liked the sounds of triumph best. She smiled fondly at him. Bless his heart. It was good to be home, and there was no denying the pleasure her presence seemed to bring him. Her first few days since returning had been busy. Although the house was in fair shape, it had needed a thorough cleaning. Then there was the restocking of the pantry. Apparently Gramps had made many meals from cold cereal, Campbell's bean-with-bacon soup and store-bought oatmeal cookies. But at least he seemed more purposeful, not as much at loose ends as she'd feared.

''Gramps?''

''What, honey?'' He looked up from the newspaper.

''Whatever happened about leasing the pond?'' She waited, heart thudding.

''It's a done deal.'' He smiled broadly.

She felt the telltale flush rising out of her collar.

''What do you mean?''

"Les and Mack have made me an offer I can't refuse."

"Have you signed anything?" A vision of the land populated with heavy artillery trained on the sky filled her mind.

"Not yet. And I won't until you look over the proposal, but I think you'll have some second thoughts."

She jabbed the needle through the button so hard she pricked her finger. *Not likely,* she thought. She bit her lip, determined not to argue with Gramps, determined to avoid the impetuous displays that had always cost her so much. Nothing was set in stone. She owed Gramps the courtesy of waiting to see what was in the proposal. Then there would be time to reason with him, maybe avoid an explosion.

Running the thread between her lips to moisten the tip, Josie carefully reinserted the damp pointed end into the eye of the needle and resumed the mechanical motions of sewing. In an effort to control her fixation with the sportsmen's-club proposal, she deliberately shifted her thoughts to the more pleasant recollection of the improvement in Amy and Les's relationship. And to her own concern, which she hadn't voiced to Amy, about the alienation she still felt in the community. But this was her home, and she hoped that just as she might find a way back to Mack, she'd also find a niche in Maizeville.

She knotted the thread in the last button, carefully folded the shirt and put the needle and thread back in the wicker sewing basket beside her. She closed the basket and set it aside. "Need any more repairs, Gramps?"

"No, honey." He peered intently at his puzzle. "What need is to finish this puzzle. Who's the author of *Kenworth?*"

Josie thought a minute. "Sir Walter Scott."

"Aha!" Gramps crowed. "That's it! *S-C-0-T-T*." He put down the newspaper and sat back, smiling in satisfaction. Then he leaned forward, peering intently at Josie. "Scott. And what about *your* puzzle?"

"My puzzle?"

"Scott. Mackenzie Scott." He flipped the lever on the side of the recliner and catapulted to his feet, giving her time to recover from his frontal assault. He crossed to the hearth, picked up a big log and threw it on the fire. With the poker, he stirred the embers to life. He turned to face her, smiling with grandfatherly affection.

"I have to believe he had something to do with your return. I hope so, anyway." He settled back in his chair, elevating his feet and lacing his fingers over his belly.

"Why do you hope so?" Josie stalled for time, the warm glow in her heart spreading in concert with the flames leaping as the new log caught in the fire.

"Honey, I've lived a long time, and the way I see it, you can run but you can't hide."

Was he going to talk in riddles all night? "I'm not following you, I'm afraid."

He chuckled. "No, I suppose not. By coming back, you've shown you don't want to hide anymore. I'm just hoping you're not going to run. From love."

"Is that what you think I've been doing?"

He straightened. "Yes, that's what I think you've been doing. For a long, long time. You've spent a great deal of your life convincing yourself you're not worthy of love. I hope—"

She interrupted him. "You're right, Gramps. That's exactly what I've been doing. I may be a slow learner, but you might say I've finally come to my senses. And I'm going after love."

"Mack?"

"Mack. I don't know exactly what to do. After all, I've made several big mistakes and I'm still not sure how we can resolve our differences about hunting, but it's worth trying to do something."

"Do you love him?"

She gulped. "Yes, Gramps. I do." In her answer was the certainty that had for so long eluded her. "I only wish I knew what to do about it."

Gramps eased back in the recliner again, a beatific smile lighting his face. "If you love him enough, something will occur to you. Yep, you'll discover what to do."

"But what if he thinks of me only as a friend?"

Gramps chuckled softly and from the table beside his chair picked up a small framed photo of MJ as a young woman. "Friend? I hope so. The very best kind of love grows between friends." A long comfortable moment of shared silence was broken only by the crackling of the fire.

Josie moved to the recliner, leaned over the back and placed a hand on Gramps's shoulder. She took the photo from him, holding it so they could both look at the image. Lost in her grandmother's loving eyes and warm smile, Josie patted Gramps absently. "Sometimes friendships go on forever, don't they, Gramps?"

He looked up, his rough gnarled hand covering the soft one on his shoulder. "They sure do, honey." His eyes found hers. "Trust him, Josie. And trust yourself."

JOSIE BOUNCED TROY against her shoulder, then shifted him in her arms so he could put his little feet on the counter and look at the colorful ties in the glass case. When Amy had suggested the shopping trip to Manhattan, Josie agreed happily. An outing together would be fun. And she adored spending time with Troy.

He had a tight hold on her heartstrings, all right. He leaned forward trying to reach the revolving display rack. "Come back here, Tiger." Josie couldn't imagine how Amy lugged him around all day. He was a handful and a half!

"What do you think, Josie?" Amy held up two ties for her inspection.

Josie considered them. "It depends. The navy with the little golfers is nice, but conservative. I kind of like the big zinnias on the other one."

"I don't know if Les'd wear it, but I like the zinnias, too. Anyway, flowers are appropriate for Valentine's Day, don't you think?"

Valentine's Day had snuck up on Josie, but at the card shop in the mall she'd bought Gramps a Valentine with geese on the front and Troy an oversize clown card, complete with real balloons.

Amy signed the charge slip and picked up the package. "Josie, I'm going to the service desk to get this wrapped. You want to come or shall I meet you someplace?"

Troy arched his back, nearly causing Josie to lose her grip on him. "You go on. I'll put Tiger here back in his stroller and we'll go for a walk. I'll meet you at the mall fountain in fifteen minutes."

The aisles and walls were festooned with streamers and pink, white and red corrugated crepe-paper hearts. Josie sighed as she maneuvered the stroller around an aisle display of men's colognes and after-shaves.

Give Your Sweetheart Some Sweet Scent, read the saccharine sign, perched amid the masculine boxes and bottles. What sweetheart? Maybe next year.

Ahead of her, the aisle was clogged by a frazzled-looking woman with a toddler on a harness and an elderly woman using a walker. "Okay, pipsqueak," she said to Troy. "Slow traffic ahead."

She leaned over and jiggled the colored plastic key ring attached to the stroller. As she straightened, she noticed they were stalled at the underwear section—men's heart-bedecked briefs, V-necked and round-necked T-shirts, athletic socks.

And then she saw them. As the traffic cleared, she approached the counter, smiling to herself, and examined the merchandise. Troy looked up expectantly, a toothless grin corroborating her intention. "I think so, kiddo. Yes, I definitely think so."

When Amy emerged from the department store, Josie was seated on the edge of the fountain, holding Troy in her lap, softly singing "This Old Man." Amy waved and hurried over. "Sorry it took so long."

"No problem. Tiger and I've had a great time."

Amy reached out for Troy and started wedging him into the stroller. A bag was lying in the seat. "Josie, can you take that out? What is it, anyway?"

Josie retrieved the bag and smiled cryptically. "Just an arrow for my bow."

"Your bow?" Amy looked at Josie as if she'd left her brain in the store.

"Well, maybe not *my* bow. Let's just say Cupid's bow."

MACK FLUNG OPEN the office door and breezed over to perch on the edge of Alice's desk. "We found the Miller kid over at the bowling alley," he said exultantly. "When he decided to run away from home, he didn't get very far."

Alice grinned at him. "I'll bet his folks were glad to see him."

"Gladys was about out of her mind. She didn't know whether to hug him or spank him when we brought him home. Of course the hugging won out."

He stood up and removed his hat. "Speaking of hugging. Stand up here, Alice, my love." Looking at him warily, Alice cautiously rose to her feet. "It's time for your Valentine's hug, sweetheart." He wrapped his arms around her waist, lifted her off the floor and twirled her around.

Her glasses slid to one side of her nose and she was breathing hard when he set her down. "Whew. I don't know what's come over you, but that's the kind of fraternization I like. Happy Valentine's Day to you, too?" The question in her voice was obvious.

He shrugged and swatted her arm with his hat. "Back to business, lady."

She picked up her pen, then paused and faced him again. "By the way, Mack. Remember the woman who brought you that envelope last summer?"

He frowned and scratched his head. "What woman?"

She pursed her lips and raised her eyebrows. "You know. The redheaded looker." She watched the light dawn and noted the gleam in his eye. "She brought you a package today. It's on your desk."

Alice feigned interest in the papers spread out before her. As he strode across the room, she swiveled in her chair to watch him.

A small package, neatly wrapped in white tissue paper and tied with a red ribbon, lay on his desk. He picked it up and carefully removed the wrapping. Holding the gift in his hands, he sank into his chair, tilted it back and crossed his feet on the desk.

There they were—one dozen monogrammed handkerchiefs. But that wasn't all. Attached to the strap binding the handkerchiefs was a tiny brass fishhook. Beneath the strap was a plain white card. As he read the message, he laughed out loud.

Thanks for not giving me a ticket. If you had, I might have needed more than one handkerchief. So here's a supply just in case. Next time you might not let me off the *hook* so easily.
Happy Valentine's Day.

Gray Honda.

Becoming aware of Alice's questioning scrutiny, he brought his chair up, planted his feet on the floor and gave her a big thumbs-up.

"Okay, nosy. Yes. I'm having a happy Valentine's Day." And he laughed again, the memory of the last time he'd seen the fishhook causing a profound stirring in his groin.

JOSIE SLIT OPEN the envelope and pulled out the official-looking letter. The Kansas Department of Wildlife and Parks had an opening for which she was suited.

Could she come to Topeka on March fourth for an interview?

Could she! She whooped and did a little jig, which sent James Cagney scurrying to safety under the kitchen table. Earlier she'd heard from the Oklahoma Department of Wildlife Conservation and was already scheduled for an interview in Oklahoma City in mid-March. She crossed her fingers and tried to stanch the surge of adrenaline on which her stomach was floating.

When she attempted to settle down to balance her checkbook, she just couldn't sit still. Instead, she ran up to her bedroom, taking the stairs two at a time. A run! That would use up some of this excess energy. She pulled on a pair of purple running pants and a purple-and-green anorak. As an afterthought, she grabbed a pair of gloves and a white wool toque.

Although the day was sunny and clear, the wind was cutting. Chicago might be the Windy City, but there was nothing quite as strong as a Kansas gale. She drew on the gloves and pulled the hat down over her ears. By the time she reached the mailbox, she was huffing and puffing. As she turned onto the dirt road, her eyes were tearing. Inside the jogging suit, she could feel her body warming with perspiration and then chilling as the cold wind sliced through her. Knowing she'd be running into the wind on the way home, she cheated and turned around before reaching the wooden bridge.

As the wind hit her full force, she lowered her head to cut the resistance. More wind-induced tears fell on her cheek, quickly evaporated by the rushing air. Sensing the onset of a sneeze, she slowed her pace, pulled one glove off and reached into her pocket for a tissue. Drat! Why was she never prepared?

Just then she heard a car behind her. Automatically she pulled over to the left edge of the road, still running and at the same time hugging herself for warmth. As the vehicle neared, it slowed until it was keeping pace with her.

She sneezed and turned to look. It was Mack. He'd rolled down his window and his face was contorted in an effort not to laugh.

"Hi, Red. Need a handkerchief?"

They stared at each other, then simultaneously broke into helpless laughter. When Mack finally regained some control, he whipped out a white monogrammed handkerchief and handed it to her.

"This time, lady, I'm going to keep track of my possessions. A certain traffic offender of my acquaintance was kind enough to provide me with a good supply of handkerchiefs, and I don't want to lose them." He reached in the back seat and tossed her a wool army blanket. "Wrap up in this and come on home with me, and I'll trade you several tissues for the handkerchief." He leaned over and opened the passenger door. "Come on."

Her face was aflame with wind, cold and embarrassment. Here was the man in all the world she most wanted to impress, and here she was, a shivering frozen lump! But this was one invitation she wasn't going to pass up, no matter what. As she climbed into the vehicle, he nodded toward the back seat. "I've just been to the store, and not only do I have Kleenex, I also have a supply of instant cocoa. Let's get you warmed up."

"I'm in no position to refuse such gallantry. I accept with pleasure." She sneezed gustily into the folds of linen. A blast of warm air from the heater spread over her feet, thawing her toes and then the rest of her. As she daintily wiped her nose, she peeked over the handkerchief to find Mack smiling to himself, his hands tapping the steering wheel to the beat of some internal music.

Her heart was pounding like a trip-hammer. It was so good to be close to him, to feel the strength emanating from his athletic body, to smell his woodsy scent again, to hear the deep honey tones of his voice. Tears, this time of happiness, welled in her eyes. *Please, please. Let me find the way back to him.*

Stranger, who'd been snoozing on the stoop soaking up the sun, raised his head as the Bronco turned in the narrow driveway. Then he jumped to his feet, leaping and running in circles. He gave Mack a cursory welcome and then jumped against Josie, his front paws planted on her chest, his tail dusting the ground in excited wags.

"Down, boy," Mack commanded. "You know you're not supposed to jump on people."

"It's okay just this once, Mack. I'm glad to see him, too." Josie knelt and ran her fingers through his thick winter coat.

Inside, true to his word, Mack took the monogrammed handkerchief from her and stuffed three tissues into her hand. "Mack," she said, "at least let me take it home and wash it."

"Nothing doing, lady. This is a valuable keepsake given me by a Valentine admirer. How could I let it out of my sight?" He winked at her and went into the kitchen to unload the groceries and start the water boiling in the kettle.

Josie glanced around the small living room. She'd wondered about his surroundings. One wall was taken up by an antique scarred wooden desk, which seemed an anachronism to the modern computer atop it. An Ansel

Adams poster hung on one wall above a sagging plaid sofa. A coffee table made out of a door stood in front of the sofa. Magazines and paperbacks littered its surface. Josie craned her neck to read the titles—Whitman's *Leaves of Grass, Sports Illustrated,* the *Atlantic, Sports Afield,* the Sunday *New York Times* and William Least Heat-Moon's *Prairyerth.* Pretty eclectic, Josie mused.

The entire wall opposite the sofa was filled with bookcases and stereo equipment. An old bentwood rocker sat in front of one bookcase and was presided over by the ugliest brass floor lamp she'd ever seen. The space next to the door was obviously Stranger's territory. His stainless-steel water dish and his food bowl were in the corner, and a plaid-covered cedar-filled dog nest was beside the door. It was, by far, the newest piece of furnishing in the house.

Josie heard the refrigerator door slam just as the kettle started to shriek. She roused herself and peered into the barely functional kitchen. "Can I help?"

Mack gestured to a cupboard. "Cups are in there. Sorry I don't have any marshmallows. I didn't know I'd be entertaining."

She produced two mugs, one with horses on it and the other advertising Zack's Gun Shop. With mock seriousness, Mack spooned precise measurements of cocoa into the two mugs, then held the kettle ceremoniously and filled the mugs. "And Mr. Mackenzie Scott poured for his houseguest, the esteemed Miss Josie Calhoun."

She nodded regally, picked up her steaming mug and sashayed into the living room, settling in queenly fashion into the rocker. Mack followed and stood leaning casually against the doorjamb, looking at her.

She felt suddenly ill at ease. Why didn't he say something? She filled the awkwardness with a sip of the cocoa. "Ouch." The darned stuff had burned her tongue.

"Too hot?" His amused eyes sought hers.

"Yes, too hot." *And not just this cocoa,* she thought.

He put his mug on top of the dog-eared *Leaves of Grass* and settled on the floor, his back against the sofa, his maddeningly attractive muscular legs stretched out in front of him, his gaze on her face.

She glanced around the room. "Er, nice place you've got here."

He kept on staring at her. "It'll do for Stranger and me."

She took another sip of the sweet chocolate. "I guess I should thank you for not giving me that ticket."

"I'm the one who needs to thank you. I appreciated the Valentine remembrance."

"It was the least I could do. And, Mack, I..." *Get hold of yourself.* "I want you to know that I'll try very hard not to leap to conclusions the way I did about your goose shooting." A sad smile flickered across her face.

He crossed his legs and leaned toward her. "Josie, the past is done. It's over. I understand."

She fought the impulse to get down on the floor beside him and curl up in his arms. She didn't dare rush things, though. She glanced at the computer and the thick sheaf of paper lying on his desk. "How's the book coming?"

His face lit up. "Well, I think. The text is finished except for a little revision, and I need only a few more photographs. Then I'll cross my fingers and hope the publishing fates smile on my efforts." He stood up as if seized by a thought. "Would you like to see some of the prints?"

She smiled. "I'd be honored."

He grabbed her by the hand and led her to a narrow door. Opening it, he helped her down the rickety wooden stairs into his darkroom. He retraced his steps to shut the door.

For a moment, the tiny room was plunged into total darkness. She stood rooted, heart thudding, as she sensed him coming toward her. His arm brushed her shoulder as he reached for the string to turn on the overhead light. For a fraction of a second, she felt him pause. She could hear her own pulse. Then he pulled the string and the enclosure was filled with a bald yellow light.

He leaned across the countertop and pulled out several manila folders. One by one he spread out the prints, commenting on each. All depicted various times of year in the Flint Hills. The play of light and shadow, the strong composition, the variety of close-ups and panoramic views all reinforced Josie's impression of his talent. Each photo, in its own way, was a gem.

"Mack, these are truly remarkable. I'm very impressed."

He gathered them up carefully and refiled them. "I'm glad you like them, Josie. Your opinion's important to me." He turned and took both her hands in his. "Very important." He searched her eyes and seemed on the brink of saying something but, instead, dropped her hands. "I've spent a lot of time in here since you left." He busied himself with the file folders.

"I can tell." She glanced around, looking at the prints hanging on the walls. In the corner was a small one of a delicate lovely blonde. She walked closer and looked at it. "Mack? Is this Sarah?"

He turned around, leaning against one of the sinks. "Yes."

Josie studied the lovely young woman with the wheat-colored hair, the honest, caring sapphire eyes, the happy natural smile. "She was beautiful." Josie turned slowly. "I hope I've grown up some since last fall. It was very wrong of me to lash out at you about Sarah." She took a deep breath. "I understand now that it was selfish of me to want you to forget her. It was my own childish need to have you all for myself."

Mack's tawny eyes encouraged her to go on. "What I've learned is that love doesn't happen on my terms. And love doesn't happen by erasing the past. Sarah was an abiding part of you, of the you who became my friend. To wish she hadn't existed and hadn't been so important to you was stupid." Her voice sank almost to a whisper. "I know that now." She lowered her gaze, praying the words had come out as she felt them in her heart.

She sensed his hand on her elbow first, then, hardly believing what was happening, she felt his arms around her pulling her against him in a warm embrace. He ran one hand over her head, caressing her hair. For a long moment all she could hear was the symphony of their breathing and heartbeats. Releasing her slowly, he held her at arm's length.

"Thank you for that, Josie. It helps. Your friendship is very important to me. I'm glad we haven't lost that."

Friendship. There was that word again. The difference now, though, lay in her new understanding of love.

"Oh, Mack, I'm very glad, too."

"To be honest with you, Josie, I don't know exactly where we go from here. But I do know being friends is a good place to start."

Just as he reached to turn off the light, she noticed something that filled her heart with the joy of a thousand firecrackers. Tacked to the inside of the door was a poster-size enlargement of a photograph. Warm giggles bubbled inside her. The photograph was of Stranger with a strawberry roan colt of a girl in a floppy camouflage hat.

Mack gestured to the door. "You really didn't think I'd forget you, did you? I also shoot dogs and people." Their joined laughter ricocheted off the darkroom walls.

JOSIE INSISTED on jogging back to the house. She needed time to think, time to embrace the sweetness of releasing guilt and pettiness, to savor the newfound maturity and ease she sensed within herself, to glory in the possibility of a new beginning with Mack.

For so long she'd been preoccupied with how people and events affected her. How blind self-absorption could be! From now on, she'd give much more attention to Mack's needs, to Gramps's needs. Maybe, just maybe, by doing more for others, her own needs would be met, too. Her introspection was interrupted by a sneeze. Damn! She'd left her tissues at Mack's.

She reached the kitchen door, tripping over the sill as she raced for a Kleenex. Another sneeze exploded. She fell into a kitchen chair, sputtering and laughing.

Trailing his newspaper, Gramps scurried into the room. "What in the world is the matter?"

She couldn't stop laughing. "No-no-thing. Achoo!" A third sneeze erupted.

"Gesundheit! Are you all right?" He peered worriedly over his spectacles.

"I'm fine, Gramps. Better than I've been in a long time." She tossed her toque onto the table. "If a cold is the price I have to pay for feeling so good, it's cheap."

Gramps, staring at her uncertainly, settled across the table from her. Josie wriggled out of her jacket and kicked off her running shoes. With the tip of his finger, Gramps tentatively pushed an oversize envelope across the table.

"What's this?" Josie picked it up.

"The sportsmen's-club proposal. Les brought it by a little while ago. I think you ought to look at it." He folded his hands on the table and waited.

The laughter died in Josie's eyes as she fingered the envelope. She'd known the moment would come. She struggled desperately to control the anger washing over her. Her beloved pond! MJ's sanctuary, turned into a seasonal battlefield. *Easy. Control yourself*. She glanced at Gramps, noting even through her agitation the hopeful expression in his eyes. What had Mack said? *He needs a purpose*.

Slowly she undid the flap of the envelope and withdrew the document, desperately trying to stem her rising anger. Spreading it out before her on the table, she forced her eyes to the words on the cover. They swam before her. She shook her head and read again:

PROPOSAL FOR
MAIZEVILLE SPORTSMEN'S CLUB WILDLIFE REFUGE
AND EDUCATIONAL NATURE CENTER

She exhaled audibly, then looked into Gramps's warm

yes. "I don't understand. I thought…" Her voice trailed off as she read the next words:

A joint project of the Maizeville Sportsmen's Club, the Maizeville High School Science Department and the Kansas State University Department of Biology.

Gramps reached over to place his warm wrinkled hand over her cold smooth one. "Sometimes things aren't what they seem. And sometimes, people and events change the look of things."

He patted her hand, chuckling softly. "Les has had a change of heart since that baby arrived. Seems he and Mack got to talking about how much scarcer the birds get with each passing generation. How important it is to preserve what they've enjoyed for their own children. Your little talk planted seeds in some other darned unlikely places, too. But the real push came from the project Mack and Wint Ferris helped Clay Johnson with. His focus was researching the dwindling local wildlife population and then educating the community about the need to preserve what we have. The whole biology class got involved." Josie shook her head in stunned amazement. "In the end, Les said, he and Mack know there are other places to hunt, but there aren't many other places where we can create a game preserve and bring schoolchildren here to learn about waterfowl and ecology."

He paused, then went on. "I think that's work worth doing. Mack and Les have already investigated securing nonprofit status and have formed a committee to raise funds and look for grant money." He squeezed her hand. "They want me to manage the facility."

Josie remained speechless, a slow grin brightening her features.

"It just could be, honey, that you had a little something to do with Mack's thinking. With a lot of folks thinking."

Josie, a delicious warmth pervading her body, picked up the proposal, bent her head over the pages and began reading.

CHAPTER FOURTEEN

JOSIE THREW her handbag into the back seat of the Honda, sank gratefully behind the wheel and began carefully maneuvering the car out of the tight parking space near the capitol building in Topeka.

Her head was throbbing and her stomach was growling ferociously. She had been far too nervous to eat before the interview. Pulling into the drive-through of the first McDonald's she saw, she ordered two cheeseburgers, a large Coke and french fries. After the first few bites she decided she'd probably live.

Once she finished the long-overdue lunch, found the interstate entrance ramp and set her cruise control, she settled down to a careful review of the exciting morning at the Kansas Department of Wildlife and Parks. Although her hands had remained clammy throughout the interviews and the Sahara Desert had taken up residence in her throat, she was pleased with most of her responses.

The personnel officer had talked with her first; then she'd spent thirty minutes with the director of the agency. She'd been impressed with his professional expertise and gracious but firm manner. When she permitted herself to think about the possibility of getting the job, her stomach fluttered. It was almost too perfect.

Her initial assignment would involve working on a federally funded project documenting the migratory patterns and population fluctuations of the snow geese in eastern and central Kansas. Since most of the job entailed fieldwork, she could operate from any home base so long as Topeka was easily accessible. That meant she could live at home, be involved with a project right down her alley—and be close to Mack!

Don't get your hopes up. Reflect on the past. How often in your life has the bird of paradise flown the coop?

Mack. She smiled to herself. After the day he'd rescued her from the freezing run, their friendship had settled into a natural comfort zone. Whether or not the relationship would lead anywhere, she couldn't be sure, but at least the first hurdle had been cleared and they were on pleasant terms.

She recalled the proposal for the Calhoun pond. Short-term, the plans called for erecting some blinds from which schoolchildren could observe the birds; long-range, the vision included an ecological nature center, complete with hiking trails, seminars and summer programs, with much of the volunteer help to come from high school students and sportsmen of all ages. She had to give Mack credit; although he'd probably always be an occasional hunter, he shared her concern for waterfowl preservation. She'd been too hasty in her judgment. If only she hadn't fouled up with him too badly; if only she could, for once in her life, be patient. But, God, how she wanted him!

One Friday, she, Gramps and Mack had attended a livestock auction. Then on Gramps's birthday, he'd invited the Haggertys and Mack for cake and ice cream. Mack had helped her with the dishes and shared stories of his tenser moments on the job. Last weekend he'd invited her to go with him to Salina to study the layout of the Grainmen's Hunting Club and look at a litter of registered Labs. As the day unfolded, they'd laughed and talked more and more naturally. In the evening, they'd stopped for dinner at the Brookville Hotel, famous for its family-style fried-chicken dinners.

Later when he'd walked her to the door, he'd imprisoned her arms in his hands, planted a chaste kiss on her cheek and then tweaked her nose with his index finger. "I'm looking forward to seeing more of you, Red. Good night."

Those words sang to Josie as she turned off the interstate toward Maizeville. If she had anything to say about it, he certainly would. The Valentine handkerchiefs had worked. Maybe it was time for something more dramatic.

She stopped in town to fill up her gas tank, pick up some clothes at the dry cleaners and buy a few groceries. Emerging from the convenience store, she bumped into a hurried young man just entering.

"Excuse me, ma'am." The teenager held the door for her. "Miss Calhoun, is that you?"

She looked into Clay Johnson's smiling blue eyes. Where had the surliness gone? "Hello, Clay."

"I heard you were back. I'm glad to see you because I need to thank you." He turned slightly red. "Because of you, I've learned a lot. I won't be killing any more geese at your pond or anywhere else."

She let out the breath she realized she'd been holding since she first recognized him. "I'm glad, Clay." She smiled. "I'm really glad." She couldn't stop smiling as she pulled away from the pumps.

When she turned off the highway by the Pioneer Oak to head for the farm, the glimmer of an idea came to her. She frowned in concentration, rolled the thought around in her mind and then nodded her head decisively. Maybe it would help her with Mack and maybe it wouldn't. But even if it didn't, it was still the right thing to do. *If* she could pull it off. She was certainly going to try. She grinned, turned the radio on full blast and yodeled along with the country-and-western singer.

The very next day after clearing the breakfast dishes, she sat down at the computer. By noon she'd sealed several neatly typed business letters. One to the Maizeville mayor, one to the state House of Representatives legislator from the Maizeville district, another to the state senator and several to various state agencies.

When Gramps came in for a quick lunch of creamed chipped beef on toast, he commented on the pile of outgoing mail. "What're you doing, honey? Sending out more résumés?"

"No. I'm escalating the stakes." She popped two pieces of bread in the toaster.

"What stakes?"

"The stakes in my campaign," she replied enigmatically.

Gramps stopped in his tracks and leaned over to look at her. "Is this another one of those things you'll tell me about when the time is right?"

"You could say that." She reached over and patted his cheek in mock condescension. "After all, it's my wise old grandpa who told me to find a way." She hummed softly to herself as she stirred the creamed chipped beef to keep it from sticking in the skillet.

BURIED UNDER A HEAP of blankets and wavering between sleep and wakefulness, Mack became slowly aware of a welcome sense of peaceful relaxation, as if his limbs were melting into the warm sheets. He shifted his feet out from under Stranger's heavy chest and rolled onto his side, pulling the pillow over his head. Burrowing deeper, he waited for sleep to reclaim him.

Instead, the obnoxiously loud cheerful voice of the early-morning local radio personality bombarded him. His mind clicked into sharp focus and moved into the action mode. Then, like a headline reeling across his brain, came the unwelcome thought. It was March eighteenth. Two years ago today, Sarah was killed.

He rolled onto his stomach, stuffing one hand under the pillow and nestling his cheek into the goose down. Sarah. He tried to picture her. Dimly he saw, like a faded photograph, a hazy image of a sweetly smiling blonde, features somewhat obscured. Though flickers of regret and sadness moved through him, they did not produce the sharp wrenching pangs or the intestinal void he'd experienced only a few months before. As he tried to capture and hold Sarah's image, it blurred and faded, receding into the gray-black edges of his consciousness.

Slowly, as if superimposed on the faint initial image, facial features began to materialize. Mack let the picture wash over him. Slowly a generous laughing mouth, lips moistened with desire, and a long freckled nose emerged. Mack, fighting the current, felt himself swimming toward some conclusion. Then as if thrown by a powerful wave onto a warm sunny beach, he saw clearly the green tidal pools of her eyes and the lustrous red of her silky curls. Josie. Josie. With a conviction born of certainty, he recognized his mourning was behind him.

He nudged Stranger off the bed with his foot. "Damnation, fella. Get out of the way. It's a new day, and I've got important things to do."

Toweling himself after his shower, Mack couldn't stop grinning. What kind of idiot was he, anyway? Why had he been fighting the truth? Josie had gotten to him. Because she had made none of her previous demands on him, he enjoyed and trusted their natural, easy companionship. From the very first day she'd returned, he had found it nearly impossible to keep his guard up. If he was honest, he had to admit he thought about her all the time. He loved her funny little gestures she made with her hands when she got excited; he found her appealing both in a lost-puppy-dog kind of way and in a seductive distinctly adult way; and she had a heart as big as all outdoors. Even her stubbornness was a result of strongly held principles. Best of all, she made him laugh.

He pulled on his briefs and leaned over the sink to brush his teeth. Glancing into the mirror, he met his reflection. He eyeballed his alter ego. "Okay, Mackenzie Scott. It's time. You want her. Go for it." He brushed vigorously.

Back in the bedroom, he pulled his uniform out of the closet and draped it across the bed. As he turned to the dresser, a small studio portrait of Sarah confronted him from its brass frame. He picked it up thoughtfully and studied it for several moments.

"Thanks, Sarah, for releasing me," he murmured. "I'll never forget you, but the time has come for me to move on." He opened the bottom dresser drawer and put the picture facedown, under his swimming trunks. "Rest in peace, dear one."

JOSIE TEETERED for a moment on the extension ladder. After steadying herself, she stretched again to scoop the dead leaves from the clogged gutter. The chore would've been much easier last fall, but she'd been too busy then. And no way was she going to let Gramps get on the ladder.

A gentle breeze fanned her perspiring face and lifted tendrils that had escaped from the ponytail. From her perch, she saw the black Bronco turn up the lane. She reached one hand into the soggy mass of wet leaves and threw them to the ground.

Mack pulled up to the yard gate and hollered out the window. "Do I give you fair warning or do I just say it?" Josie twisted her head and shot him a murderous look.

He climbed out of the Bronco and sauntered to a point just under the ladder. "Okay, here goes. Hey, Red, how's the weather up there?"

His answer came in the form of a sodden glob of vegetation directed at his head. Ducking just in time, he moved to the base of the ladder. "Missed. But how about coming down and giving me the same reward I got last time?"

She scooped up another handful, flinging it to the ground, then started down the rungs, aware of Mack's playful scrutiny of her derriere. Reaching the ground, she turned into his waiting embrace. He nuzzled her cheek and whispered in her ear, "I'm glad you decided to lower yourself to my level."

"I'm happy to rise to the occasion." Their simultaneous groans sent James Cagney scuttling for the security of the forsythia bush.

"I'm on duty later today," Mack said, "but I stopped by to see if you'd like to go fishing with me tomorrow. Thought I'd try Council Grove Lake."

Her face fell. "Oh, Mack, I wish I could, but tomorrow I have my interview with the Oklahoma Department of Wildlife Conservation. I'll take a rain check, though."

He put both hands on her shoulders and looked at her in a way that made her weak in the knees. "Count on it, Red. At the very least, a rain check."

He lowered his lips to hers and kissed her softly, gently. He pulled away slightly, then brushed her lips with a wisp of a kiss so tender it pierced her in a way the most passionate kiss could not. "See you soon, Red." He turned on his heel and strode to the Bronco.

Her hands were shaking and her breath came in ragged gasps as she waved goodbye. She clambered back up the ladder, and hope took root in her heart.

"OKAY, GRAMPS. Now what do I do?" Josie threw the letters onto the kitchen table. "Look."

Frank Calhoun settled into the chair, pushed the seed catalogs aside and picked up the letters. As he read, Josie worked hard to keep a straight face. When he began reading the second one, his face twitched with the start of a smile.

"Honey, this is great. Two job offers." Beaming, he stood up and put his arm around her shoulders. "I'm very proud of you, granddaughter. Look's like all that studying and effort finally paid off. Such talent must be in the genes."

She smiled in satisfaction. "Most definitely the paternal genes. And since you're so smart, help me with the decision. The Oklahoma job pays more, but it's primarily a desk job. The Kansas job involves the fieldwork I love, but the opportunity for advancement may not be as good. I'm so confused." She shoved a tablet of paper across the table as he sat back down. "Here's my list of pros and cons." She ran her fingers nervously through her hair as he studied the top sheet.

"Well, here's one consideration we can cross off the list. Me." He reached over and stroked her hand. "You're young. Your future's in front of you. Don't jeopardize that because of an old coot like me. I can take care of myself just fine." He perused the paper again, pursing his mouth. "It looks like you've left out one pretty serious consideration."

Josie looked up. "Oh?"

"Yep. I see nothing on this sheet about Mackenzie Scott."

Josie blushed. "There's nothing to put."

Gramps leaned forward and squinted at her. "Are you sure? What about your campaign? The truth, Josie."

She lowered her eyes, then met his unflinching gaze. "The truth? He's *the* consideration, Gramps. But it seems stupid and presumptuous to make a career decision based on the chance that a man you love will reciprocate your feelings."

"Maybe, maybe not. I'm certainly not going to tell you what to do, honey. But whatever you decide, be sure it's a decision you won't regret later. Remember that question I asked you last summer when we were looking at that first evening star? What would you wish, Josie?" Gramps scraped back his chair, planted a kiss on top of her head and went into the living room.

She shivered. She remembered. She remembered all too well. A love like Gramps and MJ had. A love strong enough to withstand pain and loss.

She pulled the tablet toward her, picked up the pencil and began the first draft of a letter to the director of the Oklahoma Department of Wildlife Conservation. "It is with regret that I must turn down your generous job offer...."

"YES!" JOSIE RAISED her fist over her head in a dramatic gesture of success. She ran down the granite steps of the state office building and danced to her parked car. She checked her watch and started purposefully in the direction of another Topeka office building.

Later, over lunch with Earl Briscoe, her state representative, she outlined her plan. He winked at her over his bowl of steaming potato soup. "Miss Calhoun, I can't tell you how delighted I am to be part of this project. Too often all we get to deal with up here are complaints, tax measures and pesky lobbyists." He reached across the table to shake her hand. "It's a pleasure doing business with you, young lady. I'll do my best to expedite this thing."

Josie favored the elderly man with a flirtatious smile. "You don't know how much I appreciate your help. I don't know how I could have pulled it off without you." The Honorable Earl Briscoe inflated before her very eyes.

THE FIRST TINGES of green poked up through the brown fields, and the trees kept a curled grip on buds poised to leaf. A blast of cold air at the tail end of March had slowed the spring blooms, but April was starting off docilely.

Mack relished the privacy of the patrol car as he headed west into the glare of the afternoon sun. He'd cringed when the sheriff had assigned him to deliver a prisoner to Topeka for evaluation at the Kansas Reception and Diagnostic Center. The prisoner babbled continual nonsense and, worse than that, smelled like the inside of a filthy zoo cage. Mack felt as if he'd gritted his teeth and held his breath for half a day. Now, relaxing on the drive back to Maizeville, he was in a more receptive frame of mind to enjoy Mother Nature's signs that spring had indeed arrived. Buttery daffodils nodded at him from farmhouse lawns, the forsythia was in golden riot, and the redbuds would burst forth any day.

The fish had started biting, especially in the early morning and late afternoon. He and Josie had gone to Council Grove Lake yesterday to fish. He smiled remembering her consternation when her "whopper" turned out to be a snapping turtle. He'd caught two small bass, which he threw back. The best part of the excursion, though, was their easiness with one another. Their relationship was undergoing a subtle yet comfortable change.

Last fall she'd sometimes been an impetuous hellion and other times a scared little girl. Then, as now, she stirred him in a wild visceral way and moved him with her tenderness and vulnerability. But she seemed less... frantic? Combative? Maybe she'd just matured. She was still perky and fun, but less adolescent. That was it! Less adolescent, more womanly. He grinned. Definitely more womanly.

Through the windshield, the harsh sun beamed directly at him. Squinting, he pulled down the visor and shifted in the driver's seat. Just a few more miles to go.

The signboards and fields sped by, and finally, cottony shreds of clouds crossed the sun, cutting the relentless glare. In the distance he saw the yellow-green tinted branches of the Pioneer Oak, delicate seedpods festooning the limbs.

Nearing the tree, he glanced quickly at it, the haunting memory only skimming through his consciousness and then quickly vanishing. He glanced back at the highway, then turned again to look at the oak. What the . . . ?

A bronzed sign had been erected at the base of the tree. He tapped the brake pedal and slowed to a halt on the edge of the road. He was too far away to read the sign. Turning off the engine, he climbed out of the patrol car. He removed his sunglasses to read the words engraved on the bronze plaque. His heart rose in his throat and he stood rooted to the spot, reading and rereading.

THE PIONEER OAK
circa 1790

May this oak always whisper "home"
to the lonely passerby.

Dedicated in loving memory of
Sarah Jane Lockton
1966–1993

Mack slowly put his sunglasses back on, but they did not mask the tears that slowly rolled down his cheeks.

CHAPTER FIFTEEN

MACK STOMPED on the accelerator, sending gravel spurting up from the rear tires of the Bronco. He couldn't wait to get home, take a shower and call Josie. Only she could have been responsible for such a fitting memorial to Sarah. Only she could have taken MJ's words of comfort and made them universal. He couldn't wait to pick her up in his arms and twirl around and crush her against him and... A devilish chuckle rattled his larynx.

He skidded to a stop in front of his house and had already shed his tie and gun belt by the time he hit the door. Stranger looked up quizzically and followed him into the bedroom where soon his clothes were lying in a crumpled heap on the floor. As Mack bellowed "You Are My Sunshine" over the noise of the shower spray, Stranger howled in accompaniment.

A towel wrapped around his waist, Mack tiptoed through the discarded clothing to the telephone. He dialed and waited, heart thudding. *Damn it, answer!*

"Hello?"

"Frank, this is Mack. Is Josie around? I'd sure like to speak with her."

"Oh, Mack, I'm sorry. She's not here right now." Mack's heart took an elevator ride to the basement. "But I expect her back any time now." Frank paused expectantly.

"Frank, I'd be much obliged if you'd have her call me as soon as she gets in."

"No problem."

Mack replaced the receiver, drawing a deep breath to replace the wind that had gone out of his sails. He wanted to see her, to talk to her, to hold her—now!

After throwing his soiled clothes into the hamper, he pulled on some faded jeans and a blue-and-gold striped rugby shirt. He walked into the kitchen, opening and closing the cabinets, peering into the refrigerator, but he couldn't seem to concentrate on supper long enough even to smear some peanut butter on a piece of bread. "Any time now," he muttered. "She'll be back any time now."

He paced into the living room, turned on the television, slumped down on the sofa, then sprang to his feet, changed the channel and paced back into the kitchen. Why didn't she call? He needed to tell her. Tell her what a dynamite thing she had done. He stopped in his tracks.

How had she done it? She must have had to talk to every government official this side of the Rockies. It couldn't be easy to get permission to erect anything on a highway right-of-way. One thing about Josie—when she was determined, a bulldozer couldn't stop her. He smiled and then walked over to the phone, willing it to ring. Stranger had given up tracking him on his laps around the house and was stretched out on the living room rug, following Mack only with his eyes.

At the sound of an approaching car, Stranger put his front paws on the window ledge and looked out. Mack leaned in behind him.

"Do you suppose it's Josie, fella? I hope so." But instead of a gray Honda, a sleek blue Lincoln pulled up to the house.

"Damn," Mack growled. "What's Beth Ann doing here?" He watched as she daintily emerged from the luxury sedan, taking care that her yellow canvas espadrilles, which matched her linen slacks and sweater, didn't encounter any dirt clods. Her blond pageboy shone in the sun as she brushed imaginary dust off her trim fanny.

Mack opened the door, standing to one side to let her enter. "What a surprise, Beth Ann. What are you doing here?"

Holding him by both arms, she smiled as if she'd just awarded him ten gold stars. "Mack, you're wonderful, just marvelous! I don't know how to thank you."

He extricated his arms from her grasp and took her birdlike hands in his. "Wonderful? Maybe. A man always likes to hear that. But 'just marvelous'? Isn't that going a little too far?"

Still clinging to him, she eyed him coquettishly. "You're being far too modest. It is the most generous loving gesture I've ever seen. Thank you, thank you!" She stood on tiptoe and planted a wet lipsticky kiss on his cheek.

"Beth Ann, you've lost me. What in the world are you talking about?"

"The sign. Sarah's sign." Her face was aglow. "I didn't do it. Ralph didn't do it. Aunt Margaret didn't do it. That leaves you."

Before she could go on, Mack put his hands on her shoulders. "Beth Ann, stop. I didn't do it, either."

"What do you mean? It had to be you."

He held her baby-doll blue eyes in his deep brown ones. "No, Beth Ann. Not me."

"Well, for heaven's sakes, who?"

"Josie."

"Josie? You mean Josie Calhoun?" Incredulity stamped itself on her features.

"Yes." He smiled broadly. "Josie Calhoun."

GRAMPS WAS SITTING on the stoop whittling as Josie walked from the car to the house. He peered up at her, grinning to himself. "Good trip to the dentist?"

She opened her mouth wide and gargled, "Look, Gramps, no cavities!"

"I'm glad."

She noticed that his grin looked suspiciously like that of a cat sitting in front of an empty canary cage.

"What's with the big grin, grandfather of mine?"

He whittled another chunk from the piece of pine in his hand. "Mack called. Sounded kind of eager. Wanted you to call him as soon as you got in. Any idea what that might be about?" He looked up inquiringly.

"An inkling, Gramps. An inkling." Then she, too, grinned like a sated feline.

"Suppose it has anything to do with that shiny new sign I saw today at the Pioneer Oak?"

"It very well could." She scrunched in beside him on the concrete step. She spoke again, softly and seriously. "Oh, Gramps, I hope I did the right thing."

He set the knife down and put his arm around her. "Josie, I can't think of a more fitting tribute to your grandmother or a grander memorial to Sarah." He hugged her to him. "MJ would be very proud of you." Abruptly he sniffed and pushed her to her feet. "Now, for Pete's sake, go call that young man of yours."

EVERY ONCE IN A BLUE MOON a day is so crystalline, so perfect, it seems to have been sent by the angels.

Josie hugged herself as she stepped onto the front porch. Wrens, cardinals, robins, chickadees, doves, all vied for solo parts in the spring chorus. Although it was early in the morning, the temperature was already sixty, and not a breath of air disturbed the dewdrops shimmering on the new green grass. Feathery trails of white gathered in the sky, then spread into spun threads of mist before dissipating into nothingness.

She clutched her old flannel robe to her chest, savoring this quiet time before the day's bustle. From the eastern horizon, rays of blue-gold spread, illuminating patches of field and woods. Then the sun burst over the land, rising quickly in the morning sky. It reminded Josie of that other sunrise, the one she and Mack had shared that autumn morning in the duck blind. She turned up the cowl collar of the bathrobe, snuggling into its soft nap. God willing, they would share many sunrises.

Sinking into the creaking wooden swing, she rocked gently back and forth. The memorial sign had been a success. After she'd telephoned Mack, he'd come right over to the house, bounded up the steps and given her a hug so tight she thought she might expire. His eyes had filled as he held her face between his hands, memorizing her features.

"Thank you for understanding and for finding just the right way to honor Sarah. You are a very special and particularly lovable woman, Josie."

The memory made her smile with pleasure. Later he'd sat her down on this very swing and made a solemn request. "You've shared your love of the geese with me.

Now I want to share with you something very important to me. Will you come with me Tuesday and let me show you my Flint Hills?"

She stopped rocking now and listened breathlessly to an instantly identifiable call. As if to put "Amen" to this glorious Tuesday dawn, a flock of Canada geese passed overhead, winging their way northward to their ancestral breeding grounds.

MACK PICKED UP a chicken leg and bit into the crisp skin. He closed his eyes in approval. Still chewing, he leaned over and handed her a thigh. "Too bad you can't cook, Red."

They were sitting on an old quilt with the picnic lunch spread around them—chicken, deviled eggs, carrot and celery sticks, cornbread and moist devil's food cake. Josie set down the crusty thigh and filled two tall paper cups with lemonade from the thermos.

"It's pretty good if I do say so myself." She looked beyond the quilt at the bank of vivid magenta redbuds clustered along the creek, swollen with the spring runoff. Above the creek, the rounded, stark curves of the hills rose, the deep bluestem creating a soothing carpet. "To tell you the truth, I don't know whether to eat or just drink in this scene." She laid a hand on his knee. "Your Flint Hills are beautiful, Mack. I'm glad you brought me."

They'd crossed two large rolling pastures before coming to a rutted truck path leading higher into the vastness of the hills. The Bronco had fulfilled its name as they jolted and bucked over outcroppings of limestone. Along the way, Mack had pointed out the flora and fauna and grew more relaxed and elated with each torturous mile.

But the destination was well worth it. She drew a deep breath of the fresh April air and sipped her lemonade. The sky was an azure dome stretching as far as the eye could see. The immensity of wave upon wave of treeless hills made her feel at once both serene and infinitesimally small.

With the main course done, Josie sliced generous pieces of the cake. She'd forgotten to bring forks, but as she jokingly remarked, "Fingers were invented first."

Mack chuckled as he watched her struggling with the gooey frosting. Every time she picked up her piece, she seemed to get another dab of frosting on a different finger. Carefully licking each finger one by one and wiping her hands on her jeans, she sat up straight and eyeballed him. "Okay, mister. What's so funny? I'm clean now."

He leaned over. "That's what you think, ma'am. Let me help you." He pulled her face toward his and nibbled at a point halfway between her mouth and chin. Still cupping her face, he grinned into her eyes.

"Mmm. You taste good. Believe I'll have me another sample," and he placed darting nips all around her chin and then on her lower lip, until he captured both lips in his, moving his tongue in flickers as if sucking chocolate from each pore.

She swooned against him, moving her tongue and lips in concert with his, drowning in the taste and feel of him. Gasping, they drew apart. Between the tiny kisses he planted on her cheeks, eyelids and forehead, he managed to mumble, "I've heard that the way to a man's heart is through his stomach—" he ran his tongue along her cheekbone "—but this is ridiculous."

He captured her lips again, and silver starbursts exploded behind her closed eyelids. Once more he pulled away. "Best chocolate cake I ever had!" He moved the picnic basket to the grass and stretched out on his back. "Come here."

He guided her head onto his shoulder, his arm wrapped lightly around her. She lay very still, listening to the chirping of birds, the gurgle of the little creek, the breeze softly whistling through the tall grass. It was a timeless place; they might be the only human inhabitants of this ancient land.

Prickles of desire coursed through her as he ran his fingers up and down her forearm. Then gently, ever so gently, he rolled her onto her side so he could look at her. She was tempted at first to look away, to demur, but something in his glance held her as if magnetized. He lifted his forefinger and tenderly traced the hairline of her forehead, then brushed each eyebrow. He trailed his finger down her cheek and over her upper lip, all the while holding her in his liquid brown gaze. His hand traced the curve of her shoulder, moved tantalizingly down her arm until he picked up her hand and brought it to his lips, grazing each finger with a kiss.

"Oh, Josie," he murmured. "God, you're beautiful."

She found the soft skin under his chin and kissed him there, then moved along his jaw to his ear. Reaching it, she twined her fingers in his hair and whispered softly, "This time, love, I believe you." And she lowered her head to rest it against his chest, her ear attuned to the rapid beat of his heart.

He bent his elbow and put one hand under his head. With the other he caressed her back, moving his fingers in lazy circling motions, beginning at the nape of her neck and moving gradually down her back.

The midday sun and Mack's gentle touch warmed Josie into a drowsy suspension between waking and sleeping. She felt as if she could lie forever in this position. Suddenly he ran his thumb up her spine, sending shock waves of delight to every extremity of her body. She lifted her head. "That woke me up, all right."

He grinned lazily and rolled her onto her back. "Let's see if this gets your attention." He slid the fingers of his left hand into her hair and began kissing each eyelid. As he gently massaged her scalp, he traced the folds of her ears with his tongue. The rest of her body was pulsing in response, aching to be kissed, caressed. She couldn't stop the involuntary thrust of her pelvis as she bent one leg and cupped the back of his head with her hand.

His kisses traveled in exasperatingly slow motion down her throat and along her collarbone. His fingers left her hair and traced the line of her jaw and fell to the top button of her shirt. As the button gave way, his warm moist mouth moved to cover the exposed flesh. She groaned with desire, powerless to stop herself, as he moved to the next button and the next. At last he pulled the tail out from her jeans and, raising up on one elbow, parted the shirt.

Tenderly he moved the fabric away from one shoulder as she slipped her arm out of the sleeve. Then he held her gently as he sloughed off her other sleeve. The vastness of the Flint Hills telescoped into the sphere of his face—his shaded cheek, his firm lips, his molasses eyes.

Her breasts thrust against the scratchy lace of her bra as his fingers fumbled with the clasp. She was on fire. Frantically she helped him with the fastener, and her breath came in shallow gasps when her breasts were freed, the nipples swollen and taut with longing. She felt his lips engulf one rosy tip in a welcome tide of warmth. She pressed her palms against each side of his head and rolled gently from side to side. He found the other nipple, flicking his tongue in electrifying strokes over the nub, first rapidly, then slowly, then accelerating in frenzied concentration.

Her body arched against his and one leg wrapped around his legs in a movement as spontaneous and natural as the flow of the spring water. She couldn't pull him close enough. She could feel the desire building in him, too, as the hardness of him nestled against her thigh.

His mouth still on her breast, he reached down and undid the fastener on her jeans. Then he plunged both his hands inside her briefs and kneaded her buttocks in a rhythm of longing. As he moaned her name, her arms wound tightly around him, and all she could see beyond his shoulder was the great canopy of blue sky. She gasped as he slowly stripped off her jeans. She lay still as he discarded them and began unbuttoning his shirt. As his muscular shoulders and chest were revealed, she convulsed with the wanton, clenching sensation deep within her. He lowered himself onto her, her thrusting nipples finding a nest against the warm skin of his chest.

"Mack, I..." The premature declaration almost tripped out. "You feel so good."

He nuzzled the hollow of her throat. "So do you, Red. So do you." Now it was she who traced the muscles and vertebrae of his back, languidly exploring him from shoulder to hip. Birds still sang and the water still danced over the stones, but she heard only the thump of their hearts.

He reached over her head and plucked a frond of prairie grass, which he trailed over her nose and lips. He feathered it over one breast, then the other, moving it in concentric circles until her nipples were teased into aliveness.

She should have felt self-conscious. She should have apologized for her freckled skin. She surprised herself by doing none of that. Instead, she felt bathed in his attention. She gloried in his tender and erotic ministrations. Beyond her, the cone shapes of the Flint Hills rose in female symbolism, and she felt truly at one with them.

Soon he was skimming the grass over her stomach and down one thigh, and then he tossed it aside, retracing its path with his lips. How could she feel both utterly relaxed and totally aroused at the same time? But she did. She drew her arms down across his back and under the waistband of his pants. She grasped his tight buttocks. He fell against her, his mouth pinning hers in an ecstasy of nipping and teasing with lips and tongue. A tidal wave of longing urged her fingers to explore his waist until she found the top button of his jeans. She writhed with the urgency to loosen him.

Lost in the intricacies of the button, at first she didn't feel him tense or hear him chuckle. Gradually she became aware of the heaving of his shoulders. What was so funny? Was he laughing at her? She opened her eyes. Mirth was exploding from his eyes.

"Mack Scott, this is no way to make a girl feel lovable. What's so damn funny?"

But all he could do was jerk his head helplessly in the direction behind her. She shoved him away and rolled over.

And then she saw them. She laughed until the tears ran down her face. For, a few feet away, staring at them and looking for all the world like woodland satyrs approving the springtime frolic, were six Hereford steers.

Mack swatted Josie's fanny and sat up. "I think they're telling us to moo-ve on." He reached for her discarded clothing and handed it to her.

"Good idea," she said, struggling into her bra. "Because I feel udderly ridiculous."

He palmed one breast. "No need, because I'm bullish on us." He enfolded her in a bear hug. And when he released her, he again held her face between his palms and looked deep into her eyes. "More than bullish." His voice thickened. "I love you, Josie Calhoun."

Her heart stopped and then tilted into orbit. The long-pent-up words burst forth. "Oh, Mack, I love you, too."

THE ARRIVAL of daylight savings time stretched the hazy spring twilight well past the dinner hour. Josie had only another two weeks before starting her job and she was making every minute count.

She'd worked in the vegetable garden all afternoon, hoeing and setting out tomatoes. A quick shower before dinner had removed all the dirt from under her fingernails and eased the soreness in her shoulder muscles. She'd tied back her curls with a bright blue ribbon and tucked her white peasant blouse into the tiered blue-and-white flowered skirt. Now, with the dinner dishes loaded in the dishwasher, she wiped her hands on a kitchen towel and joined Gramps on the porch.

She settled in the swing. Gramps was staring into the distance, looking contemplative. She gently swung, the rusty chains intermittently grinding in protest.

"A penny for your thoughts, Gramps."

"That may be all they're worth." He moved his chair so he could face her.

"I'll bet they're worth far more than a penny," she said. "They generally are."

"I was just thinking that it's the second spring since your grandmother died. I miss her. Every day."

"So do I. So do I."

"But, you know, she was right. Life goes on. One day at a time. And it's meant to be lived. The day she died, I thought my life had ended, too. Instead, you've come along, the lilacs have bloomed again and the cows have calved. Renewal. That's what it's all about." He nodded. "Renewal."

They sat in companionable silence, enjoying the fragrance of the lilacs and the breadth of the sunset. Several minutes passed. Josie stayed the swing with her foot. "Gramps, would you mind if I went for a little walk? I'd like to go up to the pasture for a while. Do you want to come?"

"No, honey. I'm just going to rock a spell more, watch some television and go to bed. You go on, though."

Josie slipped off her sandals and put on her sneakers, then started up the hill toward the stone wall. The clover was greening and the faint scent of flowers hung in the air. When she reached the wall, she gathered her skirt around her knees and sat leaning against the stones. The setting sun sent ribbons of orange across the calm surface of the pond. As the sun began to sink behind the distant hills, the first evening star twinkled in its wake.

"Star light, star bright..." Josie intoned, "...I wish I may, I wish I might, have the wish I wish tonight."

And how was her wish different from the one last August? she thought. It wasn't. The only difference was that now she knew *who* that love was. She gripped her knees in a paroxysm of delight. He loved her. He had actually said the words. Her wish was almost complete. Almost, but not quite.

He'd said no more since then, and it had been more than two months. Nothing about plans. Nothing about a future together. *Patience, Josie. Don't force the issue.* He'd said he loved her. Her, the lovable beautiful Josie Calhoun. What a long way she'd come! She could be patient. For Mack, she could do almost anything.

So lost in her thoughts was she that she failed to hear the approaching footsteps until, with a sudden plop, a fluttering white object fell into her lap. Behind her she heard a warm deep voice. "I think you dropped something, Red."

She glanced over her shoulder to see Mack, smiling with love. He vaulted the wall and settled beside her. She looked into her lap. Spread out there was a white monogrammed handkerchief. She picked it up and felt a weight attached to one corner. Knotted in that corner was a small object.

Mack ran his fingers languidly through the curls at the nape of her neck. "Go ahead. See what it is."

Gingerly she untied the stubborn knot and a tiny circlet of gold fell into the folds of her skirt. She picked it up and drew in her breath, looking at Mack with shining eyes. A solitaire diamond ring lay in her hand, the light of the setting sun catching its facets. Mack looked into her eyes and whispered solemnly, "Miss Josie Calhoun, will you be my mate for life?"

Her eyes brimmed as she nodded toward the brushy promontory sticking out into the pond. "You mean like them?" There, sitting in queenly repose on her nest, was a magnificent Canada goose. Standing guard a few feet away was the proud and vigilant gander.

"Like them," he affirmed.

"Oh, yes," she breathed, as he took the ring and slipped it over her finger. "Most definitely yes."

Later, walking arm in arm through the dusk to the farmhouse, Josie was surprised to see Gramps come out and stand, waiting, on the sidewalk. "What's he doing? He said he was going to watch television."

Mack pulled her closer and grinned. "He's probably anticipating the outcome. You see, while you were in town this morning, I stopped by to ask him for your hand. And he's the one who directed me up to the pasture just now."

Approaching the yard, they could see that Gramps held something behind his back. From a few yards away, Josie lifted her voice. "You can relax, Gramps. I said yes."

"Can't relax yet. We've got to celebrate. Here." As they approached, he handed each of them a Fourth of July sparkler. Carefully lighting the match to first one and then the other, he stood back and smiled with immense delight. "It's the sparks, Josie. I'm glad you waited for the sparks."

The *Kansas City Star*
Saturday, April 20, 1996

Local Author Reaps Success
The Changing Faces of the Flint Hills, by Kansas author Mackenzie Scott, has been selling briskly in area bookstores, according to Paul Ridner, president of the Kansas Booksellers.

A pictorial history of the change of seasons in the Flint Hills region, the book captures the elusive beauty of the moods of the hills, as well as the vast scope of the geological formations. The accompanying text evokes both the subtleties and the powerful impact of the landscape with accuracy, genuine emotion and lyricism. Text and photography combine to convey the essence of this unusual and ancient landmark.

A graduate of Kansas State University, Scott currently is an instructor in the English Department there while he pursues a master's degree and a writing career.

His next project, a photographic history of the life cycle of the Canada goose, is a collaborative effort with his wife, zoologist Josie Calhoun Scott. The book, entitled *Mating for Life,* is scheduled for late-summer publication.

The Scotts reside on a farm near Maizeville and enjoy attending retriever field trials with their two Labradors, Stranger and Friend.

HARLEQUIN SUPERROMANCE®

WOMEN WHO DARE
They take chances, make changes
and follow their hearts!

Too Many Bosses
by Jan Freed

According to Alec McDonald, Laura Hayes is "impertinent,
impulsive, insubordinate and totally lacking in self-discipline"—
all negatives in an employee. Mind you, he also has to admit that
she has the legs of a Las Vegas showgirl.

According to Laura Hayes, Alec McDonald is "a pompous
bigot who considers Kleenex standard issue for his female
employees." But while these are negatives in a boss, Laura
doesn't intend to remain his employee for long, because it's
obvious that Alec needs Laura—in his business and in his life.

Within twenty-four hours of their first meeting, Laura and Alec
are partners in a new business. *Equal* partners. Yet two bosses
is one too many for any business—especially when the boss is
falling in love with the boss!

Watch for *Too Many Bosses* by Jan Freed.
Available in May 1995, wherever Harlequin books are sold.

WWD94-7

Bestselling Author

Jasmine Cresswell

**May 1995 brings you face-to-face with her
latest thrilling adventure**

Desires & Deceptions

Will the real Claire Campbell please stand up?
Missing for over seven years, Claire's family has
only one year left to declare her legally dead and
claim her substantial fortune—that is, until a woman
appears on the scene alleging to be the missing
heiress. Will DNA testing solve the dilemma? Do
old family secrets still have the power to decide
who lives and dies, suffers or prospers, loves or
hates? Only Claire knows for sure.

MIRA The brightest star in women's fiction

MJCDD

HARLEQUIN SUPERROMANCE®

**He's sexy, he's single...and he's a father!
Can any woman resist?**

Coming in May 1995

Finding Father
By Anne Marie Duquette

Nina Delacruz, age nine, refuses to believe that her father, a world-famous mountain climber who disappeared in Alaska, is never coming back. She insists someone will find him, even though her mother, Mercedes, says it's impossible.

April Montgomery, age eleven, lost her mother as an infant, and now she's withdrawing from her father, too. April's been keeping a secret from Cass, one that she knows will hurt him deeply. If he finds out, maybe he won't love her anymore....

These two families are brought together by a dog—a dog they both claim is theirs. And as it turns out, that's the best thing that could have happened. Because, with Mercedes's help, Cass can become the father both girls need. And the lover, friend and husband *Mercedes* needs.

Look for *Finding Father* in May, wherever Harlequin books are sold.

FM-4

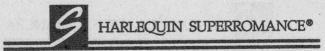

HARLEQUIN SUPERROMANCE®

presents

EVERY MOVE YOU MAKE
By Bobby Hutchinson

This May, meet the first of our FOUR STRONG MEN:

Mountie Joe Marcello. He was hot on the trail of his
man, but what he got was…a woman. Schoolteacher
Carrie Zablonski found herself in the wrong place at the
wrong time, and when Joe learned there was more to the
lady than met the eye—and she was quite an eyeful—he
assigned himself as her personal guardian angel. Trouble
was, Carrie didn't *want* his protection….

Look for *Every Move You Make* in May 1995,
wherever Harlequin books are sold.

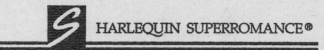

HARLEQUIN SUPERROMANCE®

presents

a new book by

Bestselling Author Janice Kaiser

MONDAY'S CHILD

Kelly Ronan was on vacation; Bart Monday was on the
lam. When the two met in Thailand, more than sparks
began to fly. Chased by a rain of bullets, they swam to
relative safety, dodging snakes and pirates on a small
but dangerous island. It wasn't Kelly's idea of a dream
vacation, but her mother had always told her she needed
a little excitment in her life....

Look for *Monday's Child* in May 1995,
wherever Harlequin books are sold.

MCHILD

HARLEQUIN®

PRESENTS
RELUCTANT BRIDEGROOMS

Two beautiful brides, two unforgettable romances...
two men running for their lives....

My Lady Love, by Paula Marshall, introduces
Charles, Viscount Halstead, who lost his memory
and found himself employed as a stableboy by the
untouchable Nell Tallboys, Countess Malplaquet.
But Nell didn't consider Charles untouchable—
not at all!

Darling Amazon, by Sylvia Andrew, is the story of
a spurious engagement between Julia Marchant
and Hugo, marquess of Rostherne—an engagement
that gets out of hand and just may lead Hugo to
the altar after all!

Enjoy two madcap Regency weddings this May,
wherever Harlequin books are sold.

REG5

Harlequin invites you to the most romantic
wedding of the season...with

MARRY ME, COWBOY!

And you could WIN A DREAM VACATION of a lifetime!

from HARLEQUIN BOOKS and SANDALS—
THE CARIBBEAN'S #1 **ULTRA INCLUSIVE**SM LUXURY RESORTS
FOR COUPLES ONLY.

Harlequin Books and Sandals Resorts are offering you a
vacation of a lifetime—a vacation of your choice at any of
the Sandals Caribbean resorts—FREE!

LOOK FOR FURTHER DETAILS in the Harlequin Books
title MARRY ME, COWBOY!, an exciting collection
of four brand-new short stories by popular romance
authors, including *New York Times* bestselling author
JANET DAILEY!

**AVAILABLE IN APRIL WHEREVER
HARLEQUIN BOOKS ARE SOLD.**

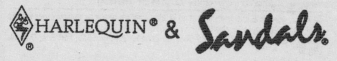

HARLEQUIN® & *Sandals*®

MMC-SANDT

HARLEQUIN®

Don't miss these Harlequin favorites by some of our most distinguished authors!
And now, you can receive a discount by ordering two or more titles!

HT #25607	PLAIN JANE'S MAN by Kristine Rolofson	$2.99 U.S./$3.50 CAN.	☐
HT #25616	THE BOUNTY HUNTER by Vicki Lewis Thompson	$2.99 U.S./$3.50 CAN.	☐
HP #11674	THE CRUELLEST LIE by Susan Napier	$2.99 U.S./$3.50 CAN.	☐
HP #11699	ISLAND ENCHANTMENT by Robyn Donald	$2.99 U.S./$3.50 CAN.	☐
HR #03268	THE BAD PENNY by Susan Fox	$2.99	☐
HR #03303	BABY MAKES THREE by Emma Goldrick	$2.99	☐
HS #70570	REUNITED by Evelyn A. Crowe	$3.50	☐
HS #70611	ALESSANDRA & THE ARCHANGEL by Judith Arnold	$3.50 U.S./$3.99 CAN.	☐
HI #22291	CRIMSON NIGHTMARE by Patricia Rosemoor	$2.99 U.S./$3.50 CAN.	☐
HAR #16549	THE WEDDING GAMBLE by Muriel Jensen	$3.50 U.S./$3.99 CAN.	☐
HAR #16558	QUINN'S WAY by Rebecca Flanders	$3.50 U.S./$3.99 CAN.	☐
HH #28802	COUNTERFEIT LAIRD by Erin Yorke	$3.99	☐
HH #28824	A WARRIOR'S WAY by Margaret Moore	$3.99 U.S./$4.50 CAN.	☐

(limited quantities available on certain titles)

	AMOUNT	$
DEDUCT:	**10% DISCOUNT FOR 2+ BOOKS**	$
ADD:	**POSTAGE & HANDLING**	$
	($1.00 for one book, 50¢ for each additional)	
	APPLICABLE TAXES*	$_____
	TOTAL PAYABLE	$_____
	(check or money order—please do not send cash)	

To order, complete this form and send it, along with a check or money order for the total above, payable to Harlequin Books, to: **In the U.S.:** 3010 Walden Avenue, P.O. Box 9047, Buffalo, NY 14269-9047; **In Canada:** P.O. Box 613, Fort Erie, Ontario, L2A 5X3.

Name: _____

Address: _____ City: _____

State/Prov.: _____ Zip/Postal Code: _____

*New York residents remit applicable sales taxes.
  Canadian residents remit applicable GST and provincial taxes.

HBACK-AJ2